It's just Joe

Lisa hated the nervous flutter that she felt when she watched Joe walk toward her. She needed to remember who he was. Her deceased fiancé's twin brother. Her son's uncle.

At one time, Joe had also been Lisa's best friend—the shoulder she'd cried on when his brother was being a jerk. But then graduation night had happened. Opportunity had awakened desire, which had led to passion. A choice with ramifications that Lisa had only just discovered.

She pushed the thought aside. She needed to deal with Joe in a businesslike manner because Maureen had warned her Joe had been asking questions about the sale of the bar.

Once Lisa had negotiations out of the way, she could bring up the possibility that for seventeen years she'd been living a lie.

Dear Reader,

Twins fascinate me. So alike, and yet often so different. Growing up, Joe Kelly and his brother, Patrick, appeared to be polar opposites—the sensitive, insightful artist versus the gregarious, self-assured athlete. But the two shared one common trait—they both loved the girl next door.

Lisa Malden lost her heart to Joe the first moment she met him—in seventh grade—but it was Patrick who pursued her and, ultimately, when Lisa discovered she was pregnant, convinced her that, despite her one, impulsive night of lovemaking with Joe, the baby had to be his. Patrick begged her to marry him. Unfortunately, he lost his battle with alcohol before they could say their vows. Grief and recriminations drove Lisa and Joe down different paths—a single mother who never left town and a celebrated filmmaker following his dream in Hollywood.

Now, seventeen years later, both Lisa and Joe have reached a crossroads. There are hard decisions to make. Truths to tell. And a teenage boy at risk of following in the footsteps of the man he thinks of as his father. But what if his real father is Joe?

In researching a book, I'm often given the opportunity to learn about new professions. I thank Daniel Heiss for walking me through the world of moviemaking and giving me a glimpse at the creative genius behind visual storytelling.

I'm thrilled to announce two upcoming releases for Harlequin's Signature Select line this fall: *Window to Yesterday*, in October, and *Betting on Grace*, in November. To find out more, visit my Web site at www.debrasalonen.com, where I have an ongoing blog about the writing life and a new contest every month. You'll also find me at www.superauthors.com and on the "Let's Talk Superromance" thread at eHarlequin.com. Or write to me at P.O. Box 322, Cathey's Valley, CA, 95306.

Happy reading,

Debra Salonen

His Real Father
Debra Salonen

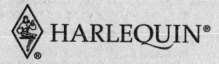

HARLEQUIN®

TORONTO • NEW YORK • LONDON
AMSTERDAM • PARIS • SYDNEY • HAMBURG
STOCKHOLM • ATHENS • TOKYO • MILAN • MADRID
PRAGUE • WARSAW • BUDAPEST • AUCKLAND

ISBN 0-373-71279-0

HIS REAL FATHER

Copyright © 2005 by Debra Salonen.

This one is for Ruth—for giving me two wonderful gifts:
undistracted days in which to write and my reward
when I'm done for the day, Malte.

Books by Debra Salonen

HARLEQUIN SUPERROMANCE

Don't miss any of our special offers. Write to us at the
following address for information on our newest releases.

Harlequin Reader Service
U.S.: 3010 Walden Ave., P.O. Box 1325, Buffalo, NY 14269
Canadian: P.O. Box 609, Fort Erie, Ont. L2A 5X3

CHAPTER ONE

"JOE'S PLACE. Name your poison."

Joe Kelly frowned. The youthful voice on the other end of the phone undoubtedly belonged to his nephew, Brandon, but what was a sixteen—or rather, recently turned seventeen-year-old doing behind a bar?

"Brandon? Is that you?"

"Uncle Joe." The boy's shout made Joe's eardrum ring. "Are you at the airport? Mom just called all p.o.ed because she couldn't find you."

He'd missed Lisa? Damn.

Joe stacked his bags and gear in a pile to keep from tripping other passengers who were exiting the Modesto airport. He looked longingly toward the parking lot where a fleet of rental cars was neatly lined up.

"The plane was late leaving LAX. A huge downpour. In mid-May. Can you believe it? I *told* your grandmother I should rent a car instead of bothering Lisa."

"Well, you know Grams," Brandon said sagely.

Did he?

Joe wasn't sure. Nothing in his thirty-five years of

being Maureen Kelly's son had prepared him for the bombshell she'd dropped when he'd called her on Mother's Day. "Well, darlin' boy, I've decided to sell the bar. And I'm getting married."

Sell Joe's Place? Joe had been too shocked to even register the other half of her announcement.

Joe's Place was a fixture in Worthington, the small, agriculture-based community in central California where Joe had grown up. His parents had owned the combination bar and grill since before Joe and his twin brother Patrick were born, and he'd never thought they'd sell it—much as he'd wanted him to. The bar had become a huge point of contention when Patrick died in an alcohol-related traffic accident the summer after the twins' high-school graduation. Joe had demanded his parents get rid of the place. His father had flatly refused.

Joe remembered their argument all too clearly. Many times since, he'd wished he could take back his hurtful words, but apologies didn't come easy to the men in his family. And, now, with his father gone two years earlier from a heart attack, there'd be no reconciliation.

"The bar was your dad's dream," his mother had added when Joe failed to comment. "I kept it going after he died because everybody said not to rush into any big changes. But when Gunny asked me to marry him I thought why not? What's keeping me here? Lisa graduates from college in a few weeks. Brandon only has one year of high school left. Everyone's life is changing, but mine."

"Marry?" Joe had managed to choke out.

"The good thing about having cancer is that you get your priorities straight," she'd said in a slightly defensive tone. "I'm tired of being alone."

Maureen had been a widow for a little over a year when she'd discovered a lump in her breast. Surgery and aggressive treatment seemed to have eliminated the disease. Joe was grateful, but he hadn't expected her recovery to lead to this. But because he hadn't really "been there" for his mother, he didn't know what to say, except, "Umm…congratulations."

Later, after the shock had worn off, Joe had given her announcement some serious thought and realized he wanted to make a movie about the bar.

Just speaking the words seemed to trigger memories. His father dispensing wisdom to a host of regulars. His mother stirring a huge vat of chili. He and his brother doing their homework on top of cases of beer.

The bar had been the center of Joe's universe for over half his life, but like every small-town watering hole he'd ever seen or heard about, it also served as a hub of social exchange, where one could take the pulse of the economy, trace the changes in societal mores and track the life—or death—of a community. Joe knew he couldn't let Joe's Place pass into other hands without documenting its history—the good and the bad.

He hadn't mentioned this aspect of his visit to his mother when he called to tell her he was coming home. In all honesty, he wasn't sure she'd approve, given his vocal antipathy toward the place. And he had no idea what to expect from the new owner since Maureen had been reluctant to share any details of the sale. "We're still negotiating," she'd told him.

Joe figured if he couldn't get her to postpone the sale for a month or two, he'd at least have a few weeks to film on-site before escrow closed. If he needed to come back to pick up any extra footage, he couldn't imagine why the new owner would object. Free publicity was free publicity, even if the movie flopped.

Documentaries were odd ducks. Some flew to mass distribution, some never got off the ground. Joe tried not to think that far ahead. At the moment, he just knew that he had to make this film. Which was why he'd brought a camera with him.

Bending down, Joe checked the locks on the silver case, which was about the size of a microwave oven. He'd shipped his tripod, portable mixing deck and laptop, which he would use to process raw footage. The hard-core post-production work would be done when he returned to L.A.

"So, is your mom coming back for me?" he asked, refocusing his attention on the present.

Lisa Malden, Brandon's mother, was Joe's "almost" sister-in-law. Unfortunately, Patrick had died before they could tie the knot.

She was part of the reason Joe didn't come back to Worthington more often. It was never easy to look your living, breathing conscience in the face.

"Yeah," Brandon said, "she was just pissed because she has so much to do before graduation."

"That's right. Mom mentioned that Lisa was graduating."

"Next Saturday," Brandon said. "'Bout time, huh?"

Lisa was the only person Joe had ever known who'd managed to drag out her college experience for nearly ten years. Although privately Joe had rolled his eyes every time his mother had mentioned Lisa's newest major, he didn't approve of the slightly deprecating tone he heard in Brandon's question.

"Well, she beat me to a degree. I dropped out of film school my final year, you know."

"So you could make movies and get rich and famous."

"Not exactly." Although that had been his intention at the time. Cocky, brash, certain he was the next Spielberg, Joe had let the small amount of fame that came from the release of his student film *Dead Drunk* lure him from the path he'd started on the first time he picked up a camera.

"Anyway, I'm here now, if she checks in with you," he said, reluctant to discuss his mistakes with a young man he barely knew. He'd made plenty over the years. Both personal and professional.

"Cool," the boy said. Brandon was a junior in high school. Joe wondered how these impending changes would affect his nephew. "Grams says you're supposed to come here for dinner. Martin is going to watch the bar while we eat."

Martin Franks. The seemingly ageless bartender who had been around for as long as Joe could remember. Maureen had told him Martin had stepped in to help run the place during her illness and recovery. Was he the mysterious buyer?

Joe had asked the buyer's name, but his mother had answered, "I'd rather not say. I don't want to jinx this."

"Great. I'm starved. Is Gunny going to be there?"

Gunner Bjorgensen, his mother's fiancé, was a man Maureen had first met in grief therapy. Since his wife had suffered from breast cancer, too, he'd been able to help Maureen negotiate some of the hurdles, both financial and emotional. Joe didn't have anything against the man, but he was worried about the timing of Gunny's proposal. Joe hoped she wouldn't regret this decision.

A honking horn startled him out of his musings.

"That could be her, Brandon. I'm hanging up."

"Wait. Did you remember my poster?"

Joe smiled. Brandon might sound grown up on the phone, but his interest in young starlets was that of a teen. "I got it."

"Cool," his nephew said.

Joe pocketed the cell phone then looked at his mountain of luggage. At first glance, one might think he was moving.

"Do you think this pilgrimage will let you set things right in your wayward past?" Modamu Davies, a composer who'd scored two of Joe's movies, had asked him last night.

"I doubt it," Joe had answered. "But Joe's Place is where my passion for filmmaking began. One of the first things I ever shot was a checkers tournament. I can still picture those grizzled old coots—cigarette in one hand and glass of beer in the other—hunched over a table that had a backgammon board on one side and a checkerboard on the other. None of them knew how to play backgammon. They called it 'that *furin* game.'"

Both men had laughed, then Joe added, "I know this movie idea sounds crazy."

"Particularly given the fact that you've avoided Worthington for so many years," Mo had interjected.

"And highly unprofitable," Joe had finished, ignoring the all-too-true comment. "But, at least I won't look back some day and wish I'd made the effort."

"Traveling down memory lane can get you in trouble, my friend," Mo had warned. "Every director I know is a control freak who spends days upon days playing with color, lighting, background and sound because this medium gives him the *illusion* of control.

"If you return to the source of your neurosis, you might *fix* what made you crazy in the first place and then where would you be?"

"Sane? Healthy? Gainfully employed?" Joe had answered, laughing.

Mo, being a true friend, hadn't mentioned Joe's recent string of bad movies, but Joe was a realist. His first film had garnered awards and been picked up for distribution by a major player. For a short time, he'd been Hollywood's golden boy. Unfortunately, his next

two productions—neither scripts of his choosing—
had reviewed well but hadn't done much at the box office. His contract hadn't been renewed, so he'd started
his own production company, where he learned the pit-
falls of business, the cutthroat nature of competition
and, above all else, humility.

Returning to the present, he hoisted the strap of his
garment bag over one shoulder, picked up his camera
case and grabbed the handle of his rolling suitcase. The
pneumatic doors opened as he approached. The parking lot was tiny by L.A. standards but pretty much
filled.

Lisa, behind the wheel of a sunshine-yellow convertible Bug, had pulled to a stop in the loading zone
and was arguing with a woman in a black uniform.

He paused. Although just six months younger than
Joe, she looked twentysomething. Her long, reddish-
blond hair was pulled through the back of a white
baseball cap. Joe couldn't read the logo above the
brim, but the symbol was hot pink, which matched her
tank top. Over that she wore an unbuttoned white shirt
with the sleeves rolled up almost to her elbows.

She pointed animatedly at her watch then nodded
toward the terminal. He knew the moment she spotted
him because she rose up on one knee and waved, her
other hand resting on the neon-pink faux-fur steering-
wheel cover.

He couldn't see her eyes because of the tortoise-
shell sunglasses she was wearing. But her smile was
all Lisa. A sudden lifting sensation in his chest made

him miss a step. He honestly couldn't tell if that was something good…or bad.

"SEE?" LISA SAID to the parking matron who'd tried to make her leave the curbside loading zone, even though she'd only just arrived. For the second time. "There he is."

The woman, who was probably ten or fifteen years older than Lisa, stared slack-jawed at the smiling man walking toward them. Some things never change, Lisa thought ruefully. That infamous Kelly charm still works.

The security guard smiled back at Joe before strolling off.

Lisa took a deep breath and wiped her hands on her denim skirt. She hated the nervous flutter in her chest. *Stop it,* she scolded herself. *This is Joe.* Her deceased fiancé's twin brother. Her son's uncle. Her old friend.

But he was also a wild card that could ruin her plans. What if he shot down her idea of buying the bar from his mother? Just the thought made her a little ill.

She'd rehearsed her spiel on the way to the airport, only to be disappointed when she'd found out his flight had been delayed. With graduation looming and a wedding to help plan, she had no time for late planes.

Lisa got out and walked to the front of the car to open the trunk. Thankfully, Modesto's airport was located on the edge of town. Instead of wasting time, she'd backtracked to a service station to fill up.

"Hi, Lisa," Joe hailed. "Sorry about the delay."

Just over six feet tall, Joe moved gracefully for a man burdened with several suitcases and a bulky silver box. His hair was the same ash blond she remembered from high school, but the style a little shaggier than she'd expected. Cargo pants, a camp shirt that needed ironing and loafers without socks completed his "rumpled artist" look.

At one time, Joe had been Lisa's best friend—the shoulder she'd cried on when his brother was being a jerk. But then graduation night had happened. Opportunity had awakened desire, which led to a choice with ramifications that Lisa had just recently discovered.

She pushed the thought aside. She needed to deal with Joe in a businesslike manner because Maureen had warned her Joe had been asking questions about the sale. Once Lisa had negotiations out of the way, she could bring up the possibility that for seventeen years she'd been living a lie.

"Brandon said you were here earlier."

Smile. Pretend everything is normal. She had too much to do. The question of her son's paternity would have to wait. Besides, as an uncle, Joe had left a lot to be desired. He probably wouldn't be any better as Brandon's father.

"No problem," she called, pushing her gym bag and running shoes out of the way to make room for his stuff.

She watched him look over her car, a 1975 VW Bug. Lisa had helped restore the car's engine during her three semesters as an automotive major. The body work and paint had been redone by a guy her mother had once dated. Lisa had unapologetically added the paisley seat covers and frivolous accessories just for the fun of it.

Brandon had been horrified. "Mom, I can't drive that car," he'd complained. "It's too girly."

She'd silently chuckled since that had been part of her plan. She didn't want her son driving a sporty convertible. Lisa was quite content to see him behind the wheel of his grandmother's older, far more sedate sedan.

"Sweet Bug," Joe said.

"Thanks."

"Is it new? Well, old, but you know what I mean."

"It was a work in progress through most of my college years," she said, running a hand over the curved fender. Lisa loved her car. It made her feel young at heart. Almost carefree. Which was an illusion, of course, but she could pretend.

"Mom mentioned that your commencement is coming up. Congratulations. How come I didn't get an announcement?"

"Thank you. I didn't see the point. Considering how long it's taken me." Suddenly embarrassed, she motioned toward the bags still sitting on the curb. "Instead of crowding everything in the trunk, why don't you put the rest in the back?"

Joe picked up his leather garment bag, which looked expensive enough to hold an Armani tux, and tossed it carelessly across the seat. The silver case he lifted as if it contained a donated heart awaiting transplant.

Lisa bit down on a smile.

"What?" he asked, apparently sensing her amusement.

"Remember when you used to zip your camera under your coat to protect it from the fog and rain? Patrick called you Mr. One Breast."

"You know, I'd forgotten that detail. Quite happily, actually."

Lisa was glad to see that Joe appeared to have done well for himself. If he was financially set, then he might not care how much his mother got for the bar. Lisa wanted to pay a fair price, but with a son going to college next year, her resources were limited.

She was nearly thirty-five. In just over a week, she'd have her bachelor of arts degree in education. And instead of applying for a teaching job, she'd decided to buy Joe's Place. At first, Maureen had been delighted by the idea of "keeping it in the family," but, now, she was dragging her feet pending Joe's okay.

Before getting in, Lisa pointed toward her ball cap and said, "There's an extra one under the seat, if the sun and wind are too much for you."

"The reduced level of smog might send my lungs into shock, but I'm willing to give it a try."

His wink took her straight back to junior high. A brand new seventh-grade student in a strange town. The principal had been showing Lisa and two other transfer students around. The first person they'd bumped into was Joe Kelly. Racing to class. Late. "Mr. Kelly," the principal had barked. "Come here."

Instead of giving Joe a lecture, the principal had introduced the new arrivals and ordered Joe to take over the tour.

The meandering expedition had been punctuated with wit and humor—Joe's trademark, she'd learned. His appreciation of the absurd, his warm, inclusive smile and wavy hair had been enough to make a girl fall in love. Which Lisa had. A fact that had turned complicated the minute she'd met his twin brother.

Once they were both seated with seat belts fastened, she put the car in gear and stepped on the gas. The sun was warm on her shoulders and thighs, but not as hot as it would be in a few weeks when summer hit the valley. Then, she'd have the top up and the air conditioner running.

Maureen wanted an outdoor wedding. The last weekend in June. The idea had Lisa sweating.

"Are we headed straight home?" Joe asked.

Lisa shifted into neutral as they waited for the light to change at the intersection. "Uh-huh. Unless you need to stop somewhere. Your mother is preparing an Irish feast. Corned beef and cabbage, red potatoes, rye bread, the works."

She happened to glance sideways and saw his pained expression. "What's the matter? You don't like corned beef?"

He shook his head. "No. I like it fine. Yum."

She recognized the lie. Joe didn't lie worth squat—

unlike his brother. Patrick and Joe had been fraternal twins. They'd shared a number of personality traits, but honesty wasn't one of them.

"Baloney. No pun intended," she said, groaning softly.

He acknowledged her lame joke with a tip of his imaginary hat. "Actually, I've been on a pretty strict diet since the holidays. Doctor's orders."

"Why?"

"I was at a party on Christmas Eve, and I started having chest pains and shortness of breath. The hostess thought I was having a heart attack and called 9-1-1. Turned out be acid reflux from too much champagne and rich food. How embarrassing is that?"

Lisa frowned. Although he tried to make the experience sound funny, she sensed that he'd been unnerved by the episode—no doubt remembering the cause of his father's death.

"Not my most pleasant holiday on record," he added.

She started to reach out to touch his arm, but a horn alerted her to the green light. She quickly shifted and shot through the intersection. A convenience store was just ahead on the right so she pulled into the parking lot. A flowering tree provided enough shade for them to sit without sweating in the sun.

"I bet you were freaked out. Your dad was only fifty-eight when he died."

Joe nodded. "My doctor says a genetic predisposition to high blood pressure is only part of my problem.

Mostly, he blamed stress, my sedentary lifestyle and poor eating habits for what happened." His full ruddy lips turned up in the corners, producing the infamous Kelly dimple in his left cheek. "He said I was lucky."

"Luck being a relative thing. When your mother finds out that you didn't tell her…"

He scrubbed a hand across his face, a gesture her son often used when he was frustrated. Lisa's stomach produced a little extra acid of its own.

"I know," he said, sinking down so his knees bumped against the dashboard. His fingers drummed an impatient tune on his thighs. "But when I saw her at my cousin Paige's wedding in November she finally seemed at peace with things. I didn't want her to worry."

Lisa and Brandon had been at Joe's cousin's wedding in the Bay area, too. Lisa had thought Joe had looked tired and unhappy. Later, Maureen told her Joe had broken up with his girlfriend of several years a few weeks earlier.

He gave her a sheepish look and added, "Plus, I knew she'd say 'I told you so.' At the wedding, she'd given me a hard time about not getting enough exercise."

Lisa understood completely. Since Maureen's medical crisis, she'd become very proactive where everyone's health—family and customers alike—was concerned.

"Since the first of the year, I've been walking to the beach from my studio every day at lunch. It's a couple of miles, and I even jog a little."

He kept talking, but Lisa's imagination lingered over the image of Joe strolling among beautiful women in skimpy bikinis. Why that bothered her, she didn't know.

"...if I sell my studio."

Lisa's heart missed a beat. "Did you say 'sell your studio'? Why would you do that?"

"Money. Remember the movie *Slippery Slope?*"

She shook her head. "Never heard of it."

"My point, exactly. It chronicled the rise and fall of Vanilla Ice. Not my idea. In fact, I tried to talk my investors out of doing it, but they insisted. And when it flopped, who'd they blame? The director, of course."

Lisa's fingers tightened on the steering wheel. "That doesn't seem fair. But that's only one movie. You've had more successes than failures. Right?"

He let out a long sigh. "The movie business has changed, Leese." Nobody had called her that in years. "Or, maybe, I've changed. I don't know. But one thing I do know, making commercial movies hasn't been fun for a long time."

Lisa knew squat about the industry, except that there seemed to be a lot of money to be made if you were good at what you did. For as long as Lisa could remember, Joe had dreamed of making movies. He'd left home to attend the prestigious Visual Arts Center in L.A., majoring in film.

His first important project, which had focused on the effect a drunk-driving death had on a family, had garnered all kinds of awards. When a national distributor had picked up *Dead Drunk,* Joe's future had seemed set.

"Are you telling me your career is over?" she asked. Sympathy warred with panic.

He extracted a pair of sunglasses from the breast pocket of his shirt. "Don't pull any punches on my account, Leese."

"Sorry. Didn't know I had to. You're the one who once told me you were destined for greatness, which was why you couldn't get out of Worthington fast enough."

He pretended to take a jab to the chin. "Good lord, I was an egotist. How did you stand me?" He didn't wait for an answer, instead saying, "The truth is I feel I'm at a crossroads in my career. Epiphany by chest pains," he said breezily. "One day I woke up and realized I wasn't a kid with a camera anymore. I was this intense, mostly unlikable, businessman creating crap for anyone who was willing to pay."

She glanced over her shoulder at the camera case sitting on the back seat. "So…you're moving home?"

"Yeah. For a while. I've decided to make a movie about Joe's Place."

"What?" The question came out as a peep, but Joe didn't seem to notice.

"I don't have the exact storyline together yet, but ideas have been percolating in my head ever since Mom called. Maybe something nostalgic using archival footage. Or with interviews of locals on the role the bar has played in the community. Or, it might take a more personal focus. I've been thinking about Dad and Patrick a lot lately."

A movie? Interviews?

"The first thing I have to do is talk Mom into postponing the sale for a while."

Lisa was speechless. *Postpone the sale?* But her loan was preapproved. And the interest rates were going up. If they waited too long, she wouldn't be able to afford to buy the place.

He lowered the shades to the end of his nose and turned to look at her. "Something wrong?"

This wasn't the first time a Kelly boy had ruined her plans. "Yes, actually." She hesitated a second then blurted out, "I'm the buyer, Joe. Your mother told me she was thinking of selling because Gunny wanted to travel and didn't want to be tied down. I had no idea you had any interest in the bar. I thought you hated Joe's Place."

He sat up sharply. "You're buying it? Good lord, why?"

"To keep Brandon gainfully employed while he goes to college. It worked for me," she added, unable to keep the pride from her tone. "I've saved enough money to pay for Brandon's college, as long as he lives at home and earns his own spending money.

"I figured that over the four years he was in college, I'd slowly fix up the place. The real-estate market is going through the roof around here. When he's done with school, I'll sell the bar and reinvest the money wherever I want."

Joe appeared shocked. "I can't believe it. You, of all people, should be overjoyed to see the damn thing gone."

Lisa knew what he meant. Joe felt the bar had contributed to Patrick's drinking problem. After Pat's funeral, Joe and his father had argued about the subject. The fight had driven a wedge between them.

"I know you think that what he saw at Joe's Place influenced your brother, but I don't agree. The bar is part of our community. Working there paid my way through college while giving me time to spend with my son.

"Brandon's been helping your mother three days a week, sweeping the floor, restocking the cooler and handling exterior maintenance. The job keeps him out of trouble and gives him enough money to pay the insurance on your folks' old car, which your mother gave him. Insurance is a big-ticket item for young drivers in California, let me tell you."

"Grunt labor? Nothing behind the bar?"

Lisa found his tone slightly judgmental. "Of course not. He helps out in the kitchen once in a while, but he can't tend bar until he turns twenty-one. And even that would depend on his grades.

"I want him to finish school the way normal people do—in four years, not ten."

Lisa had scrimped and saved to be able to pay for her son's tuition. She couldn't afford Harvard, but she could handle California State University–Stanislaus in nearby Turlock, her soon-to-be alma mater—provided Brandon did his share.

Uncomfortable with Joe's scrutiny, she tilted her wrist to look at her watch. "Oh, cripes, we'd better hurry. You know how freaked out your mother gets whenever someone is late."

Or, maybe, he didn't. He hadn't lived around his mother for nearly eighteen years. Right after Patrick's funeral, Joe had moved to L.A. Following the success of *Dead Drunk,* he'd bought a house in Topanga Canyon. He probably hadn't returned home more than a dozen times in the past eighteen years.

Lisa, on the other hand, had chosen to remain in Worthington. She'd lived with her mother most of that time. Partly to save money and partly because her mother's home shared a common fence with the Kellys, which meant two grandmothers and one grandfather in calling distance. Lisa couldn't give her son a father, but she could make sure he had plenty of extended family. Even if that meant living in the shadow of Patrick Kelly's ghost.

"ARE THEY HERE, YET?"

Brandon shifted his gaze from the television resting on an elevated stand in the far corner of the bar to his grandmother. She was transferring beer glasses from the drying rack to the lit cabinet bracketing the gold-framed mirror behind the bar. If he lived to be a hundred, Brandon knew he'd always remember her just like this. Forehead crinkled in concentration, but with lips pursed as she tunelessly whistled under her breath.

Before she got sick, Brandon would have called her short and round. Most of that extra weight was gone now. And she'd always made up for her lack of stature with a loud, commanding voice. Brandon's mother claimed the reason Grams talked so loud was from raising twins and living with a husband who was hard of hearing.

Brandon missed his grandfather. A lot. Grampa Joe had been a cool guy who'd treated Brandon fairly and never jumped on his case over little things, like his mom did. Not that Gramps was a pushover, but Brandon could read him easier and back off before Gramps reached his breaking point. Brandon used to feel that way about his mother, too, but lately, nothing he did met with her approval.

"No yellow Bug, Grams," he said, glancing over his shoulder. Two large picture windows on either side of the double doors faced Main Street, but the thick clusters of red geraniums in the outside planter boxes and the neon beer signs hanging like curtains obscured the view a bit. Of course, nothing hid his mother's car completely. "You can see that car coming five miles away."

"A hippie time capsule," his friend Rory had labeled it the other day. Just what Brandon needed—to be talked about because his mother was going through some kind of phase. He loved his mom, but just once he wished he had a *normal* family.

"Good," Maureen said, her voice easily heard over the announcers of the NASCAR qualifying race Brandon had been watching. "Bright colors are safer. I told Gunny he should paint his motor home red. He said he'd think about it. Men always say that when they're trying to humor their brides-to-be."

Brandon couldn't think about his grandmother getting married without shuddering. Old people making out. Like…why bother? They didn't actually do the dirty, did they? That was too gross to even think about. His mom was a different story. She was probably still young enough to be interested in sex. After all, she was younger than Demi Moore, who had just hooked up with an actor half her age. Plus, Mom was pretty. His pals Rory and Winston both had the hots for her, which wasn't surprising given the fact neither of them could find a girl their own age to date.

"Grams, are you sure you want to marry Gunny? He's nice and all, but he isn't as cool as Gramps."

She walked to where he was sitting and rested her elbows on the smooth surface of the bar. Today was Saturday. Cleanup day. Joe's Place didn't open until four-thirty on Saturdays. And it was closed on Sundays and Mondays, except during football season. Despite the cleaning Brandon just got done giving the place, the bar still smelled of stale beer and old smoke. Recent laws had made it illegal to smoke indoors, but that hadn't always been the case.

"Turn that off, honey boy. We need to talk."

Brandon reluctantly lifted the remote; the screen went black. He loved his grandmother and would miss her terribly when she got married and took off on her travels, but when it came to heart-to-heart talks, she wasn't Gramps.

He rocked back on the vinyl bar stool. The seat top wobbled slightly. *Crap,* he thought. His mother had asked him to tighten the screws and he'd forgotten. Brandon would hear about it later. His mother never forgot anything.

"So, kiddo, you don't think Gunny is good enough for me, huh?"

That wasn't exactly what he'd said, but Brandon nodded just the same. "He's okay, I guess."

"Gunny's a good man. He knows how hard this move is going to be for me. Saying goodbye to this place and the people I love won't be easy. He's doing his best to make this wedding as painless as possible."

Brandon faked a smile. It was on the tip of his tongue to ask, "Isn't love supposed to make you happy, not sad?" But just then, the door to the bar opened and two people walked in. His mother carried a black leather bag over one shoulder and her purse in the other hand. Following a few steps behind was his uncle wheeling a suitcase and carrying a large silver case.

Afternoon sunlight filtered through the windows. The gold and blue from a Corona beer sign cast a swath of color across the blouse his mother was wearing. And he noticed she had on a skirt.

Why was she all dressed up? Was he missing something? And what was with the serious looks on both of their faces?

Brandon had never understood the relationship between his mother and uncle. His mother occasionally criticized Joe for not calling Grams more often, but then she'd make excuses for him.

He couldn't put his finger on it, but Brandon knew there was something weird between them. He guessed it had to do with his father. But since his mother had quit talking about Patrick recently, Brandon didn't bother asking. Even if she answered, he wasn't sure he'd believe her.

But none of that mattered at the moment. The only thing Brandon had on his mind was the autographed photo his uncle had promised to get. Mandy Moore— the angel-faced hottie Rory and Winston were totally in love with.

Brandon couldn't wait to torture his friends with this new acquisition. But the main reason he'd requested the photo was to show it to Nikki Jean Cho, the coolest girl in school. Nikki planned to be an actress and last week he'd overheard her say that Mandy Moore was her inspiration.

Since Brandon tended to get all tongue-tied around girls, especially girls as fine as Nikki Jean, he figured an icebreaker would help. Granted, there were just two and a half weeks of school left, but there was always next year. Unless something—or someone— screwed things up. With his mother graduating from college and his grandmother getting married, who knew what might happen?

Worrying about the future made his mouth dry. Suddenly, he craved a beer.

CHAPTER TWO

"HI, MOM," JOE SAID as his eyes adjusted to the dimness. "I'm home. Call off the search-and-rescue team."

His mother shuffled sideways to get around a stack of cartons. Beer, he presumed. "Oh, you," she said, swatting him with the damp white towel she was carrying. "I knew you'd show up eventually. You're with Lisa. She's the responsible one. I can always count on her."

He glanced to his right to see Lisa embrace her son, who was several inches taller than his mother. The height difference really made him realize that Joe had been neglectful about visiting his family. He'd seen Brandon at Paige's wedding, but the boy hadn't looked so grown up.

After bending over to give his mother a hug, Joe extended a hand to Brandon. "How's it going, nephew?"

Lisa made an odd, almost pained sound and quickly turned away. Curious. Just as odd as her wanting to buy Joe's Place. At long last, Lisa was going to have her degree, a goal she'd had since high school. Surely she could find a more worthwhile career than running this smelly old bar.

He'd worry about Lisa and the sale later, he told himself. First, he owed his attention to his mother. As he answered questions about his flight and why he was late, it hit him that in a few short weeks, Maureen would be marrying a man Joe barely knew.

"So, Mom, is Gunny joining us for dinner?"

His mother tucked her arm through Joe's and started leading him toward the swinging saloon doors that separated the bar from the kitchen. "No. He's over on the coast, fishing with his son. He said he'd bring us back something fresh to barbecue tomorrow. His son and daughter-in-law will join us." She peered around him to ask Lisa, "Did you invite your mother?"

Joe saw the look that Lisa and Brandon exchanged.

"I wouldn't count on her," Lisa said. "She has a new boyfriend, you know. He's even single," she added for Joe's benefit.

Constance Malden, Lisa's mother, had been a source of embarrassment for Lisa for as long as Joe had known her. Connie lived by her own rules, dating whomever she pleased—even if he happened to be married. By Hollywood standards, that sort of thing happened all the time, but in Worthington, Constance's social life had provided rich fodder for local gossips.

Lisa's blasé expression appeared pasted on. He recalled a scene from high school. Lisa, Patrick and Joe had always dashed home at lunch to watch *General Hospital*—until the day Lisa had pointed at the television and burst into tears, crying, "There's my mother, the town slut."

Later, Joe had gotten Lisa to talk about what was really bothering her. She claimed that one of Constance's affairs had been with a married doctor whose daughter was the reigning homecoming queen. In a community the size of Worthington, if a woman was a social pariah, then so, by association, was her daughter.

To change the subject, Joe asked, "Is it chow time?"

"I think so," Maureen said, leading the way through the swinging doors. "Is everything ready, Martin?"

Martin Franks was a fixture at Joe's Place. Joe's father had claimed that Martin had come with the bar, which Joe and Maureen had bought with money they'd received as a wedding gift. Joe had been twenty-four at the time, Maureen just eighteen. Two years later, she'd given birth to twins.

Assuming what his father had said was true, Martin would be in his mid-seventies. But the only outward concession to time that Joe could see was the addition of silver in Martin's long black ponytail. Taller than Joe, but many pounds lighter, the man standing by the sink turned and nodded his greeting.

Prominent cheekbones created shallow, copper-toned hollows and dark eyes sparkled with humor that seldom translated to a smile.

"Martin, my old friend," Joe said, increasing his stride to reach the man. "It's good to see you."

Their hands clasped in greeting. Joe had learned years ago that Martin didn't hug.

"Hi, Martin," Lisa said, joining them. She pulled something from her purse. "How's the burn?"

"Not bad," Martin said. "The aloe you gave me helped."

"Good." After washing her hands, she unscrewed the cap of a small ointment tube and squeezed a dab onto her finger. "Mom said this will keep it from getting infected."

Martin untied the strings of the white apron knotted at his waist and pushed it aside so he could lift his green plaid shirt. A four-inch-long bright red slash paralleled one of his ribs.

Joe looked away. He'd always been a bit squeamish around blood and gore. *Maybe that's why Hollywood and I don't mix. Not enough bloodshed and violence.*

"She sent some bandages, too."

Martin tolerated the salve but waved his hand when Lisa displayed several sterile adhesive strips. "No. Air is the best medicine."

Lisa made a face. "The ointment is going to get on your shirt."

Martin looked at Joe and shrugged. "It will wash."

"Men," she said, her tone exasperated. "You all make terrible patients. Did you give your doctor this type of trouble?" she asked Joe.

Maureen made a startled sound and reached for Joe's arm to make him face her. "Doctor? What's this about?"

Lisa mouthed, "Sorry," before dashing away.

This wasn't the first time she'd gotten him in trouble. "I had a bit of a scare during the holidays," he said, taking her by the elbow when she swayed on her feet. "Nothing that diet and exercise couldn't fix. Look at me, Mom. I'm in better shape than I've ever been."

"It wasn't a heart attack. Like your dad?"

"Not even close."

"When did this happen? Why didn't you tell me?"

"Christmas Eve. That's the real reason I didn't come home." Joe had canceled because of "car trouble." In fact, he'd been in the hospital. Alone and shaken up. "I knew you'd rush down south if I told you, and when I called, Lisa said you were still a little tired from your last chemo treatments," he said, anxious to put the conversation behind him.

Maureen looked at Lisa. "Did you know about this?"

"I just found out ten minutes ago. Honest," Lisa said, handing her son a fistful of silverware to put on the table. She followed after him with paper napkins that she folded in neat triangles.

Joe studied his mother's face. More lines around her eyes and mouth, but none of the pallor he'd seen in November. She looked fit and healthy. True, she'd aged since his father had died, but Joe blamed himself for some of that. He'd been so busy wallowing in his own guilt and pain, he hadn't been much help to his mother.

He wondered what she would say about his movie. She'd always supported his dreams, but maybe she was too busy looking forward to care about the past.

LISA TURNED OFF her cell phone. Her mother had called just as Lisa had taken her last bite of dinner. She had excused herself to take the call in the bar area. Only a few regulars were present—all far enough away to afford some privacy.

Lisa hadn't minded the interruption. Maureen had started ambling down memory lane, which was always a difficult path for Lisa to trek. Her feelings had grown ambivalent over the years instead of solidifying into rosy, happy memories—especially where Patrick was concerned.

"Is everything okay?"

Lisa whirled to find Joe standing a foot away in the garish neon light coming from the CD jukebox. "Oh, yeah. Mom wanted to borrow my silk blazer for her date. She warned me not to expect her home tonight." She snickered softly. "Funny, huh? She never thought twice about staying out till dawn when I was a teenager and actually sat up worrying about her."

"Maybe this is Connie's way of showing respect to the new alpha female in the house."

Lisa couldn't prevent the laughter that bubbled up. She brushed her fingers against his arm. "That sounds like something your mother would say. Don't tell me you watch Dr. Phil, too?"

His smile looked sort of sheepish. "I was tossing around the idea of doing a movie about pop psychology and the whole plastic surgery, slice-and-dice makeover phenomenon that's going on now."

Lisa was surprised. The Joe she remembered was more into nature than human nature. Apparently, that had changed after Patrick died. "I remember when you were going to make a movie about hiking the Continental Divide."

Joe pulled back in obvious surprise. "Wow. I hadn't thought about that in years. Once I hit film school, I sorta got caught up in social issues. After *Dead Drunk* came out, I went with the flow, so to speak." He seemed slightly embarrassed.

"You don't have to apologize for being successful, Joe. I was just waxing nostalgic. Probably because of my graduation and your mother's wedding. I feel as if a chapter of my life is coming to a close."

He looked around. Lisa knew he didn't see the place the way she did—fondly, with good memories of working with Joe Sr. and Maureen.

"Dad hated my movies," he said. "He probably wouldn't want to be the focus of one, but something about this place is pulling at me to shoot it."

Lisa understood Joe's mixed feelings toward his father. She had them about hers. Her parents had divorced when Lisa was six, and she'd only seen her father a handful of times since.

"Speaking of dads, how's yours?" Joe asked, as if tapping into her thoughts.

Lisa turned to face the brightly lit jukebox, even though she had no money on her to use it. "He had surgery for prostate cancer last summer, but is doing fine."

Wayne Malden had returned to his home state of Indiana after he and Constance divorced. He'd immediately married a woman with two sons. The couple had had a daughter, Jenna, a few years later. Born with

Down syndrome, Jenna had required so much care that Wayne had quit his job in sales to stay home with her.

Lisa still had difficulty relating that kind of self-sacrifice with the man her mother spoke of with such anger—a man who'd failed to pay child support for the daughter he left behind.

"My half sister is living in a group home and doing really well, I understand. My stepbrothers are both married. I get the whole scoop in a Christmas newsletter."

Joe closed the gap between them and reached into his pocket for his billfold. He withdrew a dollar and put it in the machine. "I can't imagine what it would be like having another family somewhere on the other side of the country. Dealing with one close by is difficult enough."

Lisa watched his long fingers drum on the glass while he decided which songs to select. Joe and Patrick both had nice hands. Joe's were a bit more elegant— better fit for a pen, he'd once said. Just as Patrick's hands had been made to hold a football. Twins, but so different.

He pushed a number-and-letter combination. The first few strains of a song filled the air. A spontaneous shiver chased down Lisa's spine. *No.* Was his choice a fluke or did Joe actually remember that night as vividly as she did?

Of course not. He was a guy. A guy who'd just gotten lucky with his brother's girlfriend.

Shame brought heat to her cheeks. She started to turn away, but Joe caught her arm. "Are we ever going to talk about what happened between us or do we continue this little dance of avoidance until we're old and gray?"

Given the choice, Lisa would have picked old and gray. "I don't know what you mean."

"Of course you do. This song was playing on the car radio that night by the lake."

Lisa's heart rate sped up and a whooshing noise filled her ears—the sound of Patrick's ghost hovering?

Joe stepped closer. His voice was low, but she heard every word. "We made love, Leese. We were young. Life looks different when you're seventeen. What happened was me telling you goodbye before I took off on my big adventure. It was you telling me goodbye before you got engaged to my brother."

Lisa agreed with the goodbye part, but she also knew that her relationship with Patrick didn't figure into the equation on any level. She'd asked herself why she'd done what she had a million times over the past seventeen years—and even more often the past few weeks. There was only one answer. But how do you tell the wrong brother that you've been in love with him since the first moment you met?

Lisa tried to speak, but her words were tangled in threads of guilt. After a lifetime of growing up just one step removed from the nasty buzz of gossip, Lisa couldn't shake off the fear of what people would say if they knew what she and Joe had done on graduation night after Patrick had passed out.

Even now, years removed from that night, Lisa couldn't bring herself to explain why she'd made love to Joe when she was committed to his brother. "You were the one, Joe," she could have said. "Your brother pursued me and you didn't. He loved me, but I loved you."

Lisa had tried to tell him that after Patrick had died, but Joe had pushed her away, unwilling or, perhaps, simply unable to listen to anything once he'd learned that she'd told Patrick of their indiscretion.

"What happened was sex, Joe," she said, recalling all too vividly his hurtful remarks the afternoon of the wake. She stepped back to break his hold on her arm. "Maybe it was my mother's wayward genes kicking in. Whatever the reason, what we did took place in a parallel universe."

His hand fell to his side. She thought she read disappointment in his face, but a second later his infamous dimple was in place. "Sorry. I guess I was trying to cross over one of those bridges I burned a bit too hastily in my past. I thought as adults we might be able to start on new ground and rebuild our relationship, but apparently I was wrong."

Lisa walked into the kitchen to help clean up the dishes. She couldn't afford to hand out second chances, not until she'd finalized her business dealings with Maureen and, perhaps more importantly, figured out what to do about the issue of Brandon's paternity.

"ARE LISA AND BRANDON GONE?" his mother asked.

Joe fought to stifle a yawn. He hadn't gotten in a

run today and the lack of exercise—along with a heavy meal and the stress of returning home—had taken a toll. "Uh-huh. She said something about studying for her finals. And Brandon's going out."

Maureen closed the cupboard door and turned to face him. Her beaming smile made his heart feel lighter and not so tired. "That photo you brought him is apparently quite a coup. He's trying to impress a new girl."

"He has a girlfriend?"

His mother shook her head. "No one steady."

Joe was curious about his nephew. Brandon was a good-looking kid who had seemed pretty sociable during dinner. It struck Joe as odd that the boy didn't have girls flocking around him, like Patrick had any time he and Lisa were on the outs.

But Joe didn't know his nephew. Maybe, if things worked out, he'd be here long enough for the two of them to spend some time together. But that depended on what his mother decided about the sale.

"So, Mom, what do you think about my idea of filming Joe's Place?"

She let out a tired sigh then, taking his arm, said, "Let's go home. We can talk on the way."

Joe glanced at his watch. "But it's only nine-thirty on a Saturday night. Dad will turn over in his grave, if we close Joe's Place this early."

She swatted him gently. "He was cremated. Just like your brother. So drop that nonsense." She snapped off the kitchen light. "Martin will close up. He's had to take care of a lot since I got sick. During chemotherapy, even the smell of beer would have me rushing to the toilet."

Joe tried to hide his reaction. He couldn't think about his mother in pain, which probably explained why he'd made himself scarce during her treatment. He'd been in the waiting room throughout her surgery at Stanford, but once she'd returned home, he'd hidden out in L.A. He couldn't handle seeing his mother so weak and fragile.

"But you look great, by the way. You feel good, huh?"

His tone must have betrayed his worry, because she hugged him as she might a little boy. "Yes, dear, I'm fine. I'm getting married, aren't I? What kind of idiot would say 'I do' if she weren't healthy? Marriage is a lot of work. You have to be in good shape to survive it. Right, Martin?" she called out, with a wave to the man behind the bar.

Martin wasn't the jovial, flush-faced Irish bartender with a million stories Joe's father had been, but he was dignified and efficient. He reminded Joe of the English butler Anthony Hopkins had played in *The Remains of the Day*.

Martin didn't answer. Joe hadn't expected him to.

"Night, Martin. See you tomorrow at the barbecue," Joe said. He'd already loaded his bags into Maureen's car, which was parked beside the well-lit delivery door.

The temperature had turned brisk, a result of the Delta breeze, no doubt. Joe had always loved late spring in the valley. The fog was gone and the blast-furnace heat of summer was still a few weeks off.

Maureen walked to the passenger door of her new hybrid sedan. "Don't I need a key?" he asked, after settling into the driver's seat.

"Nope. Just push the button and put it in reverse."

Joe had known she was thinking of purchasing a new car a year ago, but after her diagnosis, all plans had been put on hold. He saw the fact that she felt well enough to invest in a big-ticket item as a testament to her good health.

"I love it. Smartest thing I ever did. You wouldn't believe the mileage I get. Did I tell you that, legally, I can drive in the diamond lane, even if I'm all by myself?"

Joe smiled. Why beating traffic in the commuter lane was important to someone his mother's age was beyond him, but he was delighted to know she was pleased with her purchase. "Is Brandon happy to have the old car?"

"Oh, heavens no," Maureen said. "He thinks his mother and I are ruining his love life by making him drive an old-lady car, but I told him he's too young to worry about love. He needs to focus on his studies."

Too young to fall in love. Joe had fallen in love with Lisa when he was younger than her son was now. Seventh grade. Her first day at a new school. Joe had been selected to show her around. There'd been a couple of other students in the group, too, but from the minute he'd seen her, Joe only had eyes for Lisa. Until his brother had staked his claim, of course. Once Patrick made up his mind to have something, everyone knew it was hopeless to fight. Patrick had been a force of nature. He'd swept through life, leaving a wake of destruction at times, benevolent gifts at others.

"How's Brandon doing in school?" Joe asked, as they exited the alley that provided access to both extra parking and the small fenced-off area euphemistically called the beer garden. The lattice-covered patio held a picnic table and half a dozen chairs for patrons who wanted to smoke.

The path home was so ingrained in his mind, Joe could probably have closed his eyes and made every turn. But instead he looked around, taking in the changes. A few new storefronts, but nothing compared to the housing developments outside the city limits. Vast tracts of land that had once produced almonds—and provided spots for Patrick and his friends to throw keg parties—were now covered with homes.

"Not bad," his mother said. "Mostly Bs. Not as good as you, but better than your brother."

Grades weren't his and Patrick's only difference. Pat had been a star athlete. Joe could barely swing a bat. Gregarious and loud, Patrick Kelly had been the center of every gathering while Joe had stayed in the background.

"Don't bother my brother," Patrick would warn people. "He's storing up information for a future screenplay."

"So tell me more about this movie you want to make," his mother said.

Joe had waited until Brandon and Lisa had left to bring up the subject, but he suddenly felt dead tired. "Does corned beef have tryptophan in it?" he asked. "I feel as if I could sleep for a month."

Maureen turned slightly in the seat. "Stop teasing, Joseph. If you don't want to tell me about it, fine."

Joe put on the blinker to pull into the driveway. A thirty-year-old square two-story with Tudor aspirations. The amber glow of the streetlight half a block away wasn't enough for him to make out the new paint and shingles that he'd paid for last summer. The gifts he'd sent while his mother was puking her guts out from chemotherapy.

"I'm sorry, Mom. This is important to me and I want to present it to you right."

Maureen didn't say anything for a minute, then she asked, "Is that the real reason you're here? Not my wedding or Lisa's graduation. You came home to re-connect with your roots?"

Was that his true goal? She made it sound so simple.

"Every movie takes a recipe and ingredients. I'm still working on my recipe, but I picture interviewing old-timers and using some of those old movies of mine I shot when I was a kid. You still have them, don't you?"

"Of course," she said, her tone offended. "They're yours. They might be valuable some day."

Joe doubted that but didn't argue. "I shipped my tripod and the rest of my editing equipment by freight.

It should be here early next week. I have until then to come up with a rough storyboard." Or at the very least, an idea of what he wanted to accomplish.

"What does Lisa think of this? She told you I've agreed to sell the place to her, right?"

Joe nodded. "She told me. I was…surprised. To say the least."

He looked at his mother. Her head was resting against the seat and her eyes were closed. Her hair had returned pure white after her treatments, and Joe still wasn't completely used to her fashionable bob. "You look exhausted. Should we table this conversation till tomorrow?"

"It's been a hectic few weeks," she said. "And there's still so much to do. First Lisa's party, then the wedding."

Joe felt his stomach muscles contract whenever that word came up. He hoped his reservations were gone by the time the couple said their vows.

She took a deep breath then opened the door. "You're right, dear. We'll talk in the morning. You know the way to your room." She got out then leaned down to add, "I'm so happy you're home. It's been too long."

Joe watched her walk up the three wide steps to the front stoop. She moved with measured grace, but none of the energy he remembered.

After pulling into the attached garage, Joe turned off the car and retrieved his luggage. When he picked up his carry-on tote, Joe remembered a second gift he'd brought for Brandon. The boy had been so thrilled by his poster, Joe had forgotten about the music CD he had for him.

Modamu Davies's new hip-hop group. Joe had heard the band's name mentioned at the last party he attended in Malibu, but he didn't know the music and was pretty sure he wouldn't like it. The thought made him feel old.

"Thirty-five is not old," he muttered, digging through the outside pocket of his suitcase. Leaving his bags in what his mother called the mud room, Joe detoured to the backyard. Hopefully, the exterior speakers he and his brother had set up still worked.

His mother's stereo sat on an oak-and-glass étagère just inside the sliding glass patio door. Joe inserted the disk and turned the knob so the only speakers playing were the ones under the eaves. A few seconds later a chest-thumping beat filled the fenced enclosure.

As he walked around, taking in the changes his mother had made to the landscaping, Joe tried to make sense of the rapper's words. Was he speaking another language?

Yeah, it's called youth, a cynical voice answered.

Joe followed a worn path in the grass and came up short when he spotted an unfamiliar gate. The Kellys shared a fence with Lisa's mother, but this entrance hadn't existed when Joe was a kid. His father must have put it in for Brandon. Maureen had told him that Joe Sr. and his grandson had been extremely close.

No mechanical latch was visible on Joe's side of the

fence—just a four-inch-long piece of string that dangled through a hole in a wooden slat. Attached to the string was a small bell.

He was tempted to walk next door and finish his conversation with Lisa. Sorely tempted. Something had sizzled between them tonight when he'd played that song.

He started back to the house, instead. Any issues between him and Lisa were best ignored. They'd screwed up once and still lived with the guilt. His feelings for Lisa were complicated. Too complicated to resolve during a brief visit home.

He'd barely taken half a dozen steps when a sound that didn't belong on the CD made him freeze midstride.

It was the tinkle of a tiny bell.

CHAPTER THREE

THE GATE OPENED with a bang. His nephew ambled through the opening.

"Hey, man, I figured it was you," Brandon said. "I heard the music. Not something Grams would play. She's into golden oldies like Joe Cocker and Rod Stewart."

Joe fought to keep from wincing. He liked that music, too. Damn, he *was* getting old.

The boy came closer, his head cocked in obvious concentration. "Who is it?"

Joe held up the jewel case that he still carried. "A new group. My friend's label. He says they're hot."

Brandon took the case from him.

"It's yours if you want it."

"Sweet," Brandon said, squinting to read the label, but the glow from the low-voltage lights was too dim.

"Let's go inside," Joe said. "If we keep the volume down, your grandmother won't mind." A gust of wind made him realize his thin shirt wasn't adequate protection from the cool night air—a fact made all the more apparent by comparison to Brandon's outfit.

"Is that a letter jacket you're wearing?" Joe asked.

"Yeah. I lettered in football and track." The boy tried to sound blasé but couldn't quite pull it off.

Joe kept his smile to himself. "I'm not surprised. Your dad was a jock, too. What about soccer? Patrick was killer at soccer."

Brandon shook his head. "I played one year, but our coach was more into flirting with my mom than teaching me the game. Kinda sucked."

Joe had wondered about Lisa's love life over the years. She was so pretty and desirable. Although his mother had never mentioned any serious attachments, Lisa must have dated. "Did she like him?"

His nephew made a wry sound. "Hell, no. She wound up getting him kicked out of the league and coached my team herself. We made it to the finals, but afterward, we both decided soccer wasn't our sport."

Joe couldn't keep from grinning.

They'd reached the patio, where the lighting was brighter, and Brandon looked at him questioningly, obviously trying to figure out what his uncle's smile was all about. To mask his true feelings, which Joe wasn't sure he understood himself, he said, "I was trying to picture what would have happened if any of *my* Little League coaches ever looked twice at Mom."

Brandon's eyes went wide. "Gramps would have kicked some serious ass."

Joe laughed. "Isn't that the truth?"

"Don't get me wrong. Gramps was a great guy. I really miss him. But he could blow up like a firecracker if you pushed him wrong."

Joe knew that all too well. Patrick had butted heads with their father all the time. The only big fight Joe had ever had with his father was the one about selling the bar. "Your son died from drinking too much. Doesn't that mean anything to you?" Joe had cried, desperately seeking someone—something—to blame.

He turned abruptly and opened the patio door. The music was a little raucous for his taste, but he planned to keep his opinion to himself. He didn't want his nephew to think he was uncool.

"This would probably sound better on a car stereo," he said, walking to the stereo where he pushed the eject button.

"Yeah, it rocks," Brandon said when Joe handed him the silver disk. "Thanks."

Joe felt pleased. "You're welcome."

They faced each other awkwardly a moment, then Joe said, "Isn't it a little early on a Saturday night for you to be home?"

"There was a party. I didn't want to go."

Joe had a feeling there was more to the story, but he didn't push. He could hardly expect Brandon to open up when they barely knew each other.

Brandon shrugged off his jacket and dropped it in a chair, then sat on the couch and plopped his feet on the cluttered oak coffee table. His sneakers were a molded design in yellow leather with no visible laces.

"Can I ask you something?"

Joe turned off the stereo then walked to the chair across from Brandon and sat down. He didn't have a lot of experience with teens, but he knew his ex-girl-friend's daughters would never have asked permission to speak. Nor would they have listened to anything he said.

"Sure. What's up?"

"Do you know why Mom never talks about him anymore?"

"Who?"

"My dad. It's like he never existed. The other day she introduced me to some lady at the grocery store as Joe Kelly's grandson. Isn't that kinda weird?"

Joe didn't know what to make of it. Was it Lisa's way of moving on? "Maybe this is what happens when a person dies young. Pat's still eighteen in everyone's mind. Too young to be the father of a boy who is nearly the same age as Patrick was when he died."

Both were quiet a moment. Then Brandon said, "I suppose it could be that. She talked about him more when I was little, but now she gets tense whenever I mention his name. Grams thinks it's because Mom is worried about me driving." He lowered his gaze and added, "And drinking."

Joe sat forward. "You don't, do you?"

"Drink?"

By Brandon's hesitation, Joe could tell the boy was tempted to lie, but after a few seconds said, "Every-body does. But I've only been drunk once. A bunch of us were at a sleepover at a friend's house. We raided his father's liquor cabinet. When his parents came home, we were all puking our guts out."

Joe and Patrick had pulled the same trick, only they'd sneaked into Joe's Place to do their drinking. The twins and three of their friends had told their parents they were staying at each other's houses. In the morning, Joe Sr. had unlocked the door to find them all passed out. To everyone's surprise, the boys' only punishment had been scrubbing the barroom floor on their hands and knees once they were well.

Joe vaguely recalled overhearing his parents arguing about letting them off too lightly.

"They're just kids," his father had maintained. "Better they drink in the bar than out on the road."

Joe frowned. Would Pat be alive if their father had come down on him harder after that first incident?

"What happened?" he asked his nephew, curious whether or not parents were tougher these days.

"His folks called everyone's parents. Mom and Grandma Constance got there first. Grandma C checked each of us out then jumped down our throats for subjecting our bodies to alcohol poisoning." He made a face. "She practically made us all sick again when she described what a liver looks like after years of alcohol abuse."

He shook his head then added, "I couldn't drive for six months and was grounded for two. Plus, I had to go to Alateen. That's Al-Anon for people my age."

In *Dead Drunk,* Joe had followed a family whose teenage son was killed in a drunk-driving accident.

The siblings of his screen family had all attended the support group for teenagers dealing with alcohol-related issues. Unlike Joe's real family, who had never acknowledged Patrick's dependency problem.

"Did you get anything out of the meetings?" Joe asked. What he really wanted to ask was "Did you quit drinking?" But Joe didn't have the right to be that nosy.

"I guess so. I mostly went for my mom's sake. She's a total narc about drugs and alcohol. When my friends ask why I'm not drinking, I tell them it's because my dad died in a DUI, but some of them don't get it."

Joe had abstained from drinking for years. "I know what you mean," Joe said, sitting forward. "I was a pariah in college. Everybody knew me as the guy whose brother died in a drunk-driving crash. They were sympathetic for a while, then they'd say things like, 'Lighten up, man. Everybody's gotta die some time, right?'"

Brandon nodded in agreement. "Exactly. My friends act like I'm a freak for not wanting to put my mom and grandma through that again."

Joe's heart went out to his nephew. "Nobody thinks what happened to Patrick will happen to them. Nobody," he repeated, shaking his head. "And you can't tell them otherwise. I tried. My movie tried. People still drink too much then get behind the wheel...and die because of it."

"Do you drink?" Brandon asked.

"Not if I'm doing the driving." Joe wasn't a complete teetotaler anymore. "I'm a big fan of taxicabs," he said. "And if you ever need a ride anywhere, you call me and I'll pay your cab fare on my credit card."

Brandon gave a small chuckle. Joe could tell he didn't believe the offer was real, but Joe meant it. "Thanks, man. You're cool." He jumped to his feet. "Well, I guess I'd better get home. Mom's probably sitting up pretending to study. I don't know what she's going to use as an excuse to wait up for me once she graduates."

Joe smiled. He liked this kid. A lot. He stood up, too. "My mother was usually sitting here sewing when Pat and I came in. On nights she really wanted to heap on the guilt, she'd be patching our blue jeans."

Brandon rolled his eyes in sympathy, then held up his CD and nodded. "Later."

He was just about to the door when he paused and looked at Joe. "I'm glad you're here. This probably sounds stupid, but it's kinda like having a piece of my dad around."

A surfeit of emotions welled up in Joe's throat, threatening to choke him. He swallowed then said, "I'm glad to be here. But you do know we weren't identical twins, right?"

"Sure. There's a photo of the three of you at the bar. Mom's got a copy, too. It's of you and my dad and her sitting on the dock at some lake. You're all three wet and laughing. You can see a lot of family resemblance."

Joe knew which photo Brandon was talking about. He had a copy, too. On his bedroom dresser.

"Actually," Brandon said looking pensive. "It's the only picture of him in the house. I asked Mom the other day why she didn't have a picture of just her and Dad."

"What did she say?"

Brandon's shoulders lifted and fell. "Something like, 'This is who we were back then. It was always the three of us.'"

The boy slid the door open. "Well, I'd better hit the sack. Grams wants me to clean the garage in the morning. She's trying to decide whether to sell this place or rent it out. I vote rent it—to me," he added with a laugh.

After he was gone, Joe locked the door and turned off the lights. His mother had left the hallway light on upstairs—as she always had when he and his brother were young. Joe trudged up each step, exhausted yet restless and unsettled. Maybe that was what coming home was all about.

"FINE."

"You know I hate that word, Lisa Janine," Constance Malden snapped.

Lisa forced herself not to roll her eyes, another bad habit her mother hated. "How does 'okay' work for you?"

Her mother's coffee cup made a cracking sound when it hit the countertop. "What's wrong with you this morning? Your classes are over and you're just two exams away from finishing college. You should be celebrating," Constance said.

Lisa stifled a sigh. Two women living under one roof was at times...challenging, to say the least. It helped that her mother had her own wing, complete with a separate entrance, but they still shared a kitchen. Some mornings the arrangement was enough to drive Lisa running from the house screaming.

"Sorry, Mom. I didn't sleep well. Brandon was late coming in. I was afraid he was out partying, but then I found out he was next door the whole time listening to music with Joe."

Constance took a sip of coffee. "That's a good thing, isn't it?"

Lisa shrugged.

"How is Joe? Is he planning to stay a while this time?"

The harmless question made Lisa turn around sharply to look at her mother. Was she interested in Joe? No. Don't be ridiculous, Lisa scolded herself. She was being neurotic.

Of course, she'd thought that before and had found out the hard way just how needy her mother was when it came to vying for the attention of attractive young men.

"Turns out he's here on a mission," Lisa said. "He plans to make some kind of movie about Joe's Place."

Constance's jaw dropped. "Really? What does that mean to your plans?"

Lisa rubbed her temple, hoping to relieve the sharp pain she felt there. "I don't know. Which is another reason I'm grouchy this morning."

Constance walked to the stove where Lisa was standing. She looped an arm supportively around Lisa's shoulders. "I'm so sorry, honey. Do you want me to talk to him for you? Get him to back off?"

It took every ounce of self-control Lisa had not to scream, "No. Stay away from him." Instead, she shook her head and said, "I plan to sit down with him today and talk this over."

Her mother poured the dregs of her coffee in the sink and placed the cup on the counter. "Well, I hope he changes his mind. You've been so happy and excited over this idea. A lovely change from the dour looks I've seen the past few months." She sighed as she walked to the door. "I know the last semester of college is a rough one, but gads, girl, you'd think someone died."

After checking her lipstick in a little mirror, Constance snapped her purse closed. "What else are you doing today?"

"Wash my car then study till it's time for Maureen's barbecue. You were invited, remember?"

"Oh, right. Did you tell Maureen I had plans? Jerry's taking me to a Celtic festival in Livermore. I swear he's the first man I ever dated who likes to do things in public." She gave a little giggle. "Well, you know what I mean. He's fun. I like him." She knocked on the wooden door trim as if for good luck, then left.

Once she was gone, Lisa took a deep breath and let it out. "It's a wonder I'm not crazier than I am."

She grinned, recalling a time when she'd said those words to Joe and Patrick. The three of them had been headed somewhere in Joe Sr.'s old truck. Joe behind the wheel and Lisa on Patrick's lap, sharing a seat belt.

Patrick had chortled and said, "Babe, you are crazy, especially in bed. Just the way I like you to be."

Lisa had buried her head in his shoulder in embarrassment, but when she peeked at Joe, she'd seen him blushing, too. She didn't know why that reaction had touched her so much. Joe was the sensitive one. He felt other people's pain in a way Patrick couldn't imagine.

Would that empathy help when it came to haggling over his parents' bar? She certainly hoped so. Because if her current plan fell through, Lisa had no idea what she was going to do. She had a stack of job applications sitting on her desk. She'd participated in several hiring fairs. Two out-of-state schools had expressed an interest in hiring her to teach at the elementary level, but Lisa couldn't bring herself to respond.

Why? She had her reasons. One of her favorites was that she didn't want to pull Brandon out of school his senior year. That made her a good mother, not a coward. Right?

JOE AWOKE TO THE SOUND of a car door. He managed to ignore it and go back to sleep, but he still heard the sound of water splashing and soon he dreamed he was frolicking on a Slip 'n' Slide with Lisa. In the buff.

When his body alerted him to the impact of such a dream, he opened his eyes, groaning. "Cripes, I haven't been home twenty-four hours and I've got a hard-on over Lisa? Pat would have gotten a laugh over that."

Not one to waste a good fantasy, Joe closed his eyes and let his imagination run. The relief was temporary, but the distraction was nice.

After a long shower and quick shave in the adjoining bathroom, Joe returned to his room and looked outside to see what the weather had in store. Shorts? Or jeans, he wondered, opening the curtain.

What he saw was his morning fantasy alive and well, which was enough to make the towel he'd tucked around his waist flutter to life. Lisa washing her car. In cutoff shorts and a sloppy white T-shirt that showed her bra. Even at a distance, he could see her nipples. "There ought to be a law against this," he muttered.

"Against what?" a voice said from the doorway.

Mortified, Joe angled his body toward the window. "Nothing."

Maureen eyed him intently with an all-knowing look then backed up. "When you're dressed, there's fruit and bagels on the counter and fresh coffee," she called. "I was just heading off on my morning walk and thought I'd see if you wanted to join me. But since you're busy ogling Lisa, I'll let you be."

Ogling Lisa? Joe stifled a groan. His erection disappeared. He tried to tell himself he was a grown man and didn't need to apologize for a natural reaction to seeing a gorgeous woman scrubbing a fender, but he gave up. A man is just a boy with big feet when his mother was in the picture, he decided.

Fifteen minutes later, armed with an oversize mug of green tea instead of coffee—another of his doctor's recommendations—he walked around the side of his parents' house and across the Greenbergs' front lawn to reach the Maldens' driveway.

He was in luck. The sound of water spraying against metal meant Lisa was still at work. He slowed to a stroll, trying to come up with a clever opening remark. Since the Greenbergs' hedge had filled in over the years, he had to detour slightly to get around it. As he approached, he was hidden from view but close enough to hear Brandon speaking to his mother.

"I'm outta here."

"Wait," she squawked. "Where are you going? Didn't you promise your grandmother you'd clean out her garage?"

Joe remembered hearing that last night.

"Later. When I come back."

"From where?"

"From where I'm going. What is this? The third degree?"

Joe bit back a smile. The boy's defensive tone reminded Joe of Patrick.

With more patience than Maureen had ever shown her sons, Lisa said, "No. It's Sunday morning. You have family obligations this afternoon, and you made a commitment to do some work for your grandmother.

I let you sleep in and now you're repaying that favor by being snippy and rude."

"Whatever," Brandon groused. "Joe gave me this new CD last night, and I want to show it to Rory. Is that a crime?"

"Not if you come right back."

"Fine," he snarled.

A car door slammed.

Joe waited until Brandon's engine was just a muffled hum in the distance before joining her. Not because he was a coward, but because he didn't want Lisa to feel embarrassed. He'd once been privy to an argument between his ex-girlfriend and her daughter and both had treated him strangely for days.

"Hi," he said, calling over the sound of water being sprayed against a hubcap. Joe had a feeling the VW's tires were getting extra attention as Lisa worked off her frustration.

She spun around in surprise. The barrel of the nozzle followed. Joe had to leap to one side to avoid getting doused.

"Oh, dang, I'm sorry," she cried, dropping her aim. "You startled me. I was thinking about my bratty son."

Joe brushed a few stray drops of water from his yellow polo shirt. "No problem. It's only water. Where's the kid?"

She pointed down the street. "He went to his friend's house. I'm hoping he'll be back soon. He has chores to do."

"Chores on a Sunday?"

"Gas money. His grandmother is more generous than I am. Around here he works for food and clothing. The money he makes cleaning Joe's Place goes straight for insurance, but Maureen takes pity on him and hires him to help out at her house any time he asks. She pays him in advance, too. Which is fine as long as he lives up to his part of the bargain."

"You're a good mother, aren't you?"

A blush claimed her cheeks and she turned around to pick up a bucket of soapy water. "I try to be consistent. Kids need that."

"Too bad more people don't. My ex had three daughters. There were many times that the eleven-year-old seemed more responsible than her mother."

"Was that Paula?" Lisa asked. "Your mother thought you were serious about her."

"Paulette," he corrected. "We broke up last fall. Neither of us wanted to pretend through the holidays."

"Pretend what?"

"That we were more than two people who liked the same restaurants."

"That's all you had in common?"

Joe took a drink of his tea. "Pretty much."

Lisa shook her head. "Wow. It took you quite a while to figure that out, didn't it?"

Joe didn't like to think about Paulette. He'd known for a long time that she wasn't the right woman for him, and he'd been certain she'd felt the same, but somehow neither had got around to ending things. "Three years."

He couldn't read Lisa's expression but still felt compelled to explain. "She's the daughter of a well-known Hollywood producer. At one time he was under the mistaken belief I was some kind of wunderkind with a camera. He and Paulette were going to coproduce one of my movies."

"What happened?"

"Nothing."

"That must have been disappointing."

Joe shrugged. "It's a crazy business, what can I say?"

She moved to another tire. "Is that the real reason behind this visit? You're tired of Hollywood?"

He wasn't ready to talk about his motives, especially since he hadn't pinned down the focus of his movie completely. "They say timing is everything and since I found myself with a little window of opportunity, I thought this was a perfect chance to spend some time with Mom before some guy whisks her away in an RV."

Lisa didn't say anything. Changing the subject, he asked, "What other kinds of chores does Brandon do?"

"He does the laundry every other week, and we all three take turns cooking, although lately Mom's been gone a lot. And since I hate grocery shopping, he and Connie share that duty."

"Wow. He sounds pretty self-reliant."

She glanced up. "I don't know about that, but some of his friends couldn't even tell you how to turn on a dishwasher."

When she bent over to apply the soapy sponge to the tires, her shirt rode up, exposing a sweet inch of bare skin. Joe had always loved the color of her skin—a warm beige that turned berry brown in the summer. The urge to touch her made his fingers tingle.

As if sensing his inappropriate intentions, she shifted to a squat and tugged down her frayed T-shirt. "What about Paulette's daughters? Didn't Maureen tell me one lives at home? Were you close?"

"Not really. The oldest is studying entertainment law at Yale. The middle girl is Brandon's age, but she's been in boarding school since before I met her mother. She's graduating early to go to Harvard. And Minnie, the youngest, is eleven. She wants to be a Laker Girl."

Lisa rocked back on her heels and laughed. "Good for her. The first two sound intensely determined not to follow in their mother's footsteps."

Like you? "That's probably their father's influence. They spend their summers with him in Italy. He's a successful actor, although he's never worked in Hollywood."

"Did they approve of you?"

Joe shrugged. "To be honest, I don't think they cared. Does Brandon like the men you date?"

Her left eyebrow rose in a questioning arch. "I've been too busy to have much of a social life." Joe wanted to ask why men weren't asking her out every weekend, but she didn't let him. "Raising children is a tough job. I'm sure your friend did the best she could with her daughters, but there comes a time when you have to admit you've lost any control you thought you had."

Her sigh competed with the sound of the hose rinsing the tire. "Brandon and I used to be pals, but there are times…like this morning…when I'm suddenly the archenemy sent to ruin his life."

Joe wondered if he should mention that he'd overheard, but Lisa distracted him by asking, "So, does Little Miss Laker Girl spend her summers in Italy, too?"

"Different father. Paulette claims he was a one-night stand on a stopover in the middle of the Pacific."

Lisa stopped scrubbing to look at him.

"I know. It sounds improbable, right? But Paulette insists that's what happened. Too many mai tais and nine months later, she has Minnie to show for it. The stranger in paradise is long gone."

An odd look of distress crossed Lisa's face. Assuming she was concerned for Minnie's sake, he added, "But Min doesn't seem the worse for it. Her grandparents spoil her rotten, and she visits her sisters every summer.

"She's a cool kid. Her accidental father doesn't know what he's missing."

Lisa spun around abruptly and applied all her attention to scrubbing one pristine hubcap. Joe felt a tension that hadn't existed before. To lighten the moment, he said, "I took Minnie to dinner to explain that her mother and I were breaking up. She said she wasn't surprised. I believe her exact words were, 'You're a nice man, Joe, but too self-absorbed to be a husband and a full-time dad.'"

Lisa's head snapped up. "She's eleven? Yikes. That had to hurt."

More than he wanted to admit. "As a friend, you're supposed to say something like, 'What do kids know?'"

"Oh, sorry," she said with a chuckle. "I'm really lousy at faking sympathy."

"I know. I remember one time when I told you I thought you'd make a good nurse and you slugged me."

"I did?"

"It was the night Patrick blacked out on the football field and they took him away in an ambulance, remember?"

She seemed to ponder the question for a moment. "Sorta. You and I hung out in the waiting room while your mom was with Patrick, right?"

Joe nodded. He could picture the moment as clearly as if he'd filmed it. Probably because he had. *I wonder if that tape is still around?* "You were giving me a hard time because I wouldn't do the twin thing and try to contact Pat telepathically."

An aha look crossed her face. "And you were doing that annoying 'cub reporter' thing that used to drive me crazy." She held the hose nozzle up to her lips and said in a deep voice, "So tell me, Miss Malden, when did you first learn that you carried the mysterious kiss-of-life gene? Is it true that by pressing your lips to my brother's you could bring him back from the brink of death?"

Joe let out a gruff hoot. "Damn fine impersonation. I really was an ass, wasn't I?"

She smiled saucily. "The only reason I didn't deck you that night was that I knew joking around was your way of hiding how scared you really were."

"Hmmm," he said taking a sip of the now tepid tea. "What other deep, dark secrets do you know about me?"

Although he'd been speaking rhetorically, her cheeks turned crimson and she stammered, "N-nothing."

Turning her back to him, she emptied the wash bucket on the pavement then picked up the hose to rinse off the bubbles.

Odd, Joe thought, watching her. They'd both had secrets back then, although his unrequited feelings were pretty obvious. He'd loved her, but she'd picked Patrick. For six years, being with Lisa had not been an option—until graduation. A memory Joe still felt guilty about. Was that the source of her embarrassment, too?

He'd tried to talk to her about the incident last night and she'd shut him down. He wasn't going to waste the effort this morning. "So," he said, once she turned off the water, "tell me about my new stepfather-to-be."

Lisa let out a small sigh. For a moment she'd been afraid Joe was going to ask her something she didn't want to answer. They needed to talk…and soon, but she didn't see how waiting until after Maureen's wedding—and the sale of Joe's Place—could hurt. Joe's mother deserved some happiness, and Lisa intended to see that her nuptials went smoothly.

"You've met Gunny, haven't you?" Lisa asked, wringing out her chamois.

She noticed that his gaze seemed fixed on her arms. His attention made her glad she'd worked out regularly at the gym all through college.

"Uh-huh. A couple of times, but I never thought they acted like two people who were madly in love. You know what I mean? I thought they were just friends."

Love? Was Maureen in love with Gunny? Lisa didn't think so. The couple's relationship seemed more about mutual loneliness and friendship than great passion. When she'd been younger, Lisa couldn't have fathomed such a thing, but now she was glad for any happiness Maureen could grab.

"What do you want to know? He's a few years younger than your mom. He retired early after selling his computer business. He has bundles of money and he treats her like a queen."

She draped the chamois over the wash bucket then started winding up her hose. "Your mom says Gunny's zest for life is good medicine for her, but, in all honesty, I get pooped when I'm around him too long."

Joe followed her to the hose bib. "Why are they getting married? Couldn't they just travel together? She's not pregnant, is she?" he asked with a wink.

Lisa gave him a get-real look, but inside she chuckled. She'd missed his wicked sense of humor. "I suggested that—the roommate part, not the pregnancy. But your mother says it wouldn't look right. Even if the world is going—"

"To hell in a handbasket," Joe finished. They'd always been the kind of friends who completed each other's sentences. "I take it that's still one of her favorite sayings?"

Lisa nodded, a little choked up for some reason. She gave her attention to the hose. After a minute, he asked, "So, we're confident this guy's not just after her money?"

She tried to smile, but the effort must not have succeeded because Joe said, "Either I'm losing my touch or you're not happy about this wedding."

The sad fact was Lisa felt closer to Maureen than she did her own mother. She honestly didn't know what she'd do with Maureen gone. Maybe that was another reason Lisa wanted to buy the bar, to keep a part of the past intact.

"I'm going to miss her. That's all," she said. "But she told me when they're not traveling, they'd live at Gunny's place on Lake Tulloch. So she'll be close by."

Joe was studying her face as if he could read something she didn't want him to see. "Be honest. Yes or no. Do you like him?"

Lisa swallowed. *Yes and no.* "Brandon thinks he's awesome because he owns a Corvette, but to me, he's the man who's taking your mom away. I guess that makes me kind of selfish, huh?"

"I know the two of you are close…"

"She's a *real* mother, Joe. You know that."

Lisa moved to the opposite side of the car. She

didn't like talking about Constance. Although her mother had reformed a bit over the years, Lisa still felt resentful about the early years when Constance's social life had seemed to take precedence over her daughter's needs.

"Is Connie serious about this new guy?" Joe's tone resonated with sympathetic understanding. He'd been privy to many of Lisa's gripes about her mother's lifestyle when they were kids. Patrick had never seemed to understand why Constance's sex life bothered Lisa so much. "So she sleeps around," he'd once said. "Big deal. Who's she hurting?"

"Me," Lisa had wanted to cry, but she'd kept the words inside. He wouldn't have understood anyway.

"I don't know. But he *is* single, at least."

"See?" Joe exclaimed. "I was right when I said that Jezebel thing was just a phase. I knew Constance would go legit someday."

Lisa's mouth dropped open. She couldn't believe he recalled a prediction he'd made nearly twenty years earlier during a game of Truth or Dare. "You remember that?"

"Of course." His grin was effused with the damnable Kelly charm that made her knees weak and her brain turn to applesauce. She carried the remainder of her car-washing implements into the garage. She needed distance to gain control of her emotions. Even though the old attraction still existed between them, she couldn't let Joe distract her from her goal. There was too much at stake—her son's future, for one thing.

Lisa had promised Brandon four years of college, and she planned to see that he got it.

Brandon was a great kid, but had turned into a teenage tyrant almost overnight after his grandfather died. He'd become secretive and touchy. He missed curfews regularly and argued about every little thing Lisa asked him to do. He even blew off his grandmother's requests for help, like this morning. And Lisa was afraid he might be experimenting with alcohol.

Lisa understood, or thought she did. She'd gone through a rebellious stage herself, and was just beginning to comprehend the results of her actions seventeen years earlier.

In one of her psychology classes, she'd learned that one's underlying beliefs colored a person's perception of the world and triggered certain unconscious responses. Lisa believed she'd slept with Joe Kelly on graduation night because he was leaving—the way her father had. The way all the men she loved did.

Because of her impulsive decision, Lisa had wound up pregnant. For reasons only Patrick could explain, he'd chosen to tell a lie—a lie that had made Lisa believe *he* was the father of her child. A lie that Lisa had wholeheartedly accepted until a casual remark from Maureen had brought Patrick's "truth" into question. If Patrick wasn't Brandon's father, then only one other man could be.

Now, Lisa was faced with the biggest decision of her life. Did she tell Joe what she suspected—and prove to the community of Worthington that, like her mother,

Lisa had no morals? After all, what kind of woman slept with one brother when she was going steady with the other?

CHAPTER FOUR

"HEY, LEESE, WOULD YOU DO ME a favor?"

Lisa was so wrapped up in her inner turmoil she'd
almost forgotten Joe's presence. She gave her head a
stern shake. *Later,* she told herself. You can figure out
the past after you take care of business.

"Sure," she said. "If it doesn't take long. I've still
got some studying to do before your mother's party.
And I told her I'd make deviled eggs."

He finished off whatever was in his cup and walked
to where she was standing. "Can you spare an hour?
I'd like to scope out the town. Driving around in your
convertible would give me good visuals, and I'm sure
you could help stir up old memories."

Scope out Worthington? Stir up memories? Was he
nuts? But no plausible excuse came to mind, so she
said, "I suppose so…if we could do it now."

He lifted his mug. "Let me run this home and leave
a note for Mom. She said she was going for a walk,
but she didn't say how long that takes."

"Usually about an hour—unless she bumps into
somebody and gets talking. And this is Sunday. She
might have stopped at the church."

The Kellys were Irish Catholic—Lisa's mother a self-professed "lapsed agnostic." When Lisa and Patrick had become engaged, Lisa had started taking classes to join the church but had dropped out after he died. Being an unmarried mother seemed contrary to church doctrine. When Maureen had offered to have baby Brandon baptized, Lisa had supported the idea, but ever since his grandfather's death, Brandon had turned his back on religion.

"Mom said something about talking business this morning. Maybe there'll be time when we get back."

Lisa's stomach made a funny noise. Lately, she'd been too tense to eat. She hoped that once the fate of Joe's Place was decided, she'd be able to stop worrying.

"It would probably be better if the two of you talked first. Maureen has my offer. A Realtor friend of Mom's drew it up for me. He's going to handle the escrow account, if Maureen decides she wants to sell to me."

Joe looked as though he wanted to say something but changed his mind. "Okay, then, I'll be back in a second. The bulk of my equipment should be arriving tomorrow, but all I need right now is my camera."

He disappeared, sprinting around the hedge like the boy he used to be.

Lisa was still standing, hands on her hips, trying to figure out how Joe's filmmaking would affect her, when Maureen walked up.

"You look perplexed."

Lisa took a deep breath and let it out. "Your son was

here. He asked me to drive him around town so he could check out all the changes."

"Really? Why doesn't he just take my car and go look for himself?"

Lisa shrugged. "Maybe he's used to having a chauffeur."

Maureen threw back her head and laughed. Her white bob bounced around cheeks that had filled out in the time since her final chemo treatment. "More likely he just wants to spend time with you. He is a single man, after all."

Lisa didn't like the speculative look in Maureen's eye. Maureen was a wise woman who had stepped into her husband's role as counselor to a great many patrons of Joe's Place, but Lisa doubted Joe had confided in her.

Joe was a relative stranger to both women—a wild card, and Lisa needed to remember that. She would keep her guard up until after escrow closed. If escrow closed. But she didn't mention that. To Maureen, she said, "Joe suggested we sit down together after our little reconnaissance mission and discuss the sale of Joe's Place."

Maureen shook her head. "Won't have time. Gunny just called." She pointed to the cell phone attached to her waist. Lisa had insisted Maureen carry it after a fainting episode last summer. "His daughter-in-law has some kind of event scheduled this evening, so he wants to do the barbecue earlier. They should be arriving around one. Are you still making your wonderful deviled eggs?"

Lisa nodded. She wanted to finalize the sale, but this was a big decision for Maureen and Lisa wasn't about to pressure her. "I already boiled the eggs. They won't take long to mix up when Joe and I get back." She looked at her watch. "But I need to review my notes for tomorrow's final at some point. When are we eating?"

"You tell me. If you need more time, Gunny's daughter-in-law will have to fend for herself."

Lisa felt a rush of emotion that almost brought tears to her eyes. Maureen's unfailing support—from baby-sitting when Lisa needed to study, to "loans" for books and supplies—was one of the reasons Lisa was graduating. She closed the distance between them and hugged her "almost" mother-in-law. "You are a treasure. I'm going to miss you so much."

Maureen hugged her back. "Well, I'm not gone, yet. We still have four more weeks together. And way too much to do. The barbecue today, your graduation party…"

"Maureen, I told you not to bother. It's almost anticlimactic considering how long it's taken me to get through college."

Joe dashed around the neighbor's hedge and joined them, flushed and boyishly cute. "Did I hear the word 'climax'?"

His mother shook her head and looked skyward as if petitioning God for strength. "No. You did not. You heard Lisa being modest and selfless, but we are ignoring her because when someone we love accomplishes a major milestone, we celebrate. Right?"

Joe looked at Lisa, his eyes behind his sunglasses unreadable. "Absolutely," he said without hesitation. "And I'll film the whole thing." He lifted the expensive-looking silver-and-black camera he was carrying, removed the protective lens cover and focused on her. "Let's start now."

Lisa put up her hands defensively. "I don't think so. Maureen, distract him while I run for cover. Good grief, I don't even have eye makeup on."

She could hear mother and son laughing as she ran toward the house. She opened the door that led into the kitchen but paused to remind Maureen, "If your guests are coming early, you'd better call Martin. And my irresponsible son is at his friend's house. If he gets home before your company arrives, grab him by the ear and put him to work. Okay?"

Maureen made a dismissing gesture with her hand. "Oh, pooh, he's just being a boy. You and Patrick were the same way, right, Joseph? Your father could never get you to help out as much as he thought you should."

Lisa jerked the door shut and leaned back against it to catch her breath. You and Patrick… All too frequently, Maureen said things like that which made Lisa feel like an absolute fraud. But was it her fault the man she trusted to do the right thing got drunk and drove his car into a canal, leaving her with an unborn child to raise alone?

She took a deep breath and pushed away from the door. Feeling sorry for herself wouldn't help matters. Neither did blaming Patrick. She was the only one who could fix this mess, and as far as she could tell, she had two choices: keep silent or tell Joe.

JOE SAT SIDEWAYS in the Bug's seat, using his knee against the door to anchor his elbow as he aimed the camera out the window. This wouldn't be great footage. His digital camcorder was an amazingly versatile workhorse, but shooting from moving vehicles would look amateurish. No matter what.

He didn't care. This morning's outing was more about scouting the landscape as he built the story in his mind. He and Lisa had been driving around for about forty minutes. He was well aware of her time constraints because his mother had pulled him aside after Lisa had gone into the house.

"Don't monopolize her time," Maureen had scolded. "She's maintained a four-point grade average the whole time she's been in college. It would break her heart to mess that up now."

Thinking about his mother's words, Joe turned to his driver and said, "Mom said you're a perfect student. That's pretty impressive. Are you valedictorian of your class?"

Lisa laughed—a familiar sound that left him a little blue and wanting something he couldn't name. "Not even close. Kids today are amazingly bright. The top three students of my graduating class came *into* college with four-point-six GPAs. I was purely a B student in high school. You were the brain."

She glanced at him and added, "My goal was to get

an A in every class. Which is partly why it took me so long to finish. Raising a child and working didn't leave a lot of time for studying, so I never took more than three classes a semester. Sometimes, if I had a particularly tough subject, I might do only one or two."

"How many classes do you have this term?"

"Four, but two were electives and I finished them early. My last two finals are with teachers who don't pull any punches. One is on testing. The other is the psychology of the young child."

"That's right. Mom said you'd changed your major to education," he said. The fact that she'd had a dozen or so majors over the years had baffled him since Joe had known from the minute he'd picked up his first still camera what he wanted to do with his life.

"Yes. My plan is to work on my foreign language skills while Brandon is in college. I thought it might be fun to teach English in a foreign country."

Lisa living in a foreign country? The idea held no appeal. He changed the subject. "The air looks particularly crappy today," he said aiming the camera toward the east. "You can't even see the mountains." He panned skyward. "Do people around here still refuse to call this brown haze smog?"

"Denial. It's easier to point the finger at agriculture than admit that the car you're driving a hundred miles a day is the culprit."

He'd almost forgotten how bright she was. He used to love to spar with her verbally. Before he could think of something clever to add, she said, "When Brandon and I lived in Turlock, we didn't even own a car. I rode everywhere on my bike with a child carrier on the back."

He turned off the camera. "When did you live in Turlock?"

She tugged down on the brim of her ball cap. "Um, when Brandon was in preschool. Constance and I had a big fight, and I moved out. For about six months. Being a single mom, working part-time and taking classes while paying for day care was tough. Plus, Brandon really missed his grandparents and they missed him. I agreed to move back on the condition that Mom build a separate suite so we could each have more privacy."

Interesting. Joe wondered what had triggered the blowup but decided it wasn't any of his business.

She put on her blinker. The green sign said 18th Street, but to locals, the six-block-long road that led straight to Joe's Place was Main.

By rising up, his knee folded under him on the seat, Joe could see over the windshield. He put the soft eye-piece to his right eye. The auto-focus gave him his first daylight look at the familiar brick front and kelly-green double doors he'd entered a million times.

Panning first left, then right, he took in the store-fronts he'd frequented as a child. Mallory's Drug. The Shoe Box. Guy's Barbershop, where Guy Pendleton held court and exchanged gossip. Guy and Joe's dad had been best friends until Guy had developed Hodgkin's lymphoma and died.

The buildings were the same, but most of the names had been changed. He turned off the camera and set it on his lap while he reached for the notebook to log the shot. "There are more shops open than I imagined there would be, but hardly any that I remember," he said, copying the time code before writing in an abbreviated shorthand very few people could interpret, "Mn St. New vers/old serv. Guy's gone now W lattice arch name Let Us Beautify You."

He studied the beauty parlor that had expanded to take over Guy's. This was where Lisa had first got her ears pierced. Patrick had had football practice that day so Joe had filled in. There, among the sharp smells and girly trappings, he'd held Lisa's hand in public. He'd shared her fear, her pain and her exhilaration. He'd even picked out the earrings she put in. Tiny gold hearts.

He looked at her ears. She wasn't wearing earrings, but, God, she was beautiful. A black ball cap. Hair twisted in place by something that looked like a gold tuning fork. Her oversize sunglasses matched the car—sunshine yellow.

"I'm glad you left your hair long. It's still beautiful."

She made a snorting sound that he used to hate. Well, at one time, when he was madly in love with her, he'd thought it was cute, but then he went through a period where everything she did pissed him off.

We're back to cute, huh? That probably wasn't a good sign.

"It's not mine," Lisa said, brushing an errant strand off her neck. It immediately dropped back against the collar of her soft-pink shirt.

"I beg your pardon?"

She made an offhand gesture. "I'm growing it for Locks of Love, a program that gives human-hair wigs to people who have lost their hair, through burns or chemo or illness. Once this mop reaches the right length—my hairdresser measures it every time I have it trimmed—I'll cut it off and send it to the group."

Joe picked up his camera. He didn't care how deserving the charity, the thought of her cutting her hair made him slightly ill. He trained the lens on Joe's Place, which was dead ahead, and pushed the On toggle.

"Do you remember when the city council talked about making my dad move so they could turn Joe's Place into the chamber of commerce or something?"

"No."

"Might have been before you moved here. They felt that having a bar at the head of Main Street gave people the wrong impression about our community."

"Oh, for heaven's sake," she exclaimed. "I bet your father had a heyday with that."

Joe grinned, picturing his father ranting about the injustice. "The city council wants to pretend that people don't drink and smoke and carouse, but the mayor is one of my best customers," he'd cried. "That's called hypocrisy, son, and if you do nothing else in your life, make damn sure you're not a hypocrite."

A sour taste rose in his throat. "Slow down," he said, adding another description in his notebook under the previous entry. By the time he was done filming, he'd have multiple logbooks filled with notations.

"Please," Lisa said.

Joe glanced sideways. "Huh?"

Her cheeks colored. "'Slow down, please.' That's what I would have said to my son. I'm still working on his manners seventeen years later."

An odd feeling—something akin to what Joe felt when things were going right when he was shooting—made him drop back down into the seat. He stared at her a moment. She was beautiful. Her skin luminous, her cheekbones dusted in blush that came from the inside out.

A thought struck him. *How could I possibly have gone so long without talking to her, without being with her?*

She gave him an exasperated look that reminded him of Brandon. "What are you staring at? Do you want me to apologize? I'm sorry. It's a terrible habit. I've even corrected complete strangers."

He took a deep breath to still the undercurrents of awareness rushing through him. *Stop. This is Lisa. Your almost sister-in-law.* He tightened his hold on the camera. "No. That's not it. I…uh, I always thought Brandon resembled Patrick, but when you make that pouty look with your lips, you look just like him. Or he looks like you. Oh, hell, you know what I mean."

He returned to his previous position and made a

show of panning the front of Joe's Place, but his mind was racing. He hadn't even been home twenty-four hours and all he could think about was kissing Lisa. Which was insane. It hadn't been right for them twenty years ago. It wasn't right now.

He zoomed in for a better view of the hand-painted billboard that spanned four feet on either side above the door. Someone had recently freshened up the green and gold.

"How's business?" he asked, casting about for a general topic of discussion.

"Steady. The regulars still show up for a pit stop after work. There are always a few who stay too long and need their spouses to come after them, but most have a beer or two then head out. After your mom came back to work, she decided to change the menu. We call the grill a bistro, now. Classy, huh?"

Joe wondered whose idea that was but he didn't ask. Since there were no cars behind them, Lisa let the car idle at a stop. He shot the building's two picture windows then turned off the camera. "I have to say, my dad would have hated the geraniums," he said as he jotted his notes.

Lisa's low chuckle sounded sexier than it had in his dream that morning. "I know. Martin and I both voted against the flower boxes, but your mother had the final say. She told us she wanted to be able to look out from behind the bar and see life." Lisa sighed. "Pretty hard to argue after all that she's been through."

Joe was glad Lisa told him the rationale behind the

ornamentation before he said something stupid that might have hurt his mother's feelings.

"So? Where now?" Lisa asked.

He checked his watch. His allotted hour was up. "Home. I don't want to jinx your perfect grade-point average."

Her grin held an element of chagrin. "I have to admit I am ready to head back. Not to study, but to see if Brandon showed up. He used to be so dependable, but lately…"

She sounded worried. Too worried. "Hey, I'm not exactly an authority, but my friends tell me the teen-age years are the roughest. A combination of hormones and the desire for independence."

"Yeah, I know. It's just that…"

"What?"

"Oh, nothing." She pointed to a popular fast-food restaurant on the corner. "This is new. Do you remember when it was an Amoco station? Look at the three-story play area. Brandon would have loved this place. Not that we could afford to eat out very often back then, but he would have gone crazy."

Joe was curious about her life. And Brandon's. It was probably too late to be a better uncle and brother-in-law, but he wouldn't mind being their friend. If Lisa would let him.

"MARVELOUS DEVILED EGGS, Lisa," Gunny said, his booming voice echoing around the Kelly's backyard.

Lisa, preoccupied with making sure her son didn't

gulp a few bites of his grandmother's delicious meal then run off, answered absently, "Thank you, Gunny. I buy the eggs from an organic farmer from Mariposa. He sells them at the local farmer's market every Saturday."

"And he's a hunk," Maureen added with a wink. "Amazing what a little fresh air and exercise can do for a body."

Her fiancé dropped his arm around Maureen's shoulders and squeezed her possessively. "How old is he?"

Maureen wriggled free. "Lisa's age, but she ignores his flirting—even when he gives her free vegetables."

Lisa felt her cheeks heat up. "He does that for all his repeat customers. Last time, he gave Maureen a vegetarian cookbook to test out some new recipes at the restaurant. Isn't this potato salad from that book, Maureen? More, Gunny?" she asked, passing the bowl his way.

Gunny's bushy white eyebrows collided. "I don't think I like the idea of my fiancée flirting with a good-looking farmer. No more Saturday markets for you, my dear."

Maureen motioned for Lisa to hand her the ceramic bowl. "Oh, for Pete's sake. The man is young enough to be my son."

Lisa sent Joe a plea for help. This was the second near-squabble between the engaged couple since Gunny and his family had arrived. The first had taken place when Gunny—no doubt in an attempt to fill the role of patriarch—had tried to light the barbecue, which even Lisa knew had a mind of its own. In fact, Patrick used to call it Pops—both as a sly reference to his father's explosive temper and because of the noise the burners made when starting.

After narrowly avoiding the scary burst of pyrotechnics, Gunny had received a tongue-lashing from Maureen. "You can't just take over, Gunner. There is protocol, and a woman's grill deserves a little respect."

No one, particularly not Gunny's son and his wife, had anything to add to that.

"Mom," Joe said, "did you say there was more bread?"

The distraction worked. Maureen went into the house without further comment.

Lisa, who was sitting beside Gunny's daughter-in-law, Christine, let out a sigh.

"She's rather feisty, isn't she?" Christine said. The woman, who bore a striking resemblance to Jodie Foster, was about Lisa's age, but that appeared to be the only thing the two had in common.

"Maureen is the most genuine person I've ever met," Lisa said in Joe's mother's defense. "You never have to wonder where you stand with her. She tells you, bluntly and honestly."

Christine's smile seemed forced. "That's um…refreshing. Michael's mother was far more old-world. She worshipped Gunny and he her. I've never seen two people more in love. Was Maureen's marriage like that?"

Lisa frowned. Maureen and Joe Sr. had been devoted to each other, but Lisa had never known two more independent souls. "They were married for nearly forty years."

"But longevity isn't a sure sign of a happy relationship, is it?"

Lisa pictured a couple of the men her mother had dated—men who had been married at the time. "No more than a ring on the finger guarantees a lasting union."

One of Christine's eyebrows rose in a perfect arch. "May I be frank? Are you and Joe comfortable with this marriage?"

Me and Joe? Did the woman have the mistaken idea that Joe and Lisa were a couple? "I have no idea how Joe feels. He only got here yesterday, and we really haven't had a chance to discuss things. I want whatever Maureen wants. If Gunny makes her happy, then I'll keep any reservations I might have to myself."

"So, you do have reservations."

Christine flicked her hand to get her husband's attention. Michael had been talking to his father, so both men looked her way. "It's not just me," Christine said triumphantly. "Linda has qualms about this wedding, as well."

"Lisa," Lisa corrected. "And I didn't say—"

Gunny gave Lisa a sour look. "What is wrong with you people? Can't two people share their twilight years in peace without their kids bickering behind their backs? If this is about your inheritance…"

Joe and Brandon turned to listen. Thankfully, Maureen was still inside. Lisa cleared her throat and said, "This has nothing to do with money. I'm not even a member of the family, legally. I simply answered Christine's question. She asked me if I was happy about you and Maureen marrying. I'll repeat what I told her to your face, Gunny.

"I love Maureen and will miss her more than I can say, but if you make her happy then she has my full support."

"I'll second that," Joe said, holding his can of soda up in a toast.

Lisa's jaw went slack. She was used to fighting her battles alone, but knowing she had backup if needed was an unusual feeling. One she liked.

"Hey, everyone," Maureen called from the porch. "Martin's here. And you'll never guess what he brought. Rattlesnake."

Christine made a gagging sound and sank back in her chair. Michael looked at his father. "Who's Martin?"

Gunny frowned. "Bartender. Works for Maureen."

Brandon pushed back from the table and hurried to meet the man who was carrying a covered plate. "Rattlesnake?" he exclaimed, whisking the cover off the dish. "Cool. Does it really taste like chicken?"

Gunny made a rude sound. "Tastes like snake." He shook his head and pushed his plate away. "Can't abide the stuff. I kill about half a dozen every summer. Chop off the heads and throw the bodies in a tree for the buzzards."

Lisa looked at Joe, who was grinning. She wondered what he found more amusing—Martin's culinary offering or Gunny's bluster?

JOE MADE A POINT OF ASKING for seconds of snake. "Amazing, Martin," he said spitting a sliver of cartilage into his napkin. "People are wrong. It tastes like chicken and fish. You should add this to the menu at Joe's Place. It would make quite the conversation piece, wouldn't it?"

Martin nodded as if considering the possibility. "Not all that easy to get, though," he said, stabbing a chunk with his fork. "This critter took up residence under my porch. I asked him to leave, but he was an ornery cuss."

His shoulders lifted and fell. "Some snakes, like some people, don't know when it's time to pack up and vamoose."

Joe blinked in surprise. That was possibly the longest speech he'd ever heard Martin make. And the intent was none too subtle, Joe decided, when he caught a glimpse of Gunny's ruddy cheeks. Martin and Gunny were acting like buck elk dueling for a doe—Joe's mother.

"Ahem." Lisa coughed pointedly. "Christine asked you a question, Joe."

Joe looked at the woman across the table from him. Pretty. Intense. Driven. He'd met dozens of women just like her. "Sorry. I didn't mean to be rude."

The woman smiled. "I once worked with a film

crew that was doing some promotion for a Tom Hanks movie. Have you ever met him?"

Joe forced himself not to groan. "No. We don't run in the same circles. But from what I hear, he's a very nice person."

"Do you like working in Hollywood?" Gunny's son asked.

Do I? "The movie business can be very frustrating, but it's also an adrenaline rush. You just have to keep your wits about you because you're dealing with egos, vast sums of money, politics and corporations."

He looked at Lisa, who appeared surprised by his candor. Actually, he'd surprised himself as well. He never would have been that frank at a party in L.A., but it was easy to be honest here.

Forty minutes later, Joe carried the last of the dishes into his mother's kitchen and found Lisa alone at the sink. "Where is everybody?"

"Upstairs. They're watching Michael install something on Maureen's computer so she can share files with Gunny's computer. I think. Brandon and Martin went to my house to check out some sound Brandon's car is making."

Joe scraped the remaining bits of snake meat into the garbage can beside where Lisa was standing. He handed her the empty plate and said, "Do you think it's a Pomo tradition to state your intentions by bringing a woman you like the meat of an animal you killed?"

The bowl she was rinsing under the faucet slipped

into the stainless-steel sink with a clatter. "You think Martin and Maureen have something going?"

"No. I think they *should* have something going. Using my highly honed observation skills," he said with a wink to show he was kidding, "I watched them today. Mom is nervous and edgy when she's with Gunny, but relaxed and herself around Martin."

"They should be relaxed around each other. They've been friends for as long as I can remember."

"Who says good friends can't fall in love and marry?"

She returned her attention to the pots and pans. She looked nervous and edgy. What did that tell him?

"He was married once, you know," Lisa said softly.

Joe's mouth dropped open. "Martin?"

Lisa glanced toward the door. "We were closing up one night and I found a photograph your dad had of Patrick. Martin could tell I was upset, so we sat down and he told me the story of how his wife left for work one morning and never came back. I don't even know if he's legally divorced."

Joe picked up a dish towel and took the pot from her when she finished rinsing it. "Someone should ask him."

Lisa scowled at him. "Why do I get the impression you think that someone is me?"

"You're a wo…wonderful diplomat."

"Nice try, but it's not going to happen. I have two tests, rehearsal and graduation coming up. That is the extent of my focus. If you want to meddle in your mother's affairs, have at it. But count me out."

Joe put the pot away then took a step closer. With her hands in the soapy water, she was trapped. He put his lips close to her ear and whispered, "I remember when you were more adventurous."

She shifted her weight to her outer foot, and then leaned in, her shoulder brushing against his chest. "I remember when you and your brother nearly got me arrested for stealing sweet corn." She brought her foot down squarely on his toes. "I've learned a lot about self-preservation since then."

Joe winced, but he took the toe-squishing like a man. Unfortunately, he was still limping when Brandon and Martin returned a few minutes later. "Stubbed my toe," he explained when asked.

Martin's smile said he didn't believe that any more than he believed that Joe liked fried rattlesnake.

CHAPTER FIVE

"I NEED HELP."

Lisa wasn't looking forward to saying those words out loud, but the truth couldn't be denied. She'd just spent half an hour with Brandon's English teacher, a woman Lisa liked and respected. When Lisa had returned from taking her test the day before, she'd found a message from Mrs. Day on her answering machine.

Short and sweet, like the woman herself, the recording said, "Brandon is in trouble in my class. We need to talk."

Lisa had set up a meeting for before school started the next morning. She hadn't mentioned the appointment to Brandon because she wanted to hear his teacher's side of the story first. Brandon had inherited his grandfather's glib tongue and could talk his way out of almost anything. Lisa wanted the facts.

And the facts were plain. Her son, who had a brilliant mind and was a fairly decent student, had, for some reason, decided not to do any of the course work in his advanced English class for the past three weeks. His teacher suggested the cause might be drugs or alcohol.

"He's in fifth period. Right after lunch. He comes in half asleep and dozes through most of the class. He used to participate in discussions. Now, nothing. Not even intelligible grunts."

Instead of pulling into her driveway and walking through the back gate to Maureen's, Lisa kept going and rounded the corner to park in front of the Kelly house. Her mother's car was still in the garage, but Lisa didn't want to discuss this problem with Constance. When it came to parenting, Maureen had a better reputation.

She rapped twice then opened the door and walked in, as was her habit, but came to an abrupt halt when she discovered a half-naked man in the foyer. "Oh, sorry," she said, trying not to stare at Joe. When did he get muscles? The Joe she'd known in high school was a proverbial ninety-eight-pound weakling compared to his brother. "I... I'm... Uh, is your mother here?"

Joe appeared amused by her flustered blather. He pointed toward the kitchen. "She's baking a cake for your party. I just came down for my shirt. She sewed a button on it last night." His brows lifted in question. "Is something wrong? You look upset."

Lisa hesitated. Telling Maureen was one thing, but Joe was practically a stranger. *A stranger with more reason to care than he knows.* "I need to talk to her about Brandon. He's messing up in school."

Joe took her elbow and guided her toward the back of the house. "Don't start until I get there. I want to help if I can."

It was tempting to say something about too little too late, but she didn't. At this point, she could use all the help she could get. Besides, she'd noticed that Brandon had sought out his uncle's company several times at the barbecue. Maybe her son craved male companionship—something missing from his life since his grandfather had passed away.

Joe left her once they reached the kitchen. She barely noticed because the smell of baking cake filled her senses. "I swear, if you could bottle that aroma, you'd make a fortune," Lisa said, pulling out a chair at the round table. "It imparts comfort."

"Good morning, dear," Maureen said, wiping her hands on the old-fashioned apron she was wearing. A patchwork background with a ruffle around the hem, the bib was embroidered with the words *Grandmothers cook with love.* "You look frazzled. Coffee and cream or tea?" She said the last with a snort of distaste and looked to where her son had been standing.

"Nothing, thanks. I just had coffee with Brandon's teacher and I'm a little jittery." She held out her hand and watched it shake. "Of course, it could be from finding out my son might flunk English."

Maureen's "What?" embodied both surprise and concern.

Before Lisa could elaborate, Joe hurried into the room. He'd tucked his neatly pressed yellow cotton shirt into the waistband of his khaki shorts. His feet were in leather sandals. He looked like a tourist on vacation.

His presence made her throat close up. Would he judge her? And Brandon? Of course, he would. People who didn't have children always thought they could do a better job of parenting. She stood up. "I just remembered something I have to do."

Joe froze mid-step. "But you said…"

Lisa looked at Maureen, who appeared equally confused. "No. Sit. You can't just pop in, say your son is trouble, then leave," Maureen said. "We need to discuss this. As a family."

Lisa felt her face heat up. "But Brandon will never speak to me again if he finds out I aired his dirty laundry in front of Joe."

Maureen glanced at her son then said, "Tough. You can blame it on me, if Brandon throws a fit. Joe has been getting by too easy for too long. He's a part of this family, and that means dealing with the messy stuff, too."

Joe put out his hands. "I want to help if I can, but if Lisa isn't comfortable with me here…" They both looked at her.

Lisa closed her eyes and took a deep breath. The weight on her shoulders at the moment seemed to be crushing her. She sank back down on the chair. "He barely speaks to me anyway. What difference does it make if he adds one more thing to his list of reasons to hate his mother?"

She sensed a presence beside her and looked up to find Joe squatting, one hand on the back of her chair. "I can't believe such a list exists, but no one is taking the blame for my actions. I'll make it clear to Brandon that I plan to be involved in all things that have to do with this family from now on. Okay?"

Lisa's heart beat double time. *Okay?* Hardly, but what could she say? No. I'm not ready for this. Since when had either of the Kelly brothers adhered to her agenda?

"He's flunking English—one of his best subjects. Apparently, he's holding his own in his other classes, but Mrs. Day, his teacher, said several other teachers have expressed concern over Brandon's attitude lately."

"Normally, he's a good student?"

"Not quite as good as you," Maureen said, joining them at the table.

Lisa braced herself to keep from flinching.

"Well, it can't be senior-itus," Joe said. He pulled out a chair for his mother then sat down across from Lisa. "I don't mean to make light. I was just trying to think back to when I was a junior in high school. Could his social life be interfering with his studies? A new girl-friend?"

Lisa and Maureen exchanged a look. "I know that he likes a girl," Lisa said. "Her name is Nikki. But from what I've heard his friends say, Brandon has yet to ask her out."

Joe looked puzzled. "Why is that? He's a good-look-ing kid. He has personality, wheels. Why doesn't he date?"

"He dates," Lisa said defensively. She didn't want

Joe to think her son was a nerd. "He just hasn't gone steady with anyone. That's probably not the term they use nowadays, but you know what I mean. There was one girl last fall that he seemed kinda serious about—remember, Maureen? She was a varsity cheerleader."

"I think she was a little too popular," Maureen said. "She'd tell more than one boy at a time that she'd go out with him."

"Late dating?" Joe asked. "She'd go to the movies with Brandon then meet someone else afterward?"

Maureen nodded. "And from what I understood, the 'afterward' usually included sex," she said, her tone caustic.

Lisa wasn't surprised. From eavesdropping on her fellow students who were just a few years older than Brandon, she'd learned that casual sex was the norm, not the exception.

"I told him girls who sell themselves short are often the most expensive in the long run," Maureen said.

"Wow, Mom, I had no idea you were such a philosopher." Joe smiled at Lisa but the look in his eyes remained serious. "So, if it's not a girl that has his head screwed on backward, then what's the problem? Mom's wedding? Your graduation? Worry about the future?"

Lisa swallowed. Her mouth was so dry she could barely say the words aloud. "His teacher thinks drugs or alcohol involved."

"No," Maureen said sharply. "I don't believe that. Not Brandon. After what happened to Patrick? He wouldn't…"

"Mom, he's a kid. You know what peer pressure is like," Joe said, throwing his hands out in a gesture that seemed to say "What do you expect?"

Lisa, who was already close to the breaking point, nearly lost it when he added, "Kids today have access to things we didn't even know existed. We'll be lucky if it's only alcohol. I—"

She jumped to her feet. The chair made a loud screeching noise on the tile floor. "*Only* alcohol?" she cried. "I can't believe you said that. You of all people should know better. You saw what alcohol did to your brother."

His cheeks flushed. "I didn't mean it that way. Yes, alcohol is a prob—"

"It's more than just a 'problem,'" she said putting air quotes around the word. "A 'problem' is when it happens to somebody else's kid. This is *my* son we're talking about. His future. His life. There's no way I'm going to sit back and watch Brandon kill himself the way Patrick did."

"I agree with you. We need to deal with this immediately. I'm just saying we shouldn't jump to any conclusions without talking to him, first. He seems like a smart kid who—"

She stopped him by leaning down till her face was inches from his. "He *is* a smart kid. He's also a Kelly, which means he's glib and verbal and clever."

Joe's brows pinched together above his nose. "I'm a Kelly and I'm not an alcoholic. Just because my brother—"

"This isn't about Patrick," Maureen said, her voice catching ever so slightly.

Lisa was reminded of how much Maureen had been through recently. She put a hand on the older woman's shoulder. "I'm sorry. I should have handled this myself. I just panicked when Mrs. Day told me Brandon might be drinking."

Maureen stood up. "I need to check on the cake."

Lisa watched her walk to the stove. She looked tired and discouraged. "I should go."

"No," Joe said firmly. "This is a family matter. If I sounded flippant before, it's because I haven't had much practice in this kind of thing, but I want to be involved. Once is enough."

Lisa knew what he meant. They'd all lived through a tragedy that had altered the course of their lives. Lisa didn't know how she'd go on if…

Joe reached out and took her hand. He gently pulled her down so she was seated again, then he let go. She had to close her fingers in a fist to keep from clinging to him.

"Let's decide on a course of action. Maybe you want to handle it differently, but I'd suggest we talk to him. Like this."

"He'll accuse us of ganging up on him and take off."

Joe shrugged slightly. "Well, then, maybe I could start a dialogue. One-on-one. In fact, the subject came up the first night I got here."

"He talked to you about drinking?" Lisa couldn't believe it. "Whenever I bring up the subject, he says something like, 'Yeah, yeah, Mom, I know all about it.'"

"He told me he sometimes feels pressured into going to parties with his friends. If he doesn't drink, they give him a hard time."

Her frustration mounting, she put her head in her hands. "Damn it. I know what that's like. Your brother was always trying to get me to drink with him. But we're not talking Friday night keggers here. This is happening in the middle of the day."

"Pat did that, too," Joe said softly just as his mother rejoined them.

"What did you say?" Maureen asked.

Lisa could see the torment in his eyes. He didn't answer right away. Finally, he said, "Patrick had a special stash of vodka that he kept in his locker at school. He'd mix it with orange juice before homeroom. Or put it in one of those little cans of vegetable drinks you used to send in our lunches."

"When he was Brandon's age?" Maureen sounded shocked.

"Younger. I think he started in middle school."

"Impossible," his mother stated. "I would have known."

Lisa tried to picture Patrick when she first met him. Would she have known? Probably not.

"I saw him, Mom. All the time. He was good at hiding it—especially from you and Lisa."

Maureen frowned. "Why didn't you tell me? Surely you knew that wasn't normal behavior."

Lisa saw the raw look of self-contrition on Joe's face and understood completely. He'd honored Patrick's wishes—just as Lisa had when Pat asked her not to tell anyone that she'd slept with his brother. "No harm, no foul, Leese-honey. This will stay between us."

"But Joe knows," she'd protested.

"Then it's just between the three of us because Joe won't tell. He's the best secret keeper of all time."

"Maureen," Lisa said gently. "Patrick had a problem, and he hid the severity of it from all of us. We can't change that."

"But Brandon is a different story," Joe said, leaning forward and taking his mother's hand. "He's not like Patrick. I can't explain how I know that, but I do."

Tears welled up in Lisa's eyes. She was half a heartbeat away from telling him the truth when Maureen said, "Well, short of grounding him for life, what's Lisa supposed to do about this?"

"I'd start by taking away his wheels," Joe said.

"Maybe he could see a counselor," Maureen suggested tentatively. "Your father never had time for such things, but after I was diagnosed with cancer, I talked to a wonderful woman who helped me a lot."

Lisa listened to their ideas without comment. She was willing to try anything, but in the back of her mind she remembered arguing with Patrick about his drinking. She'd demanded, cajoled and cried; she'd threatened to break up with him and had broken up with him more than once. He'd still driven when he'd been dead drunk.

The only thing that gave her hope was that one sentence. *He's not like Patrick.* If that were true, then, maybe her son was more like his father.

JOE DECIDED TO PUT OFF his talk with his nephew until after school. One, he wasn't looking forward to it, and two, he had a whole list of things to do before then, including going over Lisa's purchase proposal, which she'd made sure was on the table before she left.

"Mom, I'm taking this out back to read. If you need any help frosting that cake, just holler."

She swatted him away. "I told you. I'm putting it in the freezer until Saturday morning, and then I'll frost it for the party. Nobody listens to me. You're as bad as your dad was."

He paused, his hand on the sliding glass door. "Am I? I've always thought I was just like you. Everyone said Patrick was Dad's mirror image."

She smoothed a wide strip of the plastic wrap over the cake pan. "Oh, you have your share of Joe in you, too. He was the creative one, you know. The storyteller. I'm sure that's what he liked most about the bar business—getting to tell whoppers to unsuspecting customers."

"And when he wasn't telling stories, he was arguing over the news," Joe said, drawing to mind a picture of his dad behind the bar with CNN blaring.

"Joe and Patrick both shared the Kelly temper, though," she said, shaking her head. "It was never fun to be around them when they got into a battle."

Joe agreed. He could recall more than a few times when Pat and their father would get into an argument. Afterward, Patrick would storm off and get inebriated.

"Patrick was an alcoholic, Mom. You knew that, right?"

She gripped the container like a buoy on a turbulent sea. "He had a drinking problem. Your father and I disagreed on how to handle it. Joe thought Patrick would settle down once he and Lisa got married." She shook her head. "I should have fought him on that. Made Patrick get help. But you know how forceful your father could be when he thought he was right."

Joe knew. He wondered if the knowledge that he'd been wrong—dead wrong—had added to his father's steadfast determination to hold on to the bar. Giving up Joe's Place would have been tantamount to acknowledging that he'd contributed to his son's death.

"I have to put this in the freezer then head to town," his mother said. "I told Martin I'd cover for him this afternoon. If you need a car, I'm sure Lisa would lend you hers. She said she'd be studying for her last final."

Joe waited until he heard the garage door open before going outside. He let out a deep sigh as he sat down in the padded lounge chair. He was just about done reading Lisa's business plan, which had been included in the purchase offer, when he heard the back gate open.

To his immense surprise, Lisa's mother came into the yard. Blond hair pulled back in a crisp twist, she was dressed for work in white shoes, white pants and a tropical-print uniform top. Constance carried herself with the same grace and dignity as her daughter did.

"Well, hello," Joe said, scrambling to his feet. "I was wondering when I'd see you."

Constance walked to Joe with her arms open, and gave him a peck on the cheek. "It's been too long. I had a few minutes before work and thought I'd run by and say hi."

She looked him over from head to toe. "You look good, Joe. Fit and healthier than I've ever seen you."

"Thanks. You look great yourself. Dare I say happy?"

Constance pulled a chair from the patio table and sat down, motioning for Joe to do the same. "Regular sex. I highly recommend it," she said with a wink. "By that I mean sex on a regular basis. How you do it is up to you."

Joe blinked. "Pardon?"

"You heard me." Before he could react, she nodded at the paperwork he'd set aside. "I see you're looking over Lisa's proposal. What do you think?"

Joe wasn't sure how to answer, considering he hadn't discussed it with Lisa. "I'm still reading. But her business plan looks sound."

Constance shrugged. "It should. She majored in the subject for two years. Before that she was going to be a physical therapist, a social worker, a carpenter, a mechanic…oh, hell, I've lost track.

"She's graduating with a degree in education. But

is she going to put that to good use? No. Now, she wants to run a bar. Some days I just want to shake her and say, 'Make up your mind already.'"

Knowing Constance, she probably had said those words to her daughter at least twice a day.

"You think this is a bad idea?" he said, picking up the packet.

"I think she could and should be doing more with her life. Of course, I always thought that about your father, too. The man was a brilliant conversationalist, but he had the gumption of a peanut. I just never got that."

Joe was too dumbfounded to speak.

Constance seemed to sense his dilemma because she reached out and put her hand on his knee. "Don't get me wrong. I adored your dad. Would have gone after him in a heartbeat if I didn't like and respect your mother so much, but I never understood what motivated him to spend nine-tenths of his day behind a bar, dispensing wisdom and advice for free when he could have been doing the same thing as a psychiatrist on Park Avenue and made obscene amounts of money."

"My brother thought it was because at Joe's Place, Dad was King," Joe said, recalling a long-forgotten conversation. *Dad makes the rules and enforces them,* Patrick had said. *He's king of his world.*

"Could be," she said agreeably. "But that doesn't explain why my daughter wants to buy it. She's no queen."

"According to Lisa, owning Joe's Place is a temporary proposition, which will help her son through college and give her the cash she needs to buy a house wherever she chooses to relocate after she sells the place."

Constance gave him an arch look. "Oh, honey, you're still so naive. If Lisa wanted to leave Worthington, she'd have finished college the way normal people do. Instead, she chose to drag it out over nearly ten years. As far as I'm concerned, this is just another avoidance technique designed to keep her here—in bed with her ghosts."

She looked at her watch and got to her feet. "Damn. I get talking to a handsome man and lose all track of time. I've got to go before Lisa decides to take a break from studying. She'd be furious if she knew we were talking. Promise me you won't tell her."

Joe hesitated. "Why?"

Constance gave a resigned chuckle. "Because she doesn't trust me not to steal you away from her, of course. A person makes one little mistake and she's branded for life."

Joe had no idea what she was talking about, but Constance didn't appear to notice. She blew him a kiss and rushed away, closing the gate behind her.

Feeling as if he'd just danced with a tornado, he let his head fall back against the soft cushion. The day was heating up, but the sun couldn't chase away the lingering chill left by Constance's mention of ghosts. Was Lisa still in love with Patrick? That might explain why she'd never married, but Joe didn't believe it. Since his return, he hadn't detected in her even the slightest bit of hero worship for his dead brother. If anything, she seemed mad at Patrick.

Which made him wonder why.

LISA PUSHED THE BINDER AWAY. She couldn't concentrate on her notes and the study guide read like gibberish. She closed the book *Grades, Grading and Statistics*, and pushed back from her desk. *Statistically speaking,* she thought, *my life sucks.*

Lisa had converted the spare room of her mother's four-bedroom house into an office while she was majoring in construction. Each student had to complete a project as part of their final grade. Lisa had received an A-plus since her renovation had included adding the bay window where her desk sat.

She dropped her chin to her chest and rolled her head from side to side. Her hair fell forward like a curtain. She'd intended to braid it and had forgotten. Another example of her inability to concentrate.

Taking a deep breath, Lisa admitted that one reason she couldn't stay focused was the fact that Joe was only a backyard away, possibly reading her business proposal. It seemed ironic that Joe had suddenly become such an important component in her life when for years she'd been able to push his existence into a tiny corner of her mind.

"Knock. Knock."

Lisa's chin snapped up. She brushed the hair out of

her eyes and swiveled her desk chair a hundred and eighty degrees. "Hey. What are you doing here?"

"I came through the gate. The back door was open. I called your name." He held up her purchase agreement. "I knew you were anxious to talk about this, but if you'd rather I come back…"

She jumped to her feet. "No. Now is fine. I was just taking a break. In fact, I'm done studying," she said, impetuously. "If I don't know it by now, tough."

His skeptical look said he didn't buy her cavalier attitude, but his only comment was, "Nice room. I don't remember seeing it before."

"Mom used to store all her junk here. When she moved into her wing, I converted this room into my office."

"Great view of the backyard. I'd probably spend the whole time watching the birds on that awesome feeder."

She didn't tell him that she'd made it in her welding class, but his praise felt good. "Would you like a snack? How 'bout a smoothie?"

"Sure. Sounds good."

He followed her into the kitchen, making small talk while she tossed fruit and ice into the blender. Only the loud growl of the motor kept her from asking about his decision.

"Can we take these outside?" he asked when she was done pouring the thick pink liquid into two unbreakable goblets.

"Good idea. It's a gorgeous day," she said, opening

the patio door for him when he picked up both glasses. "I hope the weather stays this mild for graduation. Some of my classmates have family coming from out of state."

Joe took a sip of his smoothie, then licked his lips and said, "Very good. Sweet, but not too sweet, like the bottled kind."

Lisa smiled.

He cocked his head and said, "Why do you call your fellow graduates 'classmates' not friends? Aren't you close to any of them?"

Lisa chewed on her straw a minute. She wasn't sure how to answer. She decided to be truthful. "I have a few friends on campus. But I'm one of the oldest students in my class. Some of them come into the bar, but we don't exactly hang out."

"Oh. So, who do you hang out with?"

"My best friend is Jen McGraw. She used to be Jennifer Jensen."

"Jen-Jen?" he exclaimed. "Didn't she marry Mac McGraw a month or so after graduation? You were in her wedding."

Lisa nodded. She'd been throwing up just minutes before it was time to walk down the aisle. Morning sickness, she'd come to find out.

"She owns the beauty parlor we drove past the other day, right down from Joe's Place."

A thought suddenly hit her and she sat up straight. "Oh, my gosh, what time is it? I'm supposed to get a pedicure today."

Joe looked at his watch. "A quarter after two."

"I have fifteen minutes." She looked longingly at the stack of papers he'd set on the table. She wanted to stay and get this settled, but the pedicure was Jen's gift to Lisa. "Um…can we do this later? I have to go."

"We could talk on the way," Joe suggested. "Mom volunteered your car if I needed to go somewhere, and I'd like to check out the lighting inside Joe's Place."

Lisa stood up. "Let's go, then."

He took a big gulp of his smoothie first. He'd only taken one step when he suddenly let out a low moan and leaned forward, blindly reaching out. Lisa rushed to his side. "Joe? What's wrong?"

She slid under his outstretched arm to provide support. His weight was heavy, but familiar, just like his smell. She wrapped her arm around his waist and searched his face for a clue. "Are you okay?"

His face was scrunched in a mask of pain. "Brain freeze."

It took a second for the answer to sink in. "Oh, for heaven's sake," she said, dropping her hold. She started to move away, but Joe's grip on her shoulder tightened.

He blinked twice then looked at her and smiled. "You came to my rescue. You're my hero."

Lisa felt her face heat up. He was too close and this felt too natural. Their gazes met and something changed between them. She wasn't sure what, nor was she certain she wanted to know. Not now. She dipped her shoulder to loosen his grip and backed away. "I have to get my purse."

"And I need my billfold. Don't leave without me," he called as he left.

Lisa picked up the purchase agreement in one hand and the two sweating goblets in the other. A handwritten note was attached to the top page with a paperclip. She scanned it and her fingers went numb. Plastic tumblers fell. Peach-colored smoothie splattered across the concrete patio in every direction. Her knees seemed as substantial as the melting ice. She sat down in the chair she'd just vacated.

"Works for me. One condition: my film. Finish first?" she read aloud.

His shorthand confused her. Did it mean he wanted to complete his film *before* she took over ownership? How long would that take? Her window of opportunity was closing fast. If she didn't act soon, she'd need to reapply for a loan, which meant more money out-of-pocket and a higher interest rate.

She looked at the gate, which stood ajar. The fate of the bar was only one part of her dilemma. Joe's presence was addictive. She liked flirting with him, even though she knew it was dangerous. The longer he stuck around, the harder it would be to keep her secret from him.

And given Brandon's current problems, she was terrified what the truth might do to her son.

CHAPTER SIX

JOE RELAXED against the shiny purple hairdresser's chair and braced the soles of his sandals on the metal foot rung. Fortunately, the beautician named Marci, according to the license attached to the mirror, was off today, so Joe could observe—and film—Lisa getting a pedicure without bothering anyone.

He watched the two-inch-by-four-inch LCD screen as he panned the room and provided a play-by-play. "This is Joe Kelly, roving reporter, coming to you today from Let Us Beautify You, the shop of one Jen-Jen McGraw. Tell us, Jen-Jen, how does it feel to work on the toes of such an esteemed graduate, the venerable Lisa Malden?"

Jen, who looked about ten months pregnant, but claimed to be only six months along, cocked her head at Lisa and asked, "Doesn't venerable mean old?"

Lisa laughed. "He's got that right." She looked relaxed sitting in the oversize molded-plastic throne, which was equipped with two individual foot baths that bubbled like a witch's cauldron. Cracking open one eye, she gazed at Joe. "Turn that off. A beauty parlor is like a psychiatrist's office. What's said here stays here."

Jen erupted in giggles. "Oh, that's a good one, Lisa. Like anybody would believe that."

Joe had forgotten how much he'd liked Jen in high school. Cute and bubbly, she'd been one of those people who'd been part of the in-crowd without being popular. Sorta like Joe, who was present at all school functions but, as now, he'd hidden behind a camera.

Ignoring Lisa's request to kill the taping, he asked Jen a few questions about life in Worthington.

"My mom used to say, 'The more things change the more they stay the same,'" she said. "I never realized what that meant until my kids started pulling the same stunts I did." She shook her mane of artfully streaked hair. "Although today's kids are way more advanced than I was. Yesterday, my twelve-year-old told me she needed twenty dollars to buy art supplies. I called her teacher. Not true. Turns out she wanted to buy sex bracelets."

Lisa opened her eyes and sat upright. "Like in S and M?"

"God, no, but these are bad enough. If you wear one color, you're telling people—boys—you're interested in kissing. Another color says you'll take it a step further, and so on and so on."

Joe zoomed in on Lisa, who sucked her bottom lip in and worried it with her teeth. Her attention was aimed at her friend, so he had free reign to study her. Pert nose. Not too big, not too cute. A few freckles, but hardly the masses one might expect with such a creamy complexion. She'd secured her hair in a twisted knot on top of her head, but wavy tendrils framed her face and neck like ribbons tumbling down the side of a package.

He narrowed his focus on her neck. In high school, he'd made every effort to sit directly behind her so he could study the elegant shape of her neck. Regal. Something Greek sculptors would have fought over.

"Joe?"

He zoomed out to find her frowning at him. "Huh?" he said, lifting his gaze from the camera screen.

"Jen asked if you had any kids." Her voice was tight. He assumed she was tense about him taping her, so he panned the camera around the room, pausing at a leopard-print chair shaped like a high-heeled shoe.

"Um, no, Jen. I've left that to the professionals, like you and Lisa."

"And you never married, either?" Jen asked. "Is that due to a fear of commitment or are you gay?"

Fear of commitment? He'd been accused of that before. "Actually, I had a long-term relationship that didn't work out, so I'm considering the gay thing."

Jen laughed. "Oh, man, you're just as funny as you were in high school."

Funny? He'd been called worse.

Jen pushed herself up from the small stool she'd been sitting on and walked to a portable cart loaded with small bottles of nail polish. "Pick a color while I use the little girl's room," she ordered. "My bladder shrunk during my last two pregnancies. It'll be the size of a pea—no pun intended—by the time this babe is born."

Lisa, her feet resting on the outside edges of the now-empty basins, leaned forward to peer at her choices. "I hate this part," she said. "I can never decide."

He set his camera on the counter and walked over to the cart. Nothing appealed to him on the top rack so he lowered himself to one knee. "Maybe I can help. I picked out your first earrings. Remember?"

She blinked, her surprise obvious. "Yes, I do, but I have to admit, I'm a bit shocked that you do."

"Why? It was my first time in a beauty parlor. A boy always remembers his first time."

Her cheeks blossomed with color and Joe smiled. He loved to tease her, but in a way, he was serious. She had been the first girl he'd made love with. That night on the shore of the lake had been his first time. He'd never told her that. Or anyone. It was his secret. His guilty little secret. He'd saved himself for the woman he loved, only she belonged to his brother.

"My, my," an amused voice said, "this has a certain poetic nuance that a die-hard romantic like me just adores." Jen waddled toward them. "You're not proposing, are you? I mean, you can, of course, but I'd suggest something a little more romantic, like by the lake, or something."

Joe glanced at Lisa. Was his face as red as hers? He hoped not. To avoid Jen's discerning gaze, he pretended to study the selection of colors and impulsively picked a dark pink. "Here," he said, handing Jen the bottle before he returned to his seat.

"Labyrinth of Love," she read aloud. "I've been trying to get Lisa to try this one for months. She said it was too sexy."

Lisa scowled at her friend. "Don't tell him all my secrets."

Jen laughed. "You mean like the white knight you're still looking for?"

Lisa groaned and covered her eyes with one hand. "Jennifer."

Intrigued, Joe rocked forward, resting his elbows on his knees. "Details, Jen-Jen, details. Are we talking metaphorical or the kind on horseback?"

"Oh, hell, she'd settle for one in an SUV. Unfortunately, the only guys Lisa seems to run across either have too much baggage or not enough."

Joe shook his head. "Huh? Explain."

"Do and I'll never babysit for you again," Lisa warned.

When Jen hesitated, Joe said, "I'll babysit. I'm good with kids. Really. Brandon likes me. Just ask Lisa."

Lisa made a so-so motion with her hand, but her smile negated its effect. Jen shrugged. "I bet my kids would love to hang out with a guy who makes movies. My twelve-year-old is certain she's the next Olson twin."

Joe laughed. "So tell me what's wrong with the

men of the Central Valley that they let Lisa remain un-attached. Are they blind?"

"We call it dating-challenged," Jen said, giving Lisa a wink.

Lisa heaved a sigh. "There are a lot of good men out there. I'm sure of it, but they're not looking for a woman who is a full-time student, with a teenage son and a mother like mine." Her laugh sounded brittle. "Actually, the one guy I seriously considered keeping made a small blunder that I found out about—he slept with my mother."

Joe looked at Jen who nodded sagely. "Fortunately, Lisa found out before she'd slept with him. Can you imagine anything grosser than being in bed with a guy who could compare you to your mother?" She shud-dered. "Of course, in my case, it might make Mac ap-preciate me more. Mom's even more rotund than I am when I'm nine months pregnant."

Lisa smiled, but Joe could tell the experience still bothered her. He now understood what Constance had meant by her cryptic remark. "Do I want to know what happened to the jerk?"

"He moved away," Lisa said. "Never heard from him again."

Joe whispered, "Thank God," under his breath.

Jen waved her tiny painting wand. "I told Lisa this was good fodder for when she's behind the bar." Joe shook his head, so she'd know he missed her point. "In order to dispense advice, you gotta experience a bit of what the lovelorn are going through."

"I figure all the pain and disappointment Lisa's had in her life will help her empathize with the people who hang out at Joe's Place. You're going to keep the name the same, aren't you, Lisa?"

"Absolutely," Lisa said, but quickly added, "Um, you know it's not a done deal, yet. Joe has certain strings he wants to attach to the agreement. Don't you, Joe?"

So she'd read his addendum. "Yes, I do. But, I think after you hear my offer, Lisa, you'll agree that this is a win-win proposition."

She cocked her head. "I'm listening."

"We'll have to repeat everything to Mom."

"Oh, don't stop now," Jen cried. "I love high-stakes business deals taking place in my establishment. Makes me proud to own a beauty parlor." She looked at Joe and said, "Okay, let's hear your plan."

Joe replaced the lens cover on his camera. His stomach felt as jittery as it had the last time he pitched a story idea for a producer. "We all know how popular the television show *Cheers* was. Quirky characters in a setting people could relate to. But what if I show them the real thing? *Cheers* without the actors."

Jen and Lisa looked at each other but neither said anything at first, then Jen asked, "Would you hire locals to act in it?"

"I was thinking more along the lines of oral histories," Joe said. "But first, I have to get permission from the new owner to film inside the bar."

"Let him do it, Lisa. Please," she said recapping the

bottle. "He might need a grossly pregnant extra. This could be my one claim to fame."

Lisa started to say something, but Jen cut her off. "Stay put. You have to dry a few minutes. And I have a special little treat for the graduate. Don't move."

Lisa leaned back in the chair. "No. Please. You do enough. You did enough. If it hadn't been for your help when Maureen and Joe couldn't watch Brandon, I never would have made it to half my classes."

Jen shrugged. "Brandon is a sweetheart. He used to keep my twerps out of trouble." She paused. "Speaking of trouble, I heard some chatter from a couple of high-school kids about a big party coming up at the lake. Half a dozen kegs and hard liquor courtesy of someone with a parent in the bar business."

Lisa looked at Joe. "When?"

"This weekend, I think. It could be just a rumor, but my daughter confirmed it when I jumped all over her case about the sex bracelets."

Lisa frowned in thought. "Maybe we should schedule an inventory to make sure all of our stock is accounted for."

"And invite Brandon to help," Joe said.

"Good idea," Lisa said, directing her focus on him. "Maybe you could include that in the little talk we discussed this morning."

Jen looked from Joe to Lisa. "What's going on? He's only been in town a few days and already you have secrets?"

Lisa lowered her voice and explained. "I talked to

Brandon's teacher this morning and she's concerned that he's not doing his work. Maureen and I thought Joe might be able to get through to him."

"Good idea. He's reputedly quite cool."

"Reputedly?" Joe asked.

"My son is a year younger than Brandon and he heard it on good faith that you once dated Mandy Moore."

Joe rolled his eyes. "Good lord. She's just a year or two older than Brandon. That makes her young enough to be my child."

Lisa bent over to remove the turquoise rubber spacers between her toes. "Hey, pal, I gotta go. I promised Maureen I'd watch the bar while she cooks for the dinner crowd." She stepped down from the pedicure throne and hugged her friend. "Thanks for this. I'll see you at the party."

"Wait. Your present," Jen squealed. She waddled away and returned a second later with a small gold box. "It's a toe ring for the sexy graduate."

When Lisa hugged her friend, Jen looked over Lisa's shoulder and said, "See you around, Joe. I'm keeping my eye on you."

"I'll behave."

"I doubt that. You're a Kelly, aren't you?" Her laughter followed him out the door.

You're a Kelly, aren't you? He was, indeed. And so was Brandon. Joe had ignored his brother's problem; hell, in some cases, he'd even lied for Pat. But that wasn't going to happen this time.

LISA LIFTED HER CUP OF COFFEE to her mouth, but didn't drink—a trick she used to give people the impression she was drinking, when all she wanted to do was observe.

A small, post-dinner crowd. Mostly locals. One couple in motorcycle regalia. She'd never seen them before, but someone had whispered they were new to the area. The couple had ordered two bowls of Maureen's broccoli-corn chowder and one of Lisa's better bottles of wine.

Lisa was looking forward to experimenting with a few recipes of her own, once Maureen turned over the keys to the kitchen. An aspect of the sale Maureen didn't seem too enthused about.

When Gunny had dropped by earlier, Maureen had more or less shooed him out of the bar so she could focus on her cooking. Was Joe right? Had his mother rushed into making changes, both business- and relationship-wise, that she was going to regret?

Lisa hoped not.

"That's a very serious look you have on your face."

Lisa lowered her cup and looked to her right. Joe had slipped behind the bar without her noticing. "Am I doing the right thing buying this place?"

"Ahh, second thoughts. There's a lot of that going around these days."

She checked on her patrons—three couples at separate tables and two regulars at the far end of the bar. None appeared in need of service, so she turned to face him. "I'm worried about Brandon. What if you're right about this place contributing to Patrick's death? History has been known to repeat itself." The thought made her shiver.

"That isn't going to happen. For one thing, you're not in denial. My dad never confronted Patrick about his problems."

They happened to be standing in front of the "Rogue's Gallery," a grouping of framed photos that had hung in the same spot above the cash register for as long as Lisa could remember. She looked at one of her favorite shots—Joe Sr. and his sons, who were probably about six. "Your father did the best he could, Joe. He might have made mistakes with you and your brother, but he was great to Brandon. They were really close."

Joe removed the photo from its place on the wall and carried it to the bar, where the light was better. "I remember when this photo was taken. Dad woke us up early and took us to the river to do a little fishing before school. Pat and I were shocked, but really excited. Patrick and Dad fished and I explored. I saw a snake eating a toad."

Lisa shuddered.

"I know," he said with a smile. "It sounds gross, but to me, it was like participating in a National Geographic shoot."

Lisa touched her finger to Joe Sr.'s image. "He and Brandon went fishing a lot. Maybe I should have taken Brandon to grief counseling after your father passed away. But he'd seemed okay, and then I was so busy helping Maureen with her treatments. Maybe Brandon felt shortchanged."

"You really helped out, Lisa, which is more than I can say."

Lisa could tell this bothered him. "I figured you wouldn't be much help anyway," she said, using one of his tricks, humor, to lighten the mood. He smiled, but only for a moment.

She put her hand on his forearm. "Listen, some of the procedures—and what your mother endured after-ward—stripped Maureen of any dignity. Bad enough to share that with another woman, but your son?" She shook her head. "I do think the experience brought us closer."

Joe picked up the photograph. "How much of Bran-don's problems stem from not having a father?"

Guilt twisted inside Lisa's belly. *It's not my fault Brandon didn't have a father,* she told herself, but the excuse no longer kept her doubts at bay.

Her gaze followed Joe as he hung the picture back in place. "You can ask him when he gets here for the business meeting," she said, in answer to his question. Maureen had been too busy to discuss the transaction earlier and had asked that they all meet after the din-ner hour. "I don't think he suffered too badly. Besides, this is all he's known.

"Unlike me, who had a father for a few years then lost him when he decided he wanted a different daugh-ter."

She regretted the slip, which she knew Joe caught because he spun around to look at her. From the corner of her eye, she spotted one of the customers at the end of the bar wave his empty stein.

"Duty calls," she said and walked away. Saved by the king of beers.

"WELL, IF WE'RE ALL AGREED, then I guess we can lock up and go home," Joe said, scanning the faces gathered around the table. They'd closed Joe's Place early to formally talk about Lisa's offer and Joe's counteroffer.

Generally speaking, Joe was pleased with the way their business meeting had turned out. Short. Simple. And everyone—his mother, Lisa, Brandon and Martin—seemed to agree that what he was asking was neither punitive nor intrusive. Joe would have access to the bar and its patrons for as long as it took him to shoot the story his mind was beginning to see. In return, he would pay for Lisa's remodeling costs— within reason.

"Can I go?" Brandon asked.

Joe swallowed. This was the moment he'd been dreading. Since Brandon had made himself scarce all day, Joe had no choice but to bring this up in front of the others. But he was prepared to fail. Nothing Joe ever said had made a difference to Patrick.

"Actually, Brandon, as long as we're all together, this might be a good time to talk about what's going on with you…in school."

The boy's chin jerked backward as if slapped. "Whaddaya mean? Everything's fine in school." He turned toward his mother, his eyes narrowed suspiciously—a look Joe had seen many times on his brother's face. "Is that why you were sneaking around school today? Did that stupid cow call you?"

Lisa clasped her hands in front of her on the table. "Mrs. Day called because she's concerned about your attitude lately. You don't participate in class. You—"

He cut her off. "English lit is boring. She's boring. Ask anyone. They'll tell you. She puts us all to sleep."

"You're failing her class, honey. And you're barely making Cs in two other subjects. That isn't like you. You're too smart to flunk out."

"School sucks. I hate it. It's all a big popularity contest. If you don't hang with the right people and do the right things, you're some kind of loser freak."

Maureen leaned across the table to touch her grandson's hand, but he moved out of reach. "Sweetheart, what are you talking about? You're a star athlete, just like your daddy—"

He didn't let her finish. "No, Grandma, I'm not. I don't even like football. I only played because Grandpa was gung ho about it. He got a kick out of coming to my games and talking about them afterward down here at the bar. But he's gone, so why bother?"

Joe's mother appeared shocked.

"Football ended months ago," Joe said. "We're talking about grades. You have to do more than show up

to get a diploma. You have to study and participate.
Just ask your mother."

Brandon gave him a dirty look. "I study," he said
sulkily.

"When?" Lisa asked. "I offered to help you go over
your notes for that big algebra test, but you said you
had to finish writing a paper for English. Mrs. Day said
you never turned in that assignment."

Brandon pushed back his chair and rose, hands flat
on the table. "Now you're the study-hall narc? I did it,
but my printer doesn't work. I told you that, remember?" he said snidely. "You were too busy with your
own finals to give a shit about my stuff."

"Take it down a notch, guy," Joe said. "We're talking here, not shouting."

"And none of this addresses the issue of your
sleeping in class," Lisa said. "Brandon, your teacher
thinks this could be due to drug use or alcohol. Is she
right?"

The boy exploded in a torrent of curse words aimed
at his mother. Joe reacted without stopping to think.
He jumped to his feet and grabbed the front of Brandon's shirt in his fist. His chair made a loud clattering
noise as it crashed backward. "That's enough. Your
mother asked you a question. Are you using?"

Brandon appeared shocked by Joe's voice, but he
met Joe's gaze. Fire. Anger. And guilt.

"No."

A lie. Joe had seen the same look in Patrick's eyes
a hundred times. "Are you high?" Joe had asked his

brother. "You promised you wouldn't touch that stuff again."

"I'm cool," Patrick had claimed. "I haven't smoked dope in months."

But he had, of course. Joe had always known.

Joe felt just as impotent at this moment as he had in the past, and the frustration made him tighten his grip.

"Let go of me," Brandon said. "You're not my father."

Lisa made a strangled sound that distracted Joe long enough for Brandon to wrench free. Joe looked at her. She was as white as the papers they'd just signed.

"Brandon," she said, holding a hand toward her son.

The boy backed away from the table. "What is this? Some kind of freaking intervention? Well, forget it. I'm not a drunk," he said, giving his mother a black look. "And I don't do drugs," he added for Joe's benefit. "So get off my back."

Joe wanted to believe him, but he'd listened to the same kind of self-righteous indignation time and again from Patrick.

"Great," he said. "Then, you won't mind an occasional urine test. Just until you bring your grades up."

Brandon's jaw dropped a good two inches. The expletive that followed his look of shock had been one of Patrick's favorite comebacks—especially when he knew he was in the wrong. "Hey, I heard every excuse from my brother, Brandon. As far as I'm concerned, this is non-negotiable. You test clean, you get the keys to your car. If not, you walk."

."Mom," Brandon said, turning to Lisa. "Tell him he's full of—"

She put out her hand. "Give me your keys. Every action in life has consequences. You might as well learn that, now."

He looked astounded. And betrayed. He gave Joe a look that said *I hate you*, then tossed his keys on the table and stormed out of the room. The back door slammed with conviction a moment later.

Lisa didn't move, but she looked shattered. Joe walked to where she was sitting and put his hand on her shoulder. "That took guts. I'm proud of you."

She closed her eyes and leaned her cheek against his hand. "Thanks. I figured if you could be brave, so could I."

"For what it's worth," Martin said, from across the table, "I believe him about the drugs. I've known a lot of users, and you can see it in their eyes."

"I hope you're right," Joe said, squeezing Lisa's shoulder supportively. "But, drugs or alcohol, we all know how fast a problem can get out hand. I don't know if there's anything I could have done to help my brother. All I know for sure is that I didn't try. And I'm not going to let that happen with my nephew."

BRANDON SAT IN HIS CAR. He knew there was a spare key on a wire under the wheel well. His grandfather had put it there and showed it to Brandon. "Better safe than sorry," Gramps had explained.

He could have started the car and driven off, but he didn't. For one thing, he was too mad. He needed a minute to think about what he was going to do.

"Damn teacher," he muttered, sinking low in the seat. His knees bumped the steering wheel and he slammed it with the heel of his hand. He hated this ugly car, but he didn't make enough money to buy a new one.

It was tempting to say "Screw it" and drop out of school so he could work full-time and buy the things he wanted. But he knew his mother would have a hissy fit. She'd probably kick him out. And Grandma C was so wrapped up in her new boyfriend she probably wouldn't even notice Brandon was gone. Normally, Brandon could have counted on his other grandmother to come through for him, but Grams was getting married and leaving.

A gnawing emptiness deep in his gut made him flop sideways and reach for the glove compartment. He opened it and dug under the registration papers and insurance information until he found what he was looking for—a small, flat bottle.

Straightening up, he unscrewed the top. It had once held a kind of fruity booze some girl had brought to a party. Brandon had picked it up thinking the bottle might come in handy. He'd filled it with vodka from a bottle Grandma C's new boyfriend had left on the counter one night. Brandon had replaced the missing liquor with water so no one would notice.

He closed his eyes and took a gulp, ignoring the gag reflex that nearly made him spew. His stomach settled down after a minute and he took a second drink. Brandon didn't care what anybody said—not the counselors at school, the people at Alateen, or even his mother—booze didn't make you feel good; it just made it so you didn't feel so bad.

CHAPTER SEVEN

JOE LOOKED through the viewfinder of his digital camera and worked the toggle switch to zoom in on the line of graduates waiting to approach the dais to receive their diplomas. Lisa had insisted he leave his bulky video recorder at home. "Film me and the deal's off. Got it?" she'd threatened, with a look that said she meant it.

Considering the turbulent week they'd all had—thanks to Brandon—Joe had conceded the point.

He scanned the crowd but couldn't find her.

Stately and decorous, the protocol seemed befitting the goal that she'd worked so long and hard to accomplish.

"She looks rapturous, doesn't she?" a voice to his right said.

Joe looked at Lisa's mother. Constance was sitting beside a tall, thin man in a black suit. Joe thought the gold shirt and matching silk tie was a bit much, but Constance seemed thrilled by his presence. She'd gushed through introductions when Maureen, Gunny and Joe found the Malden party by the gate.

"I can't pick her out. Where is she?"

Constance put one hand on his arm to direct him. "Front row of the second group."

Joe squinted for another couple of seconds then nodded. "Oh."

Even from a distance, Joe could see Lisa's smile. She appeared to be talking to someone behind her— a young man a few years older than Brandon. Whatever he'd said must have been amusing because she was laughing.

Joe felt an instant reaction in his belly. It took a moment to realize that he was jealous. Making Lisa laugh was the one thing he'd been good at—except for that time after Patrick's funeral when she'd come to him upset and angry at his brother for dying. If Joe had given her a chance, would she have told him that she was pregnant?

Joe had hated her for a few years. Or wanted to. While she'd been warmly embraced by his family, Joe had felt like a pariah—booted from the Kelly family unit because of the argument he'd had with his father. Like a spoiled older child resentful of his younger siblings, Joe had blamed Lisa and Brandon for usurping his birthright.

He zoomed in and snapped the shot when she looked his way. He viewed the image on the little screen. The mortarboard hid her beautiful hair and the shiny material of the gown did nothing for her coloring, but she looked radiant. And Joe realized that he'd never stopped loving her.

Two hours later, Joe wandered around Joe's Place with a paper plate filled with hors d'oeuvres in one hand and a plastic glass of white wine on ice in the other. Twenty-five people mingled in small clusters; the largest group was gathered around the graduate herself.

Lisa glowed in her slim-fitting dress of fuchsia silk. The neckline was low enough to make Joe's throat close up. Her open-toed stiletto heels added four inches to her height and made her legs look model perfect. On one toe, a tiny silver ring sparkled.

She was more animated than he'd ever seen her. Did the validation of a diploma do that to a person, he wondered?

"Nice party, huh?"

Joe turned to greet Martin, who had been behind the bar since Joe arrived. "Hello. Taking a break?"

"Constance's gentleman friend offered to cover for me. Apparently he had experience bartending in college." Martin shrugged. "Since this is a private party, it can't hurt."

"Frees you up to dance with my mom."

Martin gave Joe a loaded look. "The way you're dancing with Lisa?"

"Touché."

Martin shook his head. "I'm an old man, what's your excuse?"

He walked away before Joe could come up with a reply. Besides, what *was* his excuse? History? The fact that she was almost, but not quite, his sister-in-law? That they'd grown apart over the years and had nothing in common?

He liked that one best, but every time he looked at her his hormones reverted back to adolescence and screamed, "Who cares, man? She's hot."

Joe scanned the room. The crowd around Lisa had dispersed for the moment and she was staring thoughtfully at the couple behind the bar—her mother and her mother's boyfriend.

He dropped his plate on a table and walked to her. "Congratulations. You look stunning, by the way."

She put a hand to her cheek. "It's the dress. A bit young for me, but Jen insisted. She said it matches the nail polish you picked out." To prove it, Lisa lifted one foot and wiggled her toes. This put her off balance and she teetered.

Joe saw this as a perfect opportunity to put his free arm around her back and pull her close. "Great shoes. Can we try that again?"

She laughed and tried to move back, but he tightened his hold. "Martin said it's time to start dancing. Everyone is waiting for someone else to break the ice."

Her eyes went wide. "Not me."

"Why not? It's your party."

"But…"

He took her hand and headed for the jukebox. "How 'bout a few golden oldies, as your son would say?"

As the first strains of a Police song filled the air, Joe led her to the corner of the room designated as the dance floor. People clapped, so Joe swept low in a fair imitation of a courtly knight. Lisa rolled her eyes before giving a mock curtsy.

Within a few seconds, six other couples had joined them. "See?" he said with a wink. "They were waiting for you to have the first dance, like at a wedding."

Lisa's smile seemed bittersweet. Did she regret the fact that she'd been deprived of that ceremony with his brother? "How does it feel to be a graduate?" he asked.

Her mostly bare shoulders lifted and fell. "The same, actually. I guess I was expecting some kind of obvious transformation, but I'm still me," she said with a self-deprecating laugh.

"Thank goodness." God, he wanted to taste her shoulder.

She looked at him a few seconds as if trying to decide if he was teasing. He changed the subject. "Mom told me you offered to handle the arrangements for her wedding."

"She's had so much on her mind lately, I was afraid she'd suffer a meltdown if I didn't step in. Did she mention that I signed you up for the work detail, too?"

He nodded, his gaze fixated on her lips, which were the color of moist cotton candy. He'd never wanted to kiss someone more.

As if sensing his intention, she broke contact with him, dancing out of his arms. The look in her eyes was both flirty and wary. Joe didn't blame her. They were adults, yes. They were attracted to each other, yes.

But they also had too much between them to make a simple fling possible.

Besides that, Joe owed her an apology. He'd spent his entire high-school years lusting after his brother's girlfriend. When Fate had granted his fondest desire, Joe had been so overwhelmed by what he felt for her, he'd assumed she felt the same. He'd pushed her to choose him over Patrick. Instead, she'd appeared mortified by what had happened between them. He'd left town in a huff and didn't see her again until Patrick's wake.

He'd flown home in shock. Eaten up by grief and guilt and self-loathing, he'd lost it when she'd admitted that she'd told Patrick the truth about what they'd done that night. Joe had accused her of laying too heavy a load on his brother's shoulders. "What the hell did you think he'd do—congratulate you on being so honest? It's no wonder he drank."

He'd been cruel. And wrong. He needed to tell her that.

When the song ended, he reached for her hand and led her toward the kitchen. "Where are you going?" she asked, resisting him.

"I noticed we were running out of chicken wings."

She looked suspicious but followed after him when he started walking again. They met Maureen and Gunny coming through the swinging doors. Gunny held one side so Maureen could exit with the tray she carried in both hands. "Having fun, dear?" she asked Lisa.

"It's the best party I've ever had, Maureen. Thank you," Lisa said, giving her a quick peck on the cheek.

Maureen looked at Joe and said, "There's another tray of pigs-in-blankets about ready to come out of the oven. Would you get them for me?"

He nodded. "Happy to help."

The twinkle in his mother's eyes made him wonder if she saw through his ploy to get Lisa alone. He nodded at Gunny, who reached into the pocket of his floral-print shirt and withdrew an envelope. "For you, sweet girl."

Lisa looked surprised, but she smiled and gave him a kiss on the cheek, too. "Thank you so much."

Moments later, they were alone in the kitchen. Joe had to let go of Lisa's hand so she could open her card. "Wow," she exclaimed. "A hundred-dollar bill. How generous!"

She looked at him a moment before sneaking a glance over her shoulder. In a soft voice, she said, "This makes me feel guilty for not being more enthused about their wedding. I like Gunny, but I don't want to see your mother leave. Selfish, aren't I?"

Joe settled his backside against the chrome prep table and crossed one ankle over the other. "Actually, you're one of the most selfless people I know. Look at everything you've done for our family."

Her cheeks turned red and her gaze dropped to the floor. "Joe, there's something you should know. I—"

He stopped her. "One confession at a time. I owe you an apology."

She looked up. "For what?"

"For being an ass the day of Patrick's funeral. I was mad at the world, and I needed somebody to blame for what happened. I didn't care who I hurt in the process. You. My dad. Hell, I probably said something nasty to my mother, too, but I don't remember." He glanced toward the door. "Don't ask her, okay? I'm a Kelly. Humbling myself once a day is all I can take."

Her lips curved upward but only for a moment. "Why are you bringing this up tonight, Joe?"

"Because ever since you picked me up at the airport I've felt like there was some ponderous weight between us. Patrick. The past. *Our* past. And, of course, my asinine behavior at the funeral. I was hoping if I apologized we might find a way to get past it."

"Why? Because we're going to be working together—well, in close proximity—for the next few weeks?"

Her tone sounded contentious. "Yes, partly."

"Because you're already bored and need a little romance to spice up your stay?"

Momentarily stunned speechless, he watched her tap the corner of the envelope to her lips. "Well, I hate to disappoint you, but it isn't going to happen. I may be a small town girl who is too afraid of life to risk leaving Worthington, but that doesn't mean I don't have plans. I do. And you aren't part of them."

Too afraid of life to risk leaving Worthington. His words came back to haunt him. The night by the lake, after they'd made love, Joe had asked Lisa to go with him. She'd refused, and he'd accused her of being too afraid to take a chance on a bigger life outside of Worthington.

"I was eighteen and full of myself. I thought I had all the answers when, in fact, I didn't even know what the questions were."

He shook his head and made a gesture toward the bar where the sound of laughter filtered under the door. "You proved me wrong, didn't you? You've met your goal of graduating from college. You have a lot of friends who think you're fabulous, and your son has turned out great—despite a few little age-related glitches. You have a lot more to show for your life than I do."

She set down the card and took a step closer. "How can you say that? You're a successful filmmaker. You're living your dream."

"I left here convinced I was going to be the next Steven Spielberg. That didn't happen."

She smiled the way she would have if Brandon had said something self-effacing. "So neither of us has set the world on fire," she said with a shrug. "I've decided there comes a time when you either embrace your life—flaws and all—or give up."

She shook her head and a lock of golden-red hair escaped from her fancy updo and danced across her shoulders. He took her by the wrist and pulled her a step closer. There bodies weren't quite touching, but he could reach her by leaning forward.

He moved slowly, giving her a chance to back away,

but she didn't. He put his mouth on hers. She didn't respond right away, but after a heartbeat her mouth opened. At first, all he could taste was the tangy flavor of the wine she'd been drinking, then her tongue touched his and memories poured into his mind. Even after all these years, she still tasted like Lisa.

This, he realized, was what he'd wanted all night. All week. Ever since he'd walked out the doors of the airport and seen her standing beside her perky little car. He needed this. He needed her.

But Lisa apparently didn't need him.

Stepping back, she held on to the table with one hand and used the other to touch her lips, as if making sure they were still there.

"I stole a kiss, not your lips," Joe said, trying to lighten the moment.

She didn't smile. "I can't do this, Joe. Not now. Not until... There's something you..." She didn't finish the thought. "I'm sorry. I have to get back to my guests."

With that, she walked out of the room.

He stared at the door. "There's what?" He started to follow her, intending to get an answer to his question, but paused when a whiff of something burning made his nose twitch.

"Oh, crap," he muttered. Grabbing a fat pot holder, he rushed to the pizza oven and pulled out a cookie sheet filled with very crispy miniature hot dogs wrapped in pastry. The overly toasted appetizers reminded him of the obvious: this was Lisa's party. Their private business would have to wait for a less public forum.

IN THE WEEK AND A HALF following her graduation, Lisa had watched her life change in ways that both thrilled and terrified her. She'd opened an escrow account to purchase the building that housed Joe's Place, signed papers at the bank that put her deeply in debt and applied to the state to transfer the liquor license to her name.

In addition, she'd spent every spare minute helping her son catch up on his schoolwork. Thankfully Brandon had passed the drug test his grandmother Constance had administered, but he'd also admitted to drinking during his lunch hour and after school. He'd returned to Alateen and seemed to be getting back on track. He was going to finish the term with *B*s and *C*s instead of *A*s, but he'd proven that he could do the work and stay sober—however resentfully. Today was the last day of school, which was mostly an open morning devoted to signing yearbooks, so she'd given him back the keys to his car on the condition he showed up for work by noon.

She checked her watch.

"If you're worried about Brandon, I could send my covert operatives to check on him. They're young. They'd pass."

Lisa looked up to find Joe leaning casually against the bar. He nodded toward a trio of college students—two men and one woman—milling around the sturdy-looking tripod that his camera was sitting atop. She pulled the cuff of her denim work shirt over her wrist. "He'll be here. He seemed genuinely interested in being part of your…um…film crew."

Frowning, she studied the threesome, who were all dressed similarly to Joe in lumpy cargo pants and baggy vests with extra pockets. Only their color schemes varied, from khaki to camouflage to solid black—the woman's.

"Tell me again. Who are these people and what, exactly, are they doing here?"

"They're film students from your alma mater. When I was at your graduation, I bumped into our high-school drama teacher. I asked him who to call if I wanted to hire some interns for a project." He motioned toward the trio. "Meet Bianca, Roger and Tim."

Lisa could tell the three, currently poring over a loose-leaf ringed binder not unlike the kind Brandon used in school, were thrilled by the chance to work with a real Hollywood director.

"Why do you need so many?"

"They're non-union."

"Huh?"

"That was a joke. They actually volunteered to work for free, but I remember being a poor college student, so I'm paying them ten bucks an hour."

"They're going to operate the camera?"

"Some of the time. To start out, they're going to log shots of your crew remodeling Joe's Place. Boring, but necessary since I picture using a time-lapsed clip.

We'll condense three or four days of footage into thirty or forty seconds worth of tape."

She vaguely remembered hearing this plan but her brain had been preoccupied with scheduling the installation of skylights, booking a venue and caterer for Maureen's wedding and quizzing Brandon on the vagaries of Hemingway. "And this is important because…"

He smiled good-naturedly. "Because a missed shot is always the best."

"Pardon?"

He stood up straight. "You can't make a movie without raw footage. I don't know yet what I'll use, but I can't use what I don't have, so we film everything."

Lisa still didn't see how a movie about a small-town bar would be successful, but according to Maureen, Joe was determined to make this movie. He'd set up his editing operation in her family room and had been copying stacks of old videos to digital format. And she'd heard from a number of sources, including Jen, that Joe and his new helpers had been all over town talking to people and taking pictures. They'd even visited the historical society.

On the positive side, that meant he was too busy to talk about what had happened between them at her graduation party. His kiss. Her near confession.

"Are you ready?"

Lisa's heart jumped in her chest. "What?"

"Your contractor just pulled up. Lights, action, camera…so to speak," he said with a teasing wink.

Lisa spun on the heel of her work boots and marched across the yellowed vinyl flooring that would be one of the first things to go. The boots felt stiff and rubbed against her ankle. She hadn't worn them since she'd switched majors from construction to finance.

She paused, hand on the levered knob, and glanced at Joe, who had joined his crew. Suddenly, the thought of having her daily progress—or lack of progress—immortalized on film made her panic.

She motioned for Joe to come to her. In a near whisper, she said, "What if my contractor doesn't want to be in a movie? Did you get a release from him? What if this whole thing takes longer than we thought? This is an old building. There could be all kinds of snags and there might be things that aren't up to code. If the building department—"

"Whoa, slow down," Joe said, rubbing her upper arms the way a coach would encourage a struggling boxer. "Take a deep breath. I've got this covered, Leese. Trust me. I've done this before."

His touch was comforting, but his tone seemed faintly condescending, which irked the heck out of her. She pushed his hands away. "Well, I haven't. And it's my money."

He cocked his head. "Actually, I'm paying for the remodeling, remember? And I already got signed releases from everybody who will be working here."

"Oh." She looked down. "I guess I'm still struggling with this whole Hollywood-production thing.

When you said filming, I pictured you in high school. Camera in hand."

"The industry has changed. Thanks to desktop editing, anyone with a decent camera and a computer can make a movie." He didn't sound happy about that, but he shrugged and added, "The good news is you can make a movie fairly cheaply."

"How cheap?" she asked bluntly. Through the window, she saw Bob Gamble, the general contractor who'd taught her building classes in college, get out of his truck.

He shrugged. "Don't worry. This is low, low budget."

She put her hand on the lever and pushed down slowly. She had one more question that needed asking. "What happens to your business in L.A. while you're up here doing what you want to do?"

He blinked. "Wow. You're full of tough questions this morning. I guess you could say I'm between jobs at the moment. I've mostly been editing other people's work for the past ten months. That pays the rent on my studio, but it's not the same as this." He made an all-encompassing gesture. "This is what I do."

Lisa looked at his camera crew. In a voice loud enough for everyone in the room to hear, she said, "Okay, but I'm not covering anybody's worker's comp injuries. And that goes double for you. I remember what a klutz you were in shop. Didn't you nearly cut off your pinkie?"

Grinning, Joe held up his right hand. "The tip is still numb. I can't believe you remember that."

"I remember the blood," she said with a grimace. Her stomach turned over, which was the real reason she couldn't have been a nurse. She got light-headed just thinking about pain and suffering.

She yanked open the door as Bob approached, flanked by his two helpers. In his mid-fifties with a solid silver mustache, the contractor was highly respected in Worthington. Lisa knew she'd only been able to afford his help because as a former student, she'd been given a discount.

"Morning, Lisa. Ready to do this?"

"Sure am," she said, kicking a rubber wedge under the door to keep it open. "You know my strategy. I don't want to be closed any longer than necessary, plus I want to retain much of the same ambience of the old Joe's Place, while giving it a fresh new look."

"Lighter and brighter," Bob said. "That means we start by installing the skylights."

Joe shook hands with all three men then said, "What about the attic?"

Bob shrugged. "Not a problem. The kind of skylight Lisa wants is designed to retrofit almost any roofline. The main thing I need you and Lisa to do is move any boxes or junk that might be stored up there. Shall we take a look?"

"I spotted a bunch of old beer signs up there," Lisa said. "They might be the kind of stuff you want for your movie, Joe. They'll take you right down memory lane."

As Joe explained his project to the contractor, Lisa

opened an eight-foot ladder under the access hole to the attic. "Well," she said, looking directly at the camera held by one of Joe's interns, "here goes nothing."

THE WORK WAS HOT AND DUSTY, which was why Joe opted to leave his camera on the main floor with two of his students at the helm. Any of the more interesting discoveries he carted down the ladder to be opened on tape.

The first trip down memory lane came when Joe opened a box marked FB and found his brother's old football uniform. He lifted the badly wrinkled jersey to his chest.

"Purple and white, fight, fight, fight," a voice called from above.

Joe looked over his shoulder. Lisa's head was poking out of the opening in the ceiling. "This looks small," he said giving the musty-smelling fabric a shake. "Wasn't Patrick bigger than me?"

"He just acted like it."

Their gazes met. Joe wondered what she was thinking. She'd made love to both brothers. Was she remembering their anatomical proportions? Her face turned red, but that could have been because she was upside down.

"Anyone ready for lunch?" a loud voice called from the kitchen. Joe had heard his mother poking around back there, but had been too busy answering questions to check up on her.

Lisa's face came back into view. "Did somebody say food? Hallelujah. Is my son here yet?"

"Yeah, I'm here," Brandon said, following his grandmother into the main room from the kitchen. His tone was a little surly, but at least he was speaking, Joe thought.

He hadn't seen much of his nephew since the big confrontation. Joe was glad the boy had come around and completed his course work for school. Whether that translated to no more drinking, he was hesitant to bet.

"Great," Lisa cried. "We need someone strong to pass these boxes to. The junk I'm tossing out the opening, but the good stuff needs a bit more care."

"Well, all of that can wait," Maureen said. "I made beef stew and corn bread."

Lisa smiled. "Bless you, but you didn't have to. You're retired, remember?"

Maureen shook her head. "I still have to eat, don't I? And I don't know how to cook for one."

Joe hurried to the ladder, which, because of the uneven nature of the flooring, was a bit wobbly. He held it until Lisa was down safely.

"Thanks," she said breathlessly.

"You're welcome." Then he motioned for his film crew to join them. "Come on, kids, the food is always the best part of filming."

Lunch was a boisterous affair. Joe was pleased to see Brandon interact with the interns. He asked them questions about college and filmmaking and showed a real interest in how to operate the camera.

"I'll show you how to run it after lunch," Tim volunteered. "If that's okay with your uncle."

Brandon looked at Joe with what Joe took as cautious optimism. "Sure. Have at it."

"Cool," Brandon said obviously trying to tone down his enthusiasm. Joe remembered feeling exactly the same way when he'd worked with his first instructor at art school.

"You know, Brandon," Joe said, "these guys are only here until two. Maybe you could take over from Tim when they leave."

"Sure," he said, his voice cracking just a bit.

Lisa, who was sitting at the end of the bar, looked at Joe with so much gratitude in her eyes he nearly choked on his mouthful of stew.

"So, Mom, I'm starting the interview portion of this next week. I notice you haven't signed up, yet."

His mother shook her head. "Now, son, you know I don't like cameras."

"But you're the key to the past. You and Martin know where all the bodies are buried."

Maureen moved away to refill someone's bowl. "Then get Martin to talk to you. I have a wedding to plan."

Joe didn't think she sounded all that happy about the prospect, but he kept still. He was certain she'd come around eventually. The movie wouldn't be the same without her input.

"Your mom told me that when you were little, you called the place 'the far,'" Lisa said, appearing suddenly at his elbow. She was carrying a basket of crackers.

"Really?" Joe asked. "I don't remember that."

"She said you never liked it here, but Patrick always asked to go to work with your dad."

She spoke softly for his benefit only. When he swiveled his seat slightly to look at her, his elbow brushed her breast and he felt a response shoot through is body.

Damn, he thought. *I can't go through the next few weeks lusting after Lisa.*

"Huh?" he said, turning to look at her.

"Remember the birthday party your parents threw for you and Patrick down here?" Lisa asked. "That caused quite an uproar, didn't it, Maureen?"

His mother chortled. "I'll say. I think every parent on the boys' list of friends called me."

Brandon, who was on the other side of Joe, asked, "Why'd you have it here, Grams?"

"Your grandpa hired a band for the party. He was so proud of himself that it never occurred to him people would be upset," Maureen explained. "And I forgot to put on the invitations that the party would take place out back. What a hoopla!"

Joe closed his eyes and tried to picture that party. Very few images from the day slipped into his mind until one hit like a wet bar rag in the face.

That afternoon he'd seen Patrick kiss Lisa.

Details came back to him. He'd been indoors trying to compose a note to Lisa—something witty and clever that would make her like him more than she liked his twin—when someone had told him his brother wanted him to come outside. Thinking it was time for cake, Joe had hurried through the storeroom, accidentally bumping into a couple locked in an embrace.

It had taken several heartbeats to realize the two were Patrick and Lisa. The instant Lisa had seen him she'd pushed Patrick away and stormed off. Patrick had laughed and boasted, "I'm gonna marry her someday." Joe hadn't doubted it for a minute and the thought had ruined his afternoon. *Was that what Pat had intended?*

FOUR HOURS LATER, Joe was filthy, tired and his shoulders felt like someone had driven over them. For the past two hours, he'd done nothing but ferry boxes from the attic to the storage room behind the bar.

"Isn't it beer time, yet?"

Lisa, who looked just as grimy as Joe felt, laughed. "Sure, why not? I think you earned it."

She walked to the hole where the ladder stood.

"Wait," Joe said. "Let me go first so I can hold the ladder for you."

She paused for half a second then shook her head and disappeared backward down the opening. Just as she had a dozen or more times that day. He chuckled under his breath.

Lisa was safely on the ground looking up. "Thanks for the offer, but you know me—the independent type." She'd taken off the cotton scarf she'd tied around her head and was using it to wipe some of the grime off her face.

Joe heard a muffled voice, then a second later she looked up at him and said, "Brandon wants to practice filming an action shot, okay?"

The college students had left several hours earlier and Joe had put Brandon in charge of keeping the log. A boring job, but an important one. "Sure. Tell Martin to starting pouring that cold one. Here I come."

He kicked the square hatch that fit into the frame closer to the opening, then lowered his feet to the second rung of the ladder—not the top, recalling Lisa's stern chastisement to the interns earlier.

Once he had his balance, he tugged the hatch in place and paused to catch his breath.

"There," he said. "Good as..."

He had no sense of falling until he hit the floor with his shoulder and cheek. His neck made a horrible sound—or was that cracking noise from the ladder that fell on him?

All he truly was aware of was Lisa's frightened cry, "Joe. Oh, God, no. Joe..." Then, her hands were touching his face. He liked her touch. He liked her. Why hadn't he told her that?

The hubbub that ensued included arguing over who would ride in the ambulance with him. Joe settled that by not letting go of Lisa's hand—even when the paramedics told him he had to. Joe pretended to be unconscious.

He was pretty sure he was going to live, but the horrible throbbing in his shoulder could mean something was broken. And his head was ringing, too. He wasn't looking forward to the pain he'd feel after the shock wore off, but, at least, Lisa was by his side.

"Joe," she said in a soft voice, her lips nearly brushing his ear. "Can you hear me, sweetheart?"

Sweetheart? Had she ever called him that before? No, he didn't think so. God, maybe he was worse off than he thought.

Her grip on his hand tightened. "Listen. I know you're going to be just fine, but when something like this happens it makes a person realize that anything could happen and what you planned to do or say somewhere down the line might not get done or said."

Huh? He mumbled something equally unintelligible.

"I'm not making sense, am I?" She sighed and pressed a tender kiss on his cheek. "I'd planned to tell you this after your mother was married. She's been through so much and then this stuff with Brandon…"

Joe's breathing stilled. Was she going to tell him that she cared for him? Maybe she still loved him. Maybe she wanted to finish what their kiss had started. Maybe they could…

"He could be yours."

Joe opened his eyes. He had to blink twice to focus against the bright light. His heart had stopped beating and he didn't have any air in his lungs to make his words come out, but somehow he managed to croak, "What?"

She moved as close as possible given the cervical collar around his neck and the presence of the paramedic beside them and whispered, "Your mother said something to me a few weeks ago that led me to question whether or not Brandon is really Patrick's. If he isn't, then you're the only other possibility."

A thousand questions crashed into his mind, but Joe wasn't given a chance to ask them. The rear doors of the ambulance opened and four hands yanked the gurney out of the vehicle. "It's show time," one of the orderlies said.

Joe watched helplessly as Lisa was directed to the waiting room while he disappeared into the E.R.

CHAPTER EIGHT

"I CAN'T BELIEVE I just said that," Lisa mumbled under her breath as she watched the gurney carrying Joe disappear behind a set of double doors marked Authorized Personnel Only. "What have I done?"

"Lisa?"

Lisa spun around so fast she almost tripped over her heavy boots. "Mom. What are you doing here? You don't work E.R."

Constance rushed forward. The concern on her face did little to ease Lisa's trepidation. If anything, her mother's presence made Lisa more nervous. What if Joe blurted out Lisa's revelation? If they gave him pain medication, he might say anything. Lisa wasn't ready for the whole world to know about her secret.

"I'm filling in for a friend. I left you a note."

Lisa made a gesture of futility. "I haven't been home. We came straight from the bar. Joe fell off a ladder. The paramedics just took him. He might have a broken shoulder or a concussion."

Her mother enfolded Lisa in her arms. To Lisa's surprise, the gesture felt honest and real, not just a nurse caring for a patient's needs. "Oh, you poor baby. You just can't catch a break, can you?"

Lisa wasn't sure what that meant, but she didn't reply. It was nice to be comforted. Something Lisa hadn't experienced in a long, long time. Most of the time growing up, Lisa had felt like the adult in the house.

"Let's go check on him," Constance said, drawing Lisa toward the emergency room doors. "I'm sure he'll be fine. He's a tough nut." She patted Lisa's shoulder and added, "When a person has something to live for, he generally recuperates a lot faster."

Lisa stopped suddenly. "What does that mean?"

Constance put her forehead to Lisa's and whispered, "He's attracted to you, silly. Smitten, I believe his mother called it. Isn't that a cute, old-fashioned word?"

She smiled, then added, "Joe isn't going to want to look like a wimp by hanging around in bed for weeks on end. He'll bounce back."

"Maureen said that?" Lisa repeated. "When did you talk to her?"

"At your graduation. She said she just wants to see you both happy. If you could be happy together then…" Constance gave her attention to pressing a certain combination of numbers on the door's keyless entry.

Lisa put her hand over the buttons. "Wait. That's crazy. Joe and I are just friends." She tried to make the words sound as though she meant them. Hell, she'd been telling herself that for so long it should sound real. But, obviously, her mother wasn't buying it.

Constance removed Lisa's hand and quickly punched in the code. "That's not true, Lisa. It's never been true, but if you want to delude yourself into believing that, then there's nothing I can do."

What could anyone do? Lisa thought, following her mother into the brightly lit room. The nurses' station to the right was busy. Constance joined the activity seamlessly. Considering all the rumors and scandals Lisa had heard over the years, she'd expected to see more of a division—like in the soap operas she'd once watched religiously.

Constance asked a few questions, looked at a chart and returned to Lisa. "They just called for the portable X-ray unit. His blood pressure is a bit high, but he's not complaining of double vision or terrible pain. Probably his shoulder took the brunt of the fall."

Lisa started to ask if she could see him, but a loud buzzing noise made her jump. Constance turned expectantly toward the door and a moment later Maureen and Brandon walked in.

Oh, lord, Lisa thought. She had to have a minute alone with Joe before his mother and Brandon saw him. She had to beg him to keep her secret a little bit longer. Just until they had some kind of game plan in place. Preferably until his mother was safely on her honeymoon.

She grabbed her mother's arm. "Where is he? I need to see him."

Constance's eyes widened at the intensity of Lisa's plea, but she nodded to her left and said, "Exam room four, the first door—"

Lisa cut her off mid-sentence, then looked at Maureen and Brandon and said, "Wait here. I'll check on him."

Lisa found Joe without a problem. Fortunately, the other two beds in the room were empty. Joe was lying unattended, his body covered by several white blankets—either to keep him from going into shock or to ward off the unnatural chill that was making Lisa wish she'd grabbed her sweatshirt before hopping aboard the ambulance.

She approached him cautiously. What did one say to a person after delivering what was probably the greatest shock possible?

Joe must have sensed her presence because he opened his eyes. And, after a tiny hesitation, smiled. "Why do they keep it so cold," he asked. "Trying to prepare people for death?"

Instead of smiling, as she was inclined to do, she walked straight to his side and asked, "Is everything a joke to you?"

His smile faded. "Not everything. And since you *never* kid around, I have to assume you meant what you said in the ambulance."

She nodded. "I'm sorry I just dumped that on you. I'd planned to tell you after the wedding. Just the two of us, sitting down, face-to-face."

"A paternity summit."

Lisa put her hand to her brow. "Don't be flip, Joe. Not now."

Joe wriggled his arm free from beneath the layers of blankets and reached out to take her hand. His was warm, hers ice cold.

"Sorry. I had somebody—a school counselor, I think—tell me humor is a defense mechanism. Patrick defended himself with his fists. I used jokes."

She relaxed slightly. His hand was strong yet gentle. He had to be as shaken up as she was, but you couldn't tell by looking at him. Something that had always pissed her off. If he'd cared for her as much as he'd claimed to that night they'd made love, why had he never once acted jealous or possessive or even passionately interested in her when she'd been dating Patrick?

Lisa pulled her hand away and stuffed it in the pocket of her jeans. "Brandon and your mother are outside. I'm begging you, Joe. Don't say anything about this matter until we've had a chance to talk. Please." When he didn't respond, she stepped closer and lowered her voice. "There's so much to explain. But you have to believe me that I didn't know."

"How is that possible, Leese?"

"Think about it. Think about Patrick. You weren't the only creative person in your family. When it came to lies, Patrick was a true genius. He told me Brandon had to be his because you'd suffered some kind of fever when you were a kid and couldn't father any children. I didn't have any reason not to believe him. Unlike me, he'd been faithful," she added softly.

Joe started to lift up, but Constance walked in at that moment and said sternly, "No, no, no. You don't get up until I say you can." She looked at Lisa and grinned. "That's not the best way to keep a man in bed, but it works in a pinch."

Lisa tried to bottle up her emotions so her mother wouldn't ask too many questions—now or later at home. She wasn't ready to talk about this issue with anyone but Joe.

"Only one visitor at a time is allowed with a patient in the exam rooms," she said, giving Lisa a curious look. "Maureen is very anxious to see her son."

Lisa looked at Joe, her plea in her eyes. His face was inscrutable. Oddly, he looked more like Patrick at that moment than she could ever remember seeing. His jaw was set, whether from pain or tension, she didn't know. After a few long seconds, he moved his head a fraction in what seemed like a nod.

Lisa tried to smile, but wasn't sure she pulled it off. "I'll be outside."

Maureen met Lisa in the hall and after a quick hug hurried into the exam room. Brandon, who was sitting on a padded chair that appeared to have come from the nurses' station, was hunched forward with Joe's movie camera cradled in his hands.

"What on earth is that doing here?" Lisa cried.

He looked up. "I didn't dare leave it behind. It's freakin' expensive. But, Mom," he said, his voice quivering with what she realized was excitement, "you won't believe it. I caught Joe's fall on tape."

She nearly stumbled. "You what?"

He motioned her closer. "I did. Really. It happened so fast, I wasn't sure, but I took a chance and looked. Wanna see it?" He sounded both proud and amazed. "You helped break his fall, Mom. If he's not hurt too bad, he can probably thank you."

"Really?" Lisa couldn't remember touching Joe on the way down. She'd thrown out her arm to stabilize the ladder, and sort of remembered feeling his body rush past her. "I don't think I did anything."

Brandon shook his head. "No. You did. See?"

He made the sequence move forward, frame by frame. Lisa had attempted to catch Joe in midair, but she'd failed. The thing that struck her most was the look on her face. Fear, of course. Even panic. But there was something in her eyes as she barked orders and gently helped him that said *love*.

She looked away, not ready to admit anything of the sort. "You're right. I tried. Too bad I'm not as strong as you are. He might not have even gotten bruised, if you'd been closer."

Brandon gave her a funny look. "What's wrong?"

She took a deep breath and reached out to touch his face. "It's my hospital phobia acting up."

His beautiful lips curled upward. Were they Joe's lips or Patrick's? Lisa didn't know anymore. "Gramma C says you have a problem with hospitals because the doctors couldn't save my dad."

Feeling a bit light-headed, Lisa grabbed his shoulder. "I need to sit down."

His smile faded and he helped her to the chair. "Are you sure you're okay, Mom?"

"Brandon, Joe wants to see what you taped," Maureen said, interrupting the moment. "I told him you caught the whole thing."

Brandon hesitated, obviously torn between staying and going. "I'm fine, sweetheart," Lisa made herself say. She wasn't thrilled to send her son in to see the man who now knew that he might be Brandon's biological father, but how could she stop him? "Go."

With a quick smile, he dashed down the hall.

Maureen followed him with her gaze. "Don't you wish he was always so excited about life? He used to be—before those damn hormones showed up. Same as it was with my boys. So loving and sweet one day and at each other's throats the next."

"I don't remember them fighting too much," Lisa said.

"Oh, heavens. There were times they made Cain and Abel look like choirboys. The only reason there wasn't bloodshed was that Joe loved his brother too much to hurt him."

Lisa didn't say anything. She was waiting to see if Joe had mentioned anything about Brandon's paternity to Maureen. "Shall we go out to the waiting room?" Maureen asked. "I hate feeling underfoot, and Constance said it's going to be a while before a doctor reads Joe's X rays."

"Okay," Lisa said, letting out the breath she'd been holding. "You go ahead. I'll tell Brandon where we are."

Lisa trudged down the hall, pausing at the doorway. The image of Joe and Brandon—heads together viewing Brandon's cinematic masterpiece—affected her almost as hard as the sight of seeing Joe fall to the floor. *Oh, God, what have I done?*

"Mom?"

Brandon hadn't expected to look up and see his mother standing in the doorway, but what really surprised him was how pale she looked. Like she'd just seen a ghost.

She'd been acting funny for weeks. He'd put it down to her graduation and finding out about his grades, but maybe it was something else. Maybe she was sick. Maybe that was the real reason she hated hospitals.

"Mom?" he repeated, his tone wobbling in a way that embarrassed him.

"Screw the rules, Lisa. Come in," his uncle said. "Brandon was just showing me his handiwork. It's amazing. He's a natural behind the camera."

Joe's praise made Brandon smile. Hell, he'd been grinning ever since he'd rewound the footage and seen for himself what he'd hoped he'd got on tape. The feeling was like catching a touchdown pass, or so he assumed. Brandon had never caught a touchdown pass. He'd tried to be the athlete everyone said his father was, but he'd never come close.

His mother made a small whimpering sound.

Brandon started toward her, but she put out her

hand. "I need to go home. I'll borrow Gramma C's car and you can ride with Grams, okay?"

Brandon nodded, but he was confused. His mother was not the kind of person who left in the middle of a crisis. A knot formed in the pit of his stomach. "What about Joe? The nurse—not Gramma C, the other one—said they probably wouldn't have to keep him over-night."

His mother's gaze dropped to his uncle and stayed for a minute. Brandon couldn't tell what she was think-ing, but she shrugged without looking at Brandon. "I'll call Martin. He'll pick Joe up, if Maureen is too tired to stay. I…I'm sorry. I…have to go," Lisa said, rushing out the door.

Brandon frowned. What the hell? Suddenly, a thought hit him. He turned to face Joe. "I bet she thinks you're going to sue her. You wouldn't, would you?"

Joe's look of surprise turned to a scowl. "Of course not. I wouldn't do anything to hurt your mother."

Brandon heard something weird in his uncle's voice. He didn't understand what it meant. Almost as though Joe liked her. But that wasn't possible. Was it?

"Hey, grandson," a voice said.

"Gramma C," Brandon exclaimed, happy to see someone who almost never lied to him or kept what she was feeling hidden. In fact, there had been a time or two when she'd been too frank. Like when she'd called his penis a penis in front of his friends.

"Believe me, boys," she'd said one time when she'd been driving Brandon and his friends some place, "if you take an anatomy class you'll discover that there is no such thing as a wee-wee. Males have penises. Get used to it."

"How's the patient?" she asked, touching some button on a monitor that was attached to the wall.

Brandon watched the lights and digital readout with interest. He'd considered becoming a doctor, but after working with Joe's film crew today he was starting to change his mind.

"My shoulder is a little sore," Joe said, "but other than that, I'm fine. Can I take two aspirin and call you in the morning?"

Brandon laughed. Gramma C pretended to look stern. "No, you may not." To Brandon, she said, "Men make terrible patients. Don't pay any attention to him. I wouldn't want him to be a bad influence on you."

Joe made a grunting sound, as if someone had just punched him in the gut.

"Mom just left," Brandon said, wishing she'd stayed.

"I know. She was going to take my car, but then Gunny showed up and she borrowed Maureen's, instead. How come you don't have a vehicle, Joe?"

"Ask my mother. She insisted I wouldn't need one."

"Aha," she said. "Probably trying to do a little matchmaking."

Between Joe and Mom? The idea was too shocking for words. He looked at his uncle, who was watching Brandon in a way that made him feel kinda sad. He didn't know why.

"I'm gonna get something from the vending machine." He didn't offer to bring anything back for his grandmother or uncle. His mother would have scolded him for his lack of manners, but Brandon didn't care. The vending machine was just an excuse to escape. He really needed to use the phone. He was supposed to meet Rory and Winston at the kegger. At this rate, he'd never get out of here.

JOE CLOSED HIS EYES and concentrated on taking long deep breaths. His blood pressure was too high and they weren't going to let him out until it was normal.

He could have told them what was causing his heart to race, his mind to churn, and—no doubt—the elevated reading on the blood-pressure cuff that was attached to his arm, but he'd promised Lisa to keep the truth to himself.

Patrick had tricked Lisa into believing Brandon was his. Why? Had Pat thought he was doing his brother a favor? After all, Joe's future had looked so bright and promising. A summer internship. A scholarship to film school. Joe wouldn't have welcomed fatherhood at age eighteen, right?

"So, how about at thirty-five?" he mumbled.

"Beg your pardon?"

Joe's eyes snapped open. "Huh?"

He lifted his head. A gray-haired woman in a white lab coat stood a foot away holding his chart. Joe hadn't even heard her come in. "Just wondering when I could get out of here," he said, letting his head fall back to the small, hard pillow.

"Now, I think. Your blood pressure has come down since we gave you the pain medication. There's no evidence of a break in your shoulder or collarbone. Head and back look fine." She snapped the file closed. "You're a very lucky man, Mr. Kelly. This could have been much worse."

You're a very lucky man. "You have no idea," he said under his breath. At her curious look, he said, "Yes, I agree. Thank you."

She gave him a wry smile. "A nurse will be right in to remove the blood-pressure cuff and blood-oxygen monitor. As soon as you're dressed, you can meet your family out front. But if you have any sharp pains or nausea in the next few hours, get your butt back in here."

Like everything else, this process took longer than Joe would have thought possible. Nearly forty-five minutes later he walked into the waiting room. His mother was sitting in a chair, her head resting on Gunny's shoulder.

Brandon, who had his legs stretched across two uncomfortable-looking benches, shot to his feet. "Hey, there he is."

Joe gave his mother a hug and shook hands with Gunny. "Sorry for all the trouble."

Gunny shook his head in his gruff way. "No problem. I came as soon as Maureen called. I tried to talk her into leaving. It's not good for her arthritis to sit like this for long periods."

His mother gave Gunny a sour look. "I'm fine. How are you, Joe? You had us worried."

"I could have saved myself a trip if I'd seen that footage Brandon shot earlier. It's pretty obvious Lisa broke my fall. How is she?" He looked around. "Has anyone talked to her since she went home?"

His mother nodded. "I was going to call her, but she left a message saying she was going to take a sleeping pill and go to bed. I missed the call because I had to turn my phone off. Hospital rules."

Joe was disappointed. He'd planned to go see her after he got home. He wanted—no, he *needed* to talk to her, but now his questions would have to wait. "Well, let's go before they change their minds. I know five-star hotels that don't charge as much as this little visit just cost me."

Gunny picked up the conversational thread by launching into a diatribe about the high price of health care and some of the many charges his wife had accrued during her illness. "Nowadays, you need to be a full-time auditor to make sense of the billings," he complained. "You wouldn't believe some of the overcharges and duplicate billings we received. My insurance company would have paid them if I hadn't raised a stink."

Ten minutes later, they were parked in front of Joe's Place to drop off Brandon, who'd left his car parked on a side street. "Bye, Grams. Thanks for the ride, Gunny. See ya later, Joe," Brandon said, obviously in a hurry to leave. He'd returned the camera to Joe as soon as they'd sat down in the back seat of Gunny's Lincoln.

As the young man disappeared around the corner, Joe looked at Joe's Place. The interior lights were still on. Then he remembered hearing Martin offer to finish up the inventory they'd started last week.

He glanced at his watch. "Is it really only midnight?" he asked, dumbfounded. So much had happened since his departure in the ambulance.

He also realized he was too wired to sleep. "Mom. Gunny. I appreciate the lift, but I think I'll get out here, too. Martin can drive me home."

Maureen turned to look at him. "Oh, Joe, are you sure? It's late. Didn't the doctor tell you to take it easy the next couple of days?"

He leaned forward and kissed her forehead. "I'm fine, Mom, but you look ready to drop. Go home. Leave the light on for me."

She smiled weakly. "I always do."

After thanking Gunny, Joe slid across the fine leather seat, picked up his camera and got out. As he watched the luxury sedan pull away from the curb, Joe took a deep breath. He was a father. Well… maybe.

The bar's door was locked, but Lisa had given him a key. Joe walked inside. The jukebox was playing a Ray Charles song, but Martin was nowhere in sight. He went to the office, where he packed his camera in its protective box then locked it in the vault. After he was done, he returned to the bar and sat down.

"So, you're still in one piece," Martin said, exiting the storeroom with a notepad in hand.

"Yep, and thirsty."

"A Guinness?"

Joe's father's favorite. "Why not?"

The nearly black liquid came with two inches of caramel-colored foam that stuck to Joe's upper lip after he took a drink. Smooth and strong. Joe hadn't tasted it in years. He'd told himself he didn't like dark beers, but in truth he was afraid he liked dark beers too much. What else had he denied himself out of fear? Lisa? A son?

"Martin, is it true that anything you tell a bartender is sacred? That it's just like spilling your guts in a confessional?"

Martin's chuckle was low and rumbling. "I guess it depends on the bar—and the confessor." He marked down Joe's beer in a little notebook Joe knew his mother kept for employees to record their purchases.

"Why?" Martin asked. "Do you have something you need to get off your chest? Did that fall finally knock some sense into your head?"

Joe vacillated. Lisa had asked him not to mention her revelation to Joe's mother or Brandon. Technically, she hadn't said anything about Martin. Joe took another sip. "On the way to the hospital, Lisa told me there's a chance that Brandon is my son, not my brother's. Pat lied to her when she found out she was pregnant. He told her I was sterile."

Martin didn't even blink. "Well, that changes things a bit, doesn't it?"

Joe looked past Martin to the wall of photographs. It only took a second to find the one he was looking for—the one Brandon had mentioned when he and Joe had first talked. Lisa sitting between the two brothers. They all three looked happy, and so young. "If it were anyone but Lisa, I'd be thinking about a paternity test, but she wouldn't lie to me."

"And would a test be able to tell you anything definite, since you and Patrick were twins?"

"Good point. I have no idea."

Martin folded his arms and leaned forward. "What are you going to do?"

"I don't know."

Neither man spoke for a few minutes. After the last of the songs was done, Martin unplugged the jukebox and returned to where Joe was sitting. He poured a cup of coffee. He sat down on the stool next to Joe.

"What happens from this point on isn't going to be easy for any of you. You and Lisa are adults. But I imagine this is going to be a real shock to Brandon."

Joe had been thinking the same thing.

"Patrick had to know his lie would come out eventually, Martin. What if I'd married and had a child? Lisa would have started asking questions. Do you think that's why he didn't try harder to stick around?"

"You're probably the only one who can answer that question, Joe. You knew him best."

Joe shook his head. "Did I? I never would have thought he was capable of this kind of deception. Martin, he cheated me out of my son's childhood."

"You didn't ask for my advice, but I'll give it to you anyway," Martin said. "Blaming a dead man is a waste of time. You can't change the past, but you can influence the future. You may have every right to barge into Brandon's life and demand that he accepts you as his father, but where will that get you?"

Joe pictured the way Brandon had blown up when confronted about his drinking. Would something like this push him over the edge? Joe's gut told him Martin was right, but Joe had to do something. He just didn't know what.

CHAPTER NINE

JOE ENTERED HIS MOTHER'S HOUSE as quietly as possible, but he was still too keyed up to sleep. A hollow sensation made him put his hand on his belly. A hunger of sorts but not the kind food or drink could appease.

After kicking off his shoes, he walked to his make-shift editing bay, which sat on his father's desk and two card tables. He turned on his computer.

Over the past week, he'd copied hours and hours of old home movies into digital format. The quality of some was so poor, he'd had to painstakingly restore the original color. He was also in the process of scanning still photographs onto his hard drive.

He pulled two photo albums from the bottom shelf of the credenza and carried them to his desk. Once seated, he opened the one marked Brandon.

Unconsciously rubbing his sore shoulder, he opened the album to the first page to see a familiar eight-by-ten. Brandon as an infant. He'd received a wallet-size copy with the birth announcement Lisa had sent him seventeen years ago.

Joe studied the face intently. Was that his nose?

No. Of course, not. It was a baby nose. And baby eyes. And fat baby cheeks. But there was *something* in the many parts of the whole that made Joe's heart race.

He slowly flipped ahead. Brandon wearing a bowl of cereal as a cap. Brandon crawling up his grandmother's stairs. The caption read Going Places at Age Nine Months. "Babies can crawl up stairs at nine months?" he mumbled under his breath.

"Some can," a voice answered. "The precocious ones."

Joe startled. He'd been so preoccupied he hadn't heard his mother's approach.

She walked to his chair and laid her hand on his shoulder. Her hair was still neatly combed, telling him she hadn't been asleep, even though she wore a nightgown and robe. A soft, feminine ensemble. White with tiny sprigs of blue-and-yellow flowers.

She didn't ask him what he was doing or why. Instead, she pulled up a chair and sat down. As Joe flipped the pages, she'd point out pictures that held special meaning to her. "This was Brandon's first day of school. Lisa and I cried so hard we had to sit on the curb after the school bus drove off. Isn't that silly? We'd been planning for that day for weeks. I'd taken him shopping for new shoes—the kind that all the cool kids were wearing, I remember."

"In kindergarten?"

She smiled sheepishly. "Brandon wouldn't have cared, but I wanted to be sure he made a good impression. Kids can be cruel, you know."

Joe did know that. He'd grown up in a traditional household with two parents and a sibling at his side to help him fight his battles, but he could remember people who hadn't fared so well. People who were regarded as "different." People like Lisa.

"Did he ever get picked on?" Joe asked, trying to keep his tone neutral. "Because he didn't have a father, I mean? Or because his mother wasn't married?"

She shook her head. "Not that I know of. He's such a sweet boy that I think he's always had a lot of friends. Brandon has a big heart. Even as a child he was very kind to others and tried hard to be liked."

"Oh, no, please tell me he wasn't a people-pleaser like me," Joe tossed out without really thinking.

His mother turned sharply to look at him. "What are you talking about?" Her tone was stern. "You were a peacemaker, not a wimp. There's a difference, you know. Sometimes peacemakers are the first ones to get punched in the face." She touched his cheek. "I saw that happen many times. Patrick's bravado would lead to a brawl, and you'd be the one to walk away with a black eye."

Joe felt a surge of emotions, probably from the painkillers the nurse had given him. He was too choked up to speak so he just turned the page.

"Peewee football," his mother said, pointing to a pint-size player in full pads and helmet. "Lisa and I were both nervous wrecks the whole season. Fortunately, Brandon almost never played. And when he did, he rarely got the ball, so he was safe."

"He wasn't a star player?" Joe asked, truly surprised.

His mother's white hair bounced from cheek to cheek. "Heavens, no. He signed up every year and earned his letter, but he spent most of the time on the bench. Which was just fine with me." She traced the W on the chest of Brandon's jersey. "I went through all kinds of hell every time Patrick got hurt."

She held up her hand and named off the different body parts Joe's brother had injured. "Concussion. Fractured wrist. Sprained ankle. Displaced kneecap. Broken ribs." She shook her head and sighed. "That boy invited calamity."

"But Brandon's never been busted up too badly?" Joe tried to make the question sound casual, but his mother cocked her head in an inquiring way before answering.

"A few bumps and bruises, but nothing his grandmother Constance couldn't fix."

Joe was glad.

He turned the page. A photograph he'd never seen before caught his eye and he pulled it free from the plastic cover. On impulse, he laid it flat on the glass of the scanner and hit a button. A light passed under it and a moment later, the image appeared on his right monitor.

Joe Sr. and Brandon sitting on the tailgate of Joe's father's old pickup truck. "They were close, huh?"

Joe thought his dad looked old and tired. What hair was poking out from under his Giants ball cap was mostly gray. Brandon was probably twelve or thirteen at the time. His legs reached nearly to the same place as his grandfather's did.

"Yes. Joe and Brandon had a special bond."

She brought her fingers close to the monitor. "This was taken on a camping trip to Shaver Lake. When Joe came home he said it was one of the best times of his life." The wistfulness in her voice reminded Joe just how much his parents loved each other.

Joe finished flipping through the pages then switched albums. His mother ran her hand over the cover and smiled—a sad smile. "I haven't looked at this one in years."

The book contained a hodgepodge of images. Old black-and-whites of distant family members were crammed in with the twins' school photos. On one page, there was nothing but panoramic views of Worthington—as seen through the eyes of a young boy.

Joe removed the one showing his father and brother standing in the doorway of Joe's Place. "Remember when I ordered this camera out of a catalog? Dad gave me a hard time about wasting my money."

His mother patted his head with a loving gesture. "Even then you were over the moon in love with taking pictures. You mowed lawns all summer to buy your first little movie camera, remember?"

Joe could picture it. He also recalled all too clearly the day his brother broke it. "It was an accident," Patrick had claimed. "I left it sitting on the fender of the car so I could film Lisa and me making out."

Patrick always knew how to get to him.

After a succession of photographic Christmases and birthday celebrations, they neared the end of the book. Joe was finally starting to unwind, until his mother said, "Do you want to tell me what's bothering you? And don't bother trying to deny it. I know when my son is upset."

"I...um..." Joe tried to think of something to use as an excuse until he could get next door and talk to Lisa.

"It's about Brandon, isn't it?"

Joe gave an ambiguous, "Hmmm."

"Lisa and I were talking a few months ago. Nothing serious. Just gabbing over coffee. She happened to mention that a friend's little boy had such a high fever his mother was afraid he might wind up sterile. The woman's doctor reassured her that scenerio was unlikely, but the story reminded me of when Patrick had a bad case of the mumps. I told her that my doctor said just the opposite. He warned me that Patrick might never be able to have children."

Joe's hand was shaking on the mouse as he named and saved the image he'd just scanned.

His mother went on. "Lisa seemed upset by this. At first, I couldn't imagine why. After all, she'd given birth to Brandon, so the doctor must have been wrong. Right?"

Joe's throat was too tight to swallow, let alone talk. He made a slight shrugging motion.

"But the more I thought about the look on her face,

the more worried I got. What if the doctors were right?"

"Did you talk to Lisa about your concerns?" Joe asked, pleased to see that his voice still worked and he sounded fairly normal. "Did you ask her what was bothering her?"

"No."

"Why not?"

"Because I was afraid she might tell me Brandon wasn't my grandson," Maureen said in a soft whisper. "I wracked my brain trying to remember any other young men Lisa had been friendly with in high school. The only one I could think of was you. And I knew you wouldn't do something like that behind your brother's back. So, I decided I was just being an old worrywart."

Joe felt his stomach drop. He felt as humiliated and ashamed as he had at age nine when he spilled grape juice on the living-room carpet then tried to clean it up with bleach. His mother had returned from work and had guessed instantly—by the smell, of course— that something was amiss. She had that same perceptive look in her eyes.

"Then you came home," she said, squeezing his hand. "And I felt something between you two. Some… history."

"Look, Mom, I wish I could talk to you about this, but Lisa asked me to—"

She cut him off mid-sentence. "I was prepared to judge you, Joe. And Lisa. But then, something happened that made me realize that nothing is black and white where a person's emotions are concerned."

The weightiness of her tone registered. He wasn't the only one in the family with secrets.

"If you and Lisa were together, son, then it was because you both cared deeply for the other. That much I do know," she said decisively.

Joe didn't confirm or deny her allegation. Instead, he asked, "What happened to change your mind?"

"Nothing that I care to get into tonight. It's late, and you should be resting."

Joe was more than happy to let the subject drop. Until he had a chance to talk to Lisa, he was going to play it cool. He'd do what he did best: observe. "And you have a big day tomorrow, don't you, Mom? Didn't Gunny say the two of you are visiting his son and daughter-in-law?"

"Yes," she said with a sigh.

"You don't sound very enthused," Joe said. "Is this something we should talk about?"

His mother got to her feet. "Just pre-wedding nerves," she said, her voice falsely perky. She waited for Joe to stand up then gave him a hug. "We're not leaving until noon, so I'll see you in the morning."

Joe kissed her cheek. "I love you, Mom."

"I love you, too, son. And no matter what happens with Lisa and Brandon, I want you to know that I understand." She put her hand flat against his chest. "You can't dictate to your heart, no matter how hard you try. Sometimes love has a mind of its own."

Joe watched her walk away. He wasn't sure how to take her cryptic message, but one thing he knew, his mother wasn't the same joyful bride-to-be who'd called him just a few weeks earlier.

LISA'S HEAD WAS POUNDING. A restless night filled with old ghosts and new worries had kept her from getting the sleep she needed. Plus, an early morning phone call from the caterer who was handling Maureen's wedding had contributed another worry to her load. The musicians the hotel usually used were already booked.

"This is the problem with last-minute plans," the caterer said. "They either fall into place or nothing works out right."

Lisa had promised to get back to the woman today with an alternate band. *Jen has a lot of connections,* Lisa thought, *maybe she can suggest somebody.*

"Why does everything have to be so complicated?" Lisa muttered under her breath as she opened the French doors off her bedroom and stepped outside.

A path of concrete stepping stones led from the patio around the side of the house. The grass needed mowing, she noticed, as she walked barefoot along the path. Keeping the yard mowed and edged was part of Brandon's chores—a responsibility he often left till Lisa got after him.

I shouldn't have to remind him. When I was his age, I took care of the yard, cooked all the meals and did most of the shopping.

"Oh, my God," she said stopping in her tracks. "I was a seventeen-year-old housewife."

Unnerved by the thought, she dashed the rest of the way to her private retreat—a place that never failed to calm her nerves. Birds chattered happily in the bright red foliage of the photinia bushes that obscured the fence. White blossoms adorned the honeysuckle vines covering the decorative trellis that had once provided privacy for her mother's hot tub.

The small square spa had been the first thing to go when Constance's new quarters were completed. Now, the shady enclave contained one padded lounge chair with a side table, to accommodate Lisa's book and iced drink when she was reading, and a two-person bench made of wrought iron and redwood for rare visitors.

Lisa sank down on the chaise and kicked out her feet. The sun felt soothing while the morning breeze hinted at the warmth to come. She closed her eyes and took a sip of herbal tea from the mug she carried. She'd forgone coffee this morning since her nerves were still on edge.

Once I get this talk with Joe out of the way, I'll be able to relax, she thought. "I hope," she murmured against the lip of the cup. "Unless he insists on doing something stupid."

She closed her eyes and rested her head against the cushion. A smart person would have stuck around and talked to him last night, rather than prolonged the worry. But at the time, she'd panicked.

After fleeing the hospital like a coward, Lisa had

returned to Joe's Place to put away all the tools and make sure everything was ready for this morning. Martin had been there doing inventory. He'd informed her that Jen and several other neighboring business owners had called to check on Joe's condition. Their concern seemed to demonstrate the fact that while Joe had been home a mere couple of weeks, already he'd reestablished a connection with the townsfolk. Her customers. Her friends.

Once home, Lisa had tossed and turned till dawn. The most pressing question seemed to be whether or not to tell Brandon about his paternity. She wanted to do the right thing for her son, but Lisa knew that if—when—the truth came out, she'd be the one branded as a harlot while sweet, affable Joe walked away with everyone's sympathy.

"I hate him," she muttered, bringing her knees up so she could rest her chin on them. "Why is everything so damn easy for Joe Kelly?"

"Which Joe Kelly would that be?" a voice asked. "Certainly not me."

Lisa's grip on her cup faltered and tea cascaded over her bare knees. She jumped to her feet, brushing lukewarm liquid from her skin.

"Oops, sorry," Joe apologized, hurrying forward. "I didn't mean to scare you. Here."

Lisa's mouth hung open. "Why are you in my yard carrying a towel?"

He held out a yellow towel that had been resting on his shoulder. Lisa recognized it as one of Maureen's.

The terry cloth was damp and smelled of Ivory soap and…Joe.

He combed his fingers through his still-wet hair. "I saw you from the bathroom window and didn't want to miss out on a chance to talk to you alone, so here I am—towel in hand."

He moved closer and dropped to one knee so he could mop up the trickles of liquid running down her shins. Lisa tried to move back but was trapped by her chair. "Don't. It's just tea. It'll dry on its own. Joe," she exclaimed sharply when his ministrations came close to the hem of her cutoff shorts. The loose, skimpy ones that she never wore in public because they were too short.

"Sorry," he said, rocking back on his heels. "I got carried away. How can you have such a perfect tan this soon in the season?"

She snatched the towel from his hand and applied it to the puddle that had collected on the cushion. "Simple," she said, easing down. "You spray it on. No sweating in the sun, no future wrinkles."

"Smart. Not as much fun as oiling you down on the swimming platform at the lake," he said with an exaggerated leer, "but it makes sense."

He walked into her small haven, which seemed to shrink with his presence. "I like what you did back here," he said, stopping to touch a luscious pink rose. "Very peaceful and serene."

With a boyish smile that brought out his dimple, he added, "But you need a water element. A little pond. With koi. I have some I'd be happy to give you."

She almost laughed at his earnest appeal, but reminded herself to be on guard. "No thanks. I have enough responsibilities without adding to the load."

Joe sat down on the settee, hunching forward so his forearms were resting on his knees. She could picture Brandon in a similar pose last night at the hospital. Except for the difference in hair color—

Lisa stopped the thought. She'd spent hours looking at Brandon's baby pictures, searching for a clue that would definitively prove which brother had fathered her child. All she'd come away with was a headache.

"How's the shoulder?"

"Not bad. Could have been ugly, if you hadn't blocked my fall."

Lisa shook her head. "I don't remember doing anything. It happened so fast."

"I agree. One minute I was on top of the ladder, the next I was on the floor looking up. Brandon did an amazing job of capturing the moment on tape. He has good instincts."

Lisa rubbed at the pain that blossomed between her eyes. "I suppose you're going to tell me that he inherited that ability from you."

When Joe didn't answer right away, she lowered her hand and looked at him. His expression seemed bemused, as if the thought hadn't struck him until just that moment. Lisa groaned. "Stop it, Joe. We have a lot of hard decisions to make that will impact my son in a huge way, so I don't want the issue muddied with emotion."

"'Muddied with emotion?' What does that mean? You're not some mechanical drone who can turn off her feelings, Lisa. This is eating you up inside, just like it is me. I can see it on your face." He cleared the distance between them, moving her feet aside so he could sit on the flat part of the chaise.

He leaned close—too close—and touched his finger to her forehead. "This line is new, isn't it? From last night I'd bet. You didn't sleep, did you? You paced and stewed and fretted."

Lisa hated that he knew her so well. "I went to the bar after I left the hospital. To put away our tools and equipment," she said truthfully.

"I know. I went there, too." He hesitated a second then added, "To talk to Martin."

Lisa heard a confession in that statement. She groaned. "You told him, didn't you?"

"Yes."

Frustration and fear made her strike out. She kicked his thigh with the heel of her foot. "Damn you. I asked you not to tell anyone."

Joe pressed his palm to her ankle, not hard but solidly enough to prevent her from kicking him again. "Actually, you said not to talk to Brandon or Mom. You didn't name Martin on that list."

She blew out an exasperated breath. "That sounds like something your brother would have said—in the seventh grade." Joe had the grace to blush. "Patrick was a master at sidestepping the truth."

He met her gaze directly and said, "Everybody

knew that about him. So, why did you believe him when he told you I was sterile?"

Lisa brought both hands up to her face, half covering her nose and mouth. "I don't know. Because he seemed so sincere? Because I couldn't imagine anyone lying about something like that?"

"Maybe you wanted to believe him because it was easier."

She sat straight. "What part was easy? The part where I told him I cheated on him? The part where he asked me to marry him and I said yes, even though…" She caught herself before she spilled her guts completely. "Before you point a finger, you should ask yourself why *you* never questioned Brandon's paternity."

The emotions she'd kept bottled up so long began to come to the surface like water from a broken main. "Why didn't you ever ask me if there was even a remote chance that Brandon was yours?"

"Well, we only did it that once."

"As opposed to the hundreds of times your brother and I made love?"

The bitterness in her voice must have been obvious because Joe frowned. "I guess so."

"Here's a news flash. Patrick liked to talk about sex a lot more than he actually got around to doing it."

The look on Joe's face said he didn't believe her. "I still have my calendar from that year," she said. "You know me—an inveterate packrat. I dug it out when your mother let slip about Patrick's mumps.

"I used to put a diagonal hatch mark through the days when Patrick and I were together, euphemistically speaking."

"And…" Joe prompted.

"And there weren't that many marks in May or June."

Joe shook his head. "I remember seeing you together all the time. You made out a lot."

"Patrick was very affectionate, especially if he thought someone was watching. But from the last week of school till the first of July, there were only four times that could have produced a baby. Four to one, Joe. That's your odds."

He put out his hands. "How was I to know that? Pat was always talking about your wild nights together. He told me you'd do anything he asked. Anywhere, any time."

Humiliation warred with anger. "That bastard. Why do men boast about conquests that never took place?"

"Not all men kiss and tell, Lisa. I used to beg Patrick to keep that aspect of your relationship to himself. I don't know why it was so important to him for me know—or at least *think*—that you were screwing every night of the week."

"I know why."

His brows lifted in the exact same way Brandon's did.

"He was jealous of you."

"Bullshit. Pat was a star athlete. Homecoming king. Everybody loved him."

She shook her head. "No. You loved him. In fact, you worshipped him, which is why he took advantage of you."

"That's crap," Joe said shooting to his feet.

"And it drove him crazy that no matter what he did, you still came out on top."

Lisa scrambled to her knees. Fueled by pent-up anger, she said, "You were the one who got a scholarship to a prestigious art school, while Patrick started driving trucks. He told everyone that was because you were an egghead and he couldn't stand being cooped up in some stupid classroom. But we all knew the real reason. Patrick wouldn't have passed any of his classes without you doing his homework."

Joe's blush told her she'd scored a hit.

"Pat was a little slow in school, but he more than made up for it on the playing field. He was brilliant," Joe said defensively.

"He was a bully. He made a great quarterback because everybody on the team knew that if they screwed up, they'd become the butt of one of Pat Kelly's nasty jokes."

Joe ran a hand through his still damp hair. "None of that really pertains to the matter at hand, does it?"

"Of course, it does. Your brother lied to us, Joe. You believed him because he was your brother, your twin. And you couldn't in a million years conceive of him doing something that despicable."

She pointed to her chest. "I bought his lie because, face it, he was staying. You were leaving. He offered.

You never did. He told me he l-loved me." She hated that her voice betrayed her. "And I promised to love him back, but apparently a wife and kid on the way weren't enough to keep him sober."

Joe made a move as if to reach for her, but Lisa pulled back, curling her arms around her knees defensively. "I tried to do the right thing. I tried to be a good mother, to keep Brandon connected to your family. But I'm tired of putting everyone else's needs first. After I send my son to college, I'm selling the bar and getting the hell out of Worthington. For good."

"I don't believe you."

"Tough. You're a stranger who's just passing through. You don't know me. Or my son. And, frankly, I think it's too late to try to pick up the pieces of a life you never wanted to live."

"I'm not a stranger. I know the person that you were," he insisted. "At one time, we were best friends. You told me all your secrets."

Lisa felt a tingle of apprehension. "Maybe. A long time ago. But that girl had little dreams. She was easily satisfied, but not me. I—"

"Used to sketch house designs inside the back of your binder. Whole floor plans with elaborate gardens." He took a step closer. "That's where I got the idea for my koi pond. From something you once drew." He pinned her in one spot with the intensity of his look. "You talked about planting roots. You said you wanted to travel, but only if you had a place to come home to."

She shivered as if he'd reached a hand into her psyche and pulled out her deepest secret.

"I don't remember telling you any of that."

His smile told her he recognized the lie. "I do. I can even tell you where and when you said it. One Saturday. We were juniors, I think. Patrick was being an ass and your mother had done something to upset you. So you packed a bag and walked to the bus depot. Where I found you."

"I was going to move to Indiana and live with my dad," she said softly. She remembered feeling humiliated to discover that the forty dollars in her pocket wouldn't get her even halfway there. She'd used the pay phone to call her father collect, and once again he'd let her down.

"I'm sorry, honey," he'd said. "But now isn't a good time. Your sister has been pretty sick, lately. The doctors want to perform surgery to fix the hole in her heart."

Lisa had screamed something rude about the hole in his head and crumpled to the ground weeping. That was where Joe had found her.

He'd made her get in his car and they'd driven to the park where he'd held her and listened to her rant. Eventually, they got around to talking about their dreams. Joe's was film school. Hers was to have a real home, a real family. He hadn't teased her or called the idea sappy, as his brother would have. And she'd rewarded him with a kiss. A comforting, friendly kiss that had ended when some friends in another car drove past and honked the horn.

"I was a kid. I was…the same age as Brandon."

He nodded. "I know. I was just thinking about how long we've known each other…and how seldom we were honest with each other. Don't you think it's time we started?"

When he took a step closer, she put out her hand to stop him. "Joe, our lives are too complicated. If you want to tell Brandon what happened between us, I can't stop you, but he's been through a lot the past couple of years. I don't know if now is the right time."

"Is that the mother in you talking or the coward?"

She clenched her fist. "Is that the judgmental asshole in you talking or just your usual big-headed self?"

Joe burst out laughing. "Oh, God, I've missed you, Leese." Hand to his heart, he tapped his chest. "Brutal honesty. That's a rare commodity in my world."

Lisa refused to be swayed by his dimple. "Oh, cut the crap, Joe. You're just as freaked out as I am. You always try to spin a situation with humor, but that isn't going to wash this time. Your brother lied, damn him. He lied on purpose. Why? I don't know, but he clearly had his own agenda. If you can forgive him for that, then you're a more generous person than I am, because, frankly, I'm furious.

"And I'm also worried as hell what this revelation will do to my son when he finds out."

"Finds out what?"

At the sound of Brandon's voice, Lisa turned so fast she bumped into Joe, who swept her into his arms and said after just the briefest hesitation, "Your mom and I are getting back together."

CHAPTER TEN

BRANDON WASN'T SURE what to make of his mother and his uncle goofing around. "How could you get back together when you never were together in the first place?" he asked.

"Joe was kidding, Brandon. You know what a joker he is. We were talking about...about what to give Maureen and Gunny for a wedding gift."

Brandon didn't believe that for a minute. Something was up. Something his mother didn't want him to know about. And Brandon was pretty sure whatever it was included Joe.

"Okay," Joe said with a careless shrug. "Maybe that was wishful thinking on my part. But speaking of gifts, what do you think about the three of us posing for a family portrait to give your grandmother?"

His mother didn't answer right away so Brandon said, "Won't there be a photographer at the wedding?"

"Brandon's right, Joe. And we have so much to do in the next two weeks I don't know when we'd squeeze in a formal sitting, but we can definitely add that to our list of things to do at or immediately after the wedding."

"As long as you put it on the agenda," Joe said.

Something in his tone sounded serious, real serious. Brandon looked at his mother who answered just as solemnly, "Just so long as we don't lose focus on your mother's big day. This is all about making her happy, remember?"

The two were like tennis players rallying, and Brandon wondered what they were *really* talking about.

"She won't be happy if we're not," Joe said.

"Well, she's not going to be happy when she finds out the band we planned to hire canceled."

Brandon lifted his hand. "Um, Mom," he said, waggling the portable phone he was holding. "Martin says Bob the contractor is at the bar. He wants to know if—"

His mother grabbed the receiver. "Oh, no. I have to go. How did it get so late?"

She looked at Joe as though he'd somehow screwed with the clocks then took off running barely sputtering, "'Bye, honey. I'll call you later." Oddly, that made Brandon breathe a little easier. Surely a person who was in love with another person didn't just run off without a kiss or something.

Brandon turned to his uncle and found Joe staring at him as if he'd never seen him before. Suddenly uncomfortable, Brandon asked, "Are you filming today?"

"No. Doctor's orders." Joe reached up and massaged his shoulder as if he'd just remembered that he'd injured it. "She told me to rest up at least twenty-four hours."

"Oh." Brandon tried to hide his disappointment, but apparently some of it showed because Joe said, "That doesn't mean we can't review footage and start cleaning up some of the shots we already have. Do you want to help?"

Brandon nearly did a back flip. He couldn't explain how right it felt to be involved in Joe's movie. He loved the feeling of the camera in his hand and looking through the viewfinder. "What would I do?"

Joe scratched his head. "I don't know exactly. We'll have to see what comes."

Brandon hesitated. He had yard work to do for his mother and he'd promised to meet Rory and Winston at the skate park. If he didn't show up, they'd think he was a loser. "I have to mow the lawn this morning. But maybe I'll come over later."

Brandon walked him as far as the gate. He wanted to ask about Joe's feelings for his mother, but he didn't want to sound like some kind of nosy jerk. "Um, you were just kidding back there, right?" Brandon said, indicating his mother's private garden. "You and Mom aren't really…"

Joe put his hand on Brandon's shoulder. "Lisa was my first love, but I was too shy to ask her out."

"So my dad did."

"Exactly. But that doesn't mean I stopped…um, caring for her."

Brandon couldn't tell if that meant he loved her or not. He hoped not. Joe was an okay guy, but his mom was…well, his mom.

"Okay, honey, have fun," Lisa said, hanging up the phone behind the bar. *Have fun. Have fun helping your uncle, or should I say, your father?*

Lisa let out a little cry and pinched the bridge of her nose. She'd been at Joe's Place for nearly an hour, but the whole time she'd wanted to turn around and hash things out with Joe.

According to Brandon, Joe had decided to spend the day editing his movie, and he'd invited Brandon to help. Whether this was a good thing or some insidious plot to get close to her son, Lisa didn't know.

Your mother and I are getting back together. The words echoed in Lisa's head like the jingle from an annoying commercial. *The man is insane,* Lisa thought, her teeth grinding in frustration. And what the heck was that about a family photo?

She was pretty sure the underlying text of their dialogue meant Joe agreed with her to put off telling Brandon the news until after the wedding. But who really knew what Joe was thinking? The man was a loose cannon. At times, he made Patrick look like the sane one.

"You okay, Lisa?" a voice asked.

She opened her eyes and dropped her hand. Martin was standing across the bar from her, a bundle of mail in hand. "Oh, sure, just thinking about all that I need to do."

"I thought Joe was going to film every step?"

She reached for the bag of disposable gloves she'd

bought to protect her hands when she started stripping the varnish off the bar. "Well, I doubt if this would make or break his movie," she said with a wink.

"Where's Brandon? Isn't he supposed to be helping you?"

"That was Brandon on the phone," she said, nodding over her shoulder. "Joe invited him to work on editing."

"The boy was all over that camera yesterday," Martin said. "Something he gets from his father, maybe?"

Lisa looked up. She knew that Martin and Joe had talked about the situation, but she wasn't ready to discuss this matter with her friend. "I don't know. I'm just happy to see him showing some interest in something. For a while there, I was afraid he was going to turn into one of those kids who hates everything."

She started to walk away but stopped when the phone rang. She picked it up. A telemarketer hoping to sell her a time-share in Hawaii. As she replaced the receiver, she remembered her first call of the morning and the fact that she still needed a band to play at Maureen's wedding.

"Damn," she muttered. "Hey, Martin, you don't happen to know any bands, do you? At this point, we'd probably be lucky to find a really bad DJ."

Martin looked bemused by her quantum leap in topic but said, "Yes, actually, my nephew plays in a band."

"*What?* Have you been holding out on me? I need names, numbers. Now."

His left eyebrow rose.

Lisa laughed and touched his arm. "Sorry. I've had a crazy morning. This feels like a sign that maybe everything will work out okay." She knew that didn't make any sense, but Lisa needed something to go right for a change.

Martin set down the mail to write a number on the back of a napkin. He handed it to her. "The band plays salsa music. That might not be what you're looking for, but they're very good. I have their CD if you'd like to listen to it."

Lisa frowned. "If they're good, they're probably booked."

He shook his head. "Carlos's wife just had a baby. He took a month off from touring, but he told me the other day that he'd like to pick up a couple of local gigs."

Lisa pressed the paper to her chest. "You are a lifesaver, my friend. I love you."

"Hello," a cheery voice called from the back of the building. A moment later, the swinging doors of the kitchen pushed outward and Maureen walked in.

Lisa was close enough to Martin to see him visibly tense. She looked at Maureen, who was dressed in white slacks, a navy-and-white striped top and a red blazer. The moment Maureen spotted Martin, her step faltered. *Curious,* Lisa thought.

"Gunny's waiting in the car," Maureen said, walking around the outside of the bar, "but I couldn't remember if Saturday's take got deposited."

"Of course it did," Martin said testily. "Don't you trust me?"

Lisa gaped. She'd never heard him speak so coldly to his employer, his friend. Lisa looked at Maureen.

"You know I do, but with everything that's been going on I thought it might have been overlooked." Maureen gave a small, halfhearted smile.

Martin crossed his arms. "Or maybe, you thought I took the entire seven hundred and forty-one dollars to Table Mountain and lost it at the craps table."

Lisa nearly swallowed the breath mint she'd just put in her mouth. She knew Martin never gambled at the nearby casino. He'd said many times that money was too hard to come by to risk on a game of chance.

Maureen looked at the ceiling and heaved a great sigh. Then she turned on one heel and marched away.

Neither Lisa nor Martin spoke for a good minute, then Lisa said, "Well, I don't know what that was about, but I'm pretty sure it didn't involve gambling."

Martin picked up the mail that he'd set on the bar next to the jar of maraschino cherries. "Not the kind you mean, anyway."

After sorting the bills from the flyers, he walked to the office and left a minute later. Lisa thought about calling Maureen to find out what was going on between her and Martin, but instead she called the number Martin had given her. She figured some days you were better off picking music over drama.

NINE DAYS HAD PASSED since Joe's conk on the head and shoulder. He'd avoided climbing any more ladders and he hadn't picked up any power tools just in case Lisa was right when she'd called him a klutz. But when he wasn't busy working with his students—and Brandon—he'd found other ways to contribute to the remodeling effort that didn't involve electricity or leaving the ground. Like washing windows.

The exercise had increased the mobility in his sore shoulder, but that didn't mean he enjoyed the work. "I hate this job," he muttered, applying a spray cleaner to a section of plate glass.

"Whiner."

Lisa's tone held a teasing quality he'd missed hearing since their big confrontation. For the most part, she gave him a wide berth, but today she was tackling the window to Joe's left.

She and Brandon had removed the large neon signs from both windows the day before when Joe's film crew was present. Joe had been surprised by what a difference that small change made to the place. The main barroom, already made lighter and brighter thanks to the clean walls and new skylights, seemed fresher and more welcoming.

Was Joe comfortable with the change? He wasn't sure, but, at least, Lisa seemed happy with the progress they'd made—renovation-wise. She also seemed content to avoid talking about their relationship.

Joe wasn't sure that was a good thing, either. But after blurting out that he wanted to get back together with her and having Lisa shoot that suggestion out of the air with a very annoyed "He's kidding," Joe was reluctant to broach the subject.

The only real positive in Joe's life was his blossoming relationship with Brandon, who seemed genuinely enamored of all aspects of moviemaking.

Joe didn't delude himself into believing that Brandon's friendly attitude would remain the same if... *when* he learned the questions surrounding his paternity, but Joe was prepared to deal with that later. He hoped right after his mother's wedding.

Which was a week from today. The last Saturday in June.

"Tomorrow's Father's Day," Lisa said.

"I know. Gunny is spending the weekend with his kids, which is why Mom decided to use the time to take Brandon shopping for a new suit. They'll spend the night in the city and come home tomorrow."

Joe unrolled a few sheets of paper towels then set the roll back on the floor between them. He aimed his bottle of blue liquid at another section of glass. "I was a little surprised that he agreed to go with her. Patrick and I used to hate shopping for clothes. Was it because she let him drive her car?"

"Probably. But Brandon's a good shopper. We never had a lot of money, so I used to drag him all over to find the best deals."

He didn't like thinking about Brandon and Lisa struggling on a budget while he was spending big bucks to fit the Hollywood image of a successful moviemaker. He remembered hearing someone say that in the film industry fame is measured in cat years. If you're out of the limelight for a year or two...

"Joe."

"Huh?" he said, looking over to see Lisa staring at him. "Sorry. I was daydreaming."

"I asked if you feel bad because we haven't told him yet? This is another Hallmark moment you're missing."

Her question irked him. It somehow implied that he had a choice in the matter. "You set the agenda and I've chosen to go along with it because I'm the outsider here. You know Brandon better than I do."

She wiped a section of glass with short, focused movements. The sunlight coming through the window made her skin luminous. "And I appreciate that. I guess I'm feeling ambivalent because as a child I hated this holiday. I just knew that somewhere in the world some little girl was going out to brunch with her daddy or walking hand in hand with him at the zoo and my dad never even bothered to call."

Joe heard the tremor in her voice and knew how badly she missed having a relationship with her father. "I don't think Brandon would like me holding his hand at the zoo."

She picked up the window cleaner and lifted it as if she intended to pitch it at him. Instead, she shook her head and said, "No, I don't think he would."

Joe put out his hand for the bottle. He held it to the window and sprayed. "Maybe it's different with guys," he said. "I used to send my dad a card if I thought about it, but I can't remember doing anything big unless Mom set it up."

He wadded up a few sheets of paper towel and tackled the wet area with a vengeance. When he was done, he stepped back to look for streaks. The bright red blossoms from the geraniums in the window box seemed to invite the outside in. Wouldn't his dad have hated all this light and beauty? Joe's Place was supposed to be the kind of place where people escaped from the real world to forget their problems, not to celebrate the sunny cheer of the day.

"Do you know what's stupid? I still send my dad a card every year. I never hear back from him, but I always waste half an hour picking out just the right sentiment—not too mushy, not too generic, then write a few words and send it off. Dumb, huh?"

He turned to look at her. The sunlight made her hair glisten like gold. Her brow was wrinkled in a way that made Joe want to hold her and kiss away her sadness. But he didn't dare. Not until they had things settled with Brandon.

As if reading his mind, Lisa looked at him and said, "Maybe we should discuss what we're going to tell Brandon. I'm afraid that the closer he gets to you, the more of a shock it's going to be."

"You're the one who suggested we wait until Mom is safely on her honeymoon," Joe said testily. "If you'd prefer I take out an ad in the paper, just say the word."

"Are you two fighting again?" a voice asked.

Lisa gave a little peep and spun around. Constance was standing in the doorway of the kitchen.

"Mom," Lisa exclaimed. She gave Joe a look that told him she hadn't discussed the matter of Brandon's paternity with her mother. "What are you doing here?"

Constance was dressed in her nurse's uniform, but with the top two buttons open. "I thought I'd stop on the way home and say goodbye. I won't see you until next Friday."

Joe blinked in surprise. He hadn't heard any mention of a trip. "Where are you going?" he asked.

"Back east to meet Jerry's family," she answered with a grimace. "His mother and two of his brothers live in Massachusetts. I'm pretty sure they'll hate me on sight." She made a motion of nonchalance with her hand. "But at least I'm getting a free trip out of it."

Lisa put down her cleaning supplies and walked across the room to where her mother was standing. "Stop thinking so negatively. They're going to love you. Just like Jerry does."

Constance seemed a bit tearful and uncertain. "You really think he loves me?"

Considering the friction Joe usually detected between mother and daughter, he was surprised when Lisa put her arm around her mother's shoulder. "He wouldn't be taking you home to meet his family if he didn't. Now, quit worrying."

Constance gave a wobbly smile. "I'll try."

"Good. Are your bags packed?"

She nodded. To Joe, Constance said, "Lisa let me

raid her closet in case they're ultraconservative people. Jerry likes what he calls my avant-garde look, but I didn't think bold colors and leather were a good idea."

Joe grinned. If Lisa's closet was empty, did that mean she had nothing to wear? His grin faltered when it dawned on him that with Constance leaving town Lisa would be alone until Maureen and Brandon returned.

Oh, God.

"Huh?" Joe said, realizing the women were looking at him and expecting an answer. "Sorry. My mind was wandering." *No. Don't go there. Only an idiot would play with that kind of fire.*

Lisa was frowning. She couldn't read his mind. Right?

"Mom asked if you wanted to use her car while she's gone."

"That's very generous of you, Constance. I'd appreciate it. Every time I suggest renting a car, Mom has a fit. She says I should walk more."

"I'll leave the key on the kitchen counter," Constance said. She waved goodbye then turned to leave. Lisa walked her out. They were talking too softly for Joe to catch their words. He did notice that Constance was grinning, while Lisa was not.

After Lisa returned to the barroom, Joe asked, "Do you think this thing with Jerry is serious? Your mother seems pretty invested, emotionally."

Lisa stopped in the middle of the room and looked

up at the new skylights. Her smile told him she liked what she saw. "To tell you the truth, I've never seen Mom act like this. She's giddy and nervous when they're together, and she pouts when he doesn't call.

"In the past, Mom set the rules when she was dating a man. Jerry doesn't appear to play by her rules, and believe it or not, Mom seems to be okay with that."

"Maybe it's love."

Lisa met Joe's gaze. She took a breath and slowly let it out before answering. "Maybe it is."

Joe had never known Lisa to cut her mother any slack when it came to men. He wasn't sure why, but he felt oddly heartened by Lisa's admission.

"What time does Martin come in?" he asked. Since the bulk of the remodeling was done, they'd re-opened the bar. His good intentions were warring with the image of a romantic dinner—steaks on the grill, a little music, some candles.

"He isn't working tonight."

"What?" His fantasy evaporated.

Lisa returned to the window, snatching a scrap of paper towel as she passed by him. Rubbing at a speck too small for Joe to see, she told him, "He asked for the night off, which, frankly, has me a little worried. Have you noticed how quiet Martin's been lately? I think something's bothering him."

"Martin broods. It's part of his image." When she made a scoffing sound, he added, "Hey, I've known him since I was a little kid. He's always been inscrutable."

Lisa gave him a look that told him he was a fool. "Your mother read me a review of one of your movies a few years ago. I can't remember which, but it said you had a 'keen eye for the details of life' or something to that effect."

Joe felt his cheeks heat up. "What's your point?"

"Maybe those details only apply to life outside of Worthington."

Joe took a step toward her. "You're a brat. You know that?"

She laughed saucily. "That sounds like something your brother would have said." Sobering, she added, "Martin is your friend and he's in pain. I didn't think he'd open up to me, but you're a guy. The least you could do is ask."

Joe watched her walk through the swinging doors into the kitchen. She was right. He'd been so wrapped up in his personal dilemma—and filming his movie— he hadn't been paying attention to those closest to him.

But it wasn't too late to change. Starting with Lisa.

LISA LOOKED AT THE CLOCK and stifled a yawn. Less than an hour to go. Thank God. It had been a long, busy night. Joe had proven to be a big help. Instead of conducting interviews, he'd filled in wherever needed—waiter, dishwasher, cashier and doorman.

She glanced sideways. He was perched on a stool behind the bar, one elbow resting on the counter below the mirror as he attempted to read the operational manual for the new beer glass washer that she'd had installed. The light was poor in that part of the bar, but she didn't invite him to come closer to the cash register. Lisa needed the space to help diffuse the sexual tension between them.

Only an idiot would try to pretend the edgy little tingle she felt every time Joe touched her didn't exist. Lisa wasn't dumb. Nor was she blind to the fact that her son was out of town tonight. With Brandon and Maureen on their shopping trip and Constance winging it east, Joe and Lisa had two empty houses to choose from if they wanted to make up for lost time.

If.

"You look pooped," Joe said, taking her by surprise. "Do you want me to close up so you can go home?"

She hopped off her stool and stretched. "No, thanks. I was just thinking about Brandon. I told him not to pick out anything too expensive, but your mother spoils him."

"She was that way with me and Patrick, too," Joe said with a smile. "Dad would have a fit every August when we went shopping for school clothes. He'd say, 'It stays hot around here until October, whatcha spending all that money for now?'"

Lisa could picture it. Joe's father had been generous to her in many ways, but he was a conservative spender. She was one of the few employees who stuck around for long at Joe's Place. Except for Martin.

Martin's relationship with the family had always

seemed a given and she honestly hadn't questioned it until now.

Before she could bring up the subject, the door crashed open and four bodies stumbled in, laughing and tripping over each other's feet.

"College boys," Lisa told Joe. "Good money, but not without a few…um, challenges."

"Leeesaaaa," the tallest of the four—a Nordic god minus the armor—sang. "Hey, baby, I'm here," he said, breaking free of the cluster to stagger to the bar.

Lisa could feel Joe's questioning gaze and fought to control her blush. Surely he didn't think she had anything going with a boy only a few years older than her son. "Hi, Jeremy. Taking a little break before summer school starts?"

His answer was lost in the hubbub created when his friends joined him, pushing and jostling to get the best stool. To Joe, she said, "I call them the Js."

"Why?"

"You'll see."

The four were so loud and obnoxious it took nearly five minutes for them to quiet down enough that Lisa could take their orders. "What will it be tonight, boys? Beer with a water chaser?"

The four looked at each other and roared as if she were a real comedian. Lisa sensed heads turning. Her other patrons had no doubt been enjoying the quiet. Lisa had no control over who entered her establishment, but she could set a limit on how unruly they became.

Jeremy shushed his friends then asked, solemnly, "Did you miss us?"

"Absolutely," Lisa said, crossing her fingers out of sight behind the bar. "I actually thought you might have gone home for the summer." She kept her tone friendly, but added seriously, "You know I can't serve you unless you have a designated driver."

A round-faced boy with spiky hair that was already showing evidence of male-pattern baldness raised his hand. "I stopped drinking two bars ago, Lisa. I'm fine. Honest."

"Good for you, Jordon. How 'bout a mocha?"

"Cool."

Lisa looked at Joe and said, "Will you get Jeremy, Josh and Jacob their beers while I go to the kitchen for Jordon's mocha?"

Joe's lips twitched and he mouthed, "The Js." Aloud, he said, "Three brewskies coming up."

The young men laughed at the passé term.

Lisa spotted Joe's annoyed frown, but kept walking. She had to quit looking at Joe, wondering if what she'd seen in his eyes when he'd learned that her mother was going out of town meant what she thought it did. She'd purposely not mentioned the trip because she hadn't wanted him to get the wrong idea.

She told herself they would be foolish to even consider "hooking up," as her college-student friends called it. But, damn, if her traitorous body wasn't tingling all over at the prospect.

When she returned with a large paper cup filled

with the mocha, she had to go looking for the Js. They were grouped around the pool table, which was off to one side of the building.

Good place for them. Was that Joe's idea or theirs? she wondered.

"Thanks, Lisa. We paid the new guy," Jordon said, taking the hot drink from her. The other three pushed colored balls around the green felt, missing more often than they connected, which seemed to delight them no end.

After checking on the patrons at her other tables, Lisa was on her way back to the bar when a hand suddenly grabbed her arm and pulled her up against a solid chest. The muscles showed the kind of toning that came from years of water polo.

"I've been missing you, Lisa," Jeremy said. The *Se*s came out as a "sh" sound that made her name sound like Leesha.

"Oh, that's sweet, Jeremy," she said, trying to extricate herself from his clammy grip.

His right arm plopped across her shoulder—dead weight that almost made her stumble. She stuck the damp, smelly bar rag that she used to wipe off the empty tables directly under his nose.

His head fell back and his grip faltered, but before Lisa could step away, he jumped sideways as if plucked from behind by the hand of God.

"What the f—?"

Jeremy's rude epithet was cut short when a fist bunched the material of his Hooters T-shirt right under his throat and squeezed.

"Don't ever…put your hands…on Lisa…again." Joe's sentence was slow and emphatic.

Jeremy's eyes went wide for a moment, and then narrowed belligerently. He tried to take a swing at Joe, but Lisa blocked the punch. On a less-impaired day, Jeremy could have done bodily harm to any opponent.

"Js," she said, giving them her sternest mother look. "Don't do anything stupid that gets you banned from the bar. You know the rules. No fighting."

"Tell that to him. He started it," Jeremy whined.

Joe dropped his hold and stepped back, but she could tell by the set of his shoulders he didn't trust his opponent not to try something foolish.

"Well, boys," Lisa said, "that's the thing. When Joe is working, he gets to set the rules."

Lisa wasn't sure which rule they'd broken. A brand new one that said no male customer was allowed to touch her?

The four Js looked at each other and seemed to come to some kind of silent consensus. "We're out of here," one of them said. They turned to leave, Jeremy in the lead. Only Jordan lingered. "Sorry about that, Lisa," he said, chin down.

She gave him a one-arm hug. "Don't sweat it. Joe and I were your age once. Sometimes the beer gets away from you. Come back next weekend and I'll buy you one. No, wait," she corrected herself. "We're closed next weekend for Joe's mother's wedding."

Jordon looked momentarily surprised then made a motion that seemed to say he understood. "You're *that*

Joe," he said looking at the man beside her. "Now, I get it. Mrs. Kelly told us that you and Lisa had a thing for each other." He smiled broadly. "That'll make Jeremy feel better. He'd never poach another guy's turf."

He saluted them both with his paper cup then hurried after his friends.

"Turf?" Joe repeated.

"They're kids," Lisa said, purposely trying to keep the conversation's focus off anything personal. "And scaring away customers is not the best way to run a business. You could prove to be a liability."

He took her arm in a much gentler manner, but his touch was far more meaningful than Jeremy's had been. "Or, perhaps, I'm an underutilized asset."

"What does that mean? Do you really think I couldn't defend myself from a tipsy twenty-one-year-old?"

"Not at all. You're obviously a pro at deflecting unwanted attention. I'm talking about us."

"Which us is that, Joe? Old friends? Co-workers? Near-miss in-laws?"

"How 'bout the us that feels an undeniable attraction for each other?"

Joe ran his finger down the side of her face and tilted her chin upward so they were looking directly into each other's eyes. She captured his hand and held it away from her skin. She couldn't think when he was touching her. She dropped his hand and walked to the bar.

Joe took the seat Jeremy had used when he'd come in earlier. "Tell me to leave and I will. Honest. I know as well as you do what a mistake this probably is, but…I want to be with you, Lisa. I have since the first moment I saw you at the airport." He chuckled. "Hell, since the first day of seventh grade."

Lisa felt a bit woozy. Like she'd walked into a time warp or something. She'd made the wrong decision once before and it had come back to haunt her. Would this time be any different?

"Just because we have a small window of opportunity doesn't mean we should take it." Although she wanted to. So badly she could almost taste it.

"I agree," he said solemnly. "This isn't about getting lucky, although being with you—even just sitting here talking to you—makes me feel like the most fortunate of men. It's about coming full circle."

"I don't know what you mean."

"Yes, you do. You just don't want to admit it."

"Admit what?"

"That you're my soul mate and I've spent the last seventeen years trying to outrun my destiny."

Lisa laughed. She had no choice. Because if he was serious then she might be tempted to believe him. And she didn't dare do that. "Quit messing with my head, Joe, or you'll be sleeping alone."

He didn't smile. If anything, the gravity of the look in his eyes intensified. Then a moment later, his mouth pulled to one side and his dimple appeared. Lisa's heart turned over.

"Did you just ask me to spend the night with you?" he asked in a low, sexy whisper.

Her cheeks grew so warm she almost picked up an ice cube to cool them down. "Um…yes."

He rose up on his forearms and leaned across the bar to pull her into a kiss. "Is it closing time yet?"

Lisa shook her head. Now, this Joe she remembered all too well. Serious one minute, joking the next. Was she just a trifle disappointed that he didn't push harder to find out how Lisa truly felt about him? Maybe. But another part of her was already planning ahead.

CHAPTER ELEVEN

JOE ENTERED LISA'S ROOM SLOWLY, trying to see every-thing at once. He felt like a monk being allowed en-trance to a holy shrine, although his body's response to Lisa was anything but monk-like.

"Nice," he said smiling at the whimsical mix of color. Two walls were sunshine yellow, the other two salmon. The fluffy comforter was a swirling mix of the two shades against a white background. He fingered a sheer turquoise scarf draped over a lampshade with a beaded fringe. "I like the gypsy overtones."

She laughed. "My mother calls it a waste of glam-our since I never entertain here."

As if regretting that revelation, she hurried to a bed-side table and bent over to withdraw a small box of matches from its drawer. She used several to light half a dozen votive candles scattered around the room.

When Joe moved to give her access to a chest-high dresser, he noticed the framed photograph resting atop it. The one Brandon had mentioned that first night after Joe had returned home, the same shot that was hanging in the bar.

He picked it up. Three friends, mugging for the camera, on a perfect summer day. They'd spent the entire day at the lake, swimming and pigging out on junk food. Lisa sat between the two brothers.

Joe studied his brother's face. So familiar and, yet, a stranger. A fact that still hurt.

Not now, he told himself. *This is about Lisa and me, not Patrick.*

Lisa blew out the match she held and dropped it in a trash can, then took the photo from him and turned it face down. "No ghosts allowed," she said, echoing his unspoken sentiment.

Her hazel eyes seemed all-knowing. Could she read his mind? "These candles are special," she said. "Good for exorcism." Her tone told him she was joking.

Joe shook his head and chuckled. "And I thought all the kooks were in southern California."

He pulled her into his arms. She threaded her fingers through his hair, studying it. "I like your hair long."

"Jen-Jen made me promise I'd come in and get it styled before the wedding."

She cocked her head and said in a low, sexy voice, "Then, I'd better make the most of tonight. I always fantasized about making love with a tortured artist."

Joe's heart did a midair flip. He wanted her so badly he was half-afraid he might embarrass himself before he even opened the condoms they'd picked up at an all-night pharmacy. As if sensing his dilemma, Lisa slowed things down by stepping away. She turned off the overhead light then walked to a bookcase that held a small stereo and a compact television. She selected a CD and pushed a button.

Joe recognized the singer. Norah Jones. He'd seen her perform at a cast party in L.A. a few years ago.

Lisa turned to face him, then she reached up to remove the clip from her hair. "I probably smell like Joe's Place," she said, ruffling the locks with her fingers. "Do you want to shower fir—"

He cut her off by closing the distance between them and kissing her. "You're perfect," he said. "Just the way I remember."

Her smile seemed tremulous. "The only time we were together was at night, Joe. And we'd been drinking."

"No," he said firmly, lifting a lock of hair to his lips. "Patrick was drinking. I was completely sober, which made it all that much harder to live with my conscience."

When her lips turned down in a frown, he added, "But the only regret I have now is that I never told you how much that night meant to me. How much I loved you. And how beautiful you were."

She brought her hands up between them. "We can't change the past, Joe. So, let's leave it out of this room tonight. Okay?"

Her request surprised him. He'd been about to suggest the idea himself, but hearing Lisa set parameters was something new. In high school, she'd been more of a follower than a leader. He liked this new Lisa. A lot.

He bowed his head and kissed her temple, inhaling the scent of her skin. A subtle mix of soap and lotion blended with the smells of Joe's Place. The combination was surprisingly powerful and made him want to lap her up.

"I desire you more than you could possibly know," he murmured running his hand down her back. He loved the supple flow and sweet curve of her hip.

Her shape had changed since the last time they'd been together. But so had his. A tad more girth around his middle, but at least he'd sharpened a few muscles after his near-miss in December.

"I like what you've done with your body, Joe," Lisa said, running her hands up under his shirt.

Joe felt a lightness rush through his body. An energy that quickened his breath and gave him the strength to bend down and gather her up in his arms. She tensed in surprise then laughed. "What are you doing?"

"Something I've wanted to do ever since you dragged me to that revival of *Gone With the Wind*."

In three steps, he reached the bed where he gently placed her. She cooperated fully with just a hint of shyness as he removed her clothing. The candlelight gave the room a mellow, golden hue. Lisa's body was womanly perfect, but there was something new. Something he'd not seen before.

He ran the tip of his finger across the thin silver scar just below her bikini line. "Cesarean?"

She nodded.

"Why didn't I know that?"

Her shoulders rose and fell. "You didn't ask?"

Guilt stabbed him and he must have winced visibly because she let out a low "Oh…" and put her hands on either side of his face. "I love this scar, Joe. It reminds me of Brandon, who is the best thing that ever happened to me."

He pressed his lips to the scar, spreading slow, purposeful kisses along the entire length. "Thank you," he said, looking up through misty eyes. "Thank you for giving us Brandon."

He watched the tears form in her eyes but she dashed them away and smiled. "No one ever said that to me."

"I'm notoriously late, remember?" he said, drawing her hand to his lips.

"You sent flowers."

He didn't remember that. In fact, all he remembered from the nine months following his brother's death was burying himself in his work.

She turned on her side. Drawing him closer, she brushed back his hair and kissed his forehead. "You were the only one. Maureen brought a big basket of baby clothes and my mother bought a car seat. Your dad gave him a football," she said with a smile. "I was just so relieved because everyone seemed so happy to welcome my son into the world, but you're the only one who sent something to me."

Joe gathered her into his arms. "Oh, sweetheart, I hate to admit this, but we're being honest, right?"

She pulled back slightly, her eyes wide.

"The flowers weren't from me. Maybe mom sent them and put my name on them. I don't know." He rested his forehead against hers. "I was a self-centered jerk at the time. But I've improved over the years. Can you forgive me?"

She took a deep breath. "Your brother never would have admitted that." When she looked at him, Joe knew that the slate had been wiped clean.

He covered her hand with his and said, "Do you know what the doctor said when he looked at the ultrasound of my chest?"

She shook her head.

"He said, 'This isn't Joe's heart, it belongs to Lisa.'"

He watched her lips quiver as she tried to hold in her laughter. When he winked, she couldn't control herself any longer. "That is the sappiest thing I've heard. How can you make jokes at a time like this?"

When her giggles died down, he moved closer and took her face in his hands. "You know me, Leese. You know that's what I do when things get too serious. I hide behind humor.

"But, in complete and utter honesty, I want more than anything to make love with you tonight. Can we do that?"

She hesitated for a fraction of a second then said, "Do you see all these candles, Joe? I've had them around for ages. If you look closely, you'll see that each one says 'Save for Joe.' So, I guess that means…"

Joe let out a whoop and flattened her body beneath

him. "Jokes. How can you make jokes at a time like this?" He kissed her until the laughter turned to passion. Until the humor that had always been a part of their relationship gave way to the desire they'd only allowed to surface once before.

LISA STARED AT THE CEILING and listened to the sound of Joe sleeping. He didn't snore, but his breathing was deeper than hers. It invaded her space. And she loved it. She loved him.

She had no regrets about last night. They'd played and laughed and burned up in each other's heat. He was a kind and thoughtful lover. And he was still here.

After the second time they'd made love, Lisa had expected him to get dressed and walk home, but he'd snuggled next to her and let out a long, relaxed sigh. "You don't mind if I stay, do you?" he'd asked.

She'd been too overcome with emotion to speak. He'd apparently taken her silence as an okay. As he'd drifted off, she'd wept. Not because she was sad, but because she needed to. The men she loved left. Her father. Patrick. Even Joe, although she couldn't blame him since she'd never asked him to stay.

Would he stick around if she asked now? His business, his home, his life was in Los Angeles. And hers was here for the next five years, at least. What would that mean to their relationship? And what exactly was their relationship going to be? Good friends who had sex? The separated parents of a college student who communicated regularly but didn't live together?

She didn't know because they hadn't spoken of the future.

She turned on her side and studied Joe's face. He liked to sleep on his stomach, apparently. No pillow. His left arm was thrown overhead, his right still touched Lisa's upper thigh.

Did I ever stop loving him? The answer was no. Although there had been many times when she wanted to hate him. Like when she was struggling to pay the bills and his mother would relate some story of Joe's high-profile lifestyle. She'd stomp around and kick innocent pieces of furniture until she stopped feeling sorry for herself.

Joe made a snuffling sound and flopped to his back, his arm covering his eyes to keep out the thin, silvery light of dawn. Through the open windows, Lisa could hear the pesky bird that had built a nest in the ornamental pear tree. "Who-wee," it said, over and over.

She wondered what "who-wee" meant in bird.

With the sheet bunched between them, Lisa had an opportunity to study his torso. Her fingers hovered over a small, raised scar the shape of a half moon just above his heart. She couldn't imagine what had caused it, but as she tentatively touched the mark, it occurred to her that they'd both fought their battles alone.

But what about the future? She wished she were the kind of person who could leave the worry about tomorrow to someone else, but that wasn't her nature.

"You're frowning," Joe said, peeking out from under his arm. "I wish you wouldn't do that when my penis is in view."

She chuckled and reached down to touch said body part. "Would it make you feel better if I told you your body is significantly more endowed than your brother's?"

His left brow rose. "Yes, but I don't believe you. I probably saw Patrick naked as often as you did. We even had pissing contests. He always beat me."

Lisa squeezed him in a way that made his body jerk in response. "I'd forgotten how competitive you two were. Unless Patrick needed your help to clean up some fix he'd gotten in."

"Maybe. A couple of times."

"Oh, pooh," she said, running her hand up his belly. "Patrick had a big mouth. He was always on somebody's bad side."

Joe rose up on one elbow and fluffed his pillow so he could sit up against the headboard. "We're talking Patrick. Does that mean the rule against bringing in the past is lifted?"

Lisa flopped back and focused on the ceiling. They'd have to talk about this stuff some time, right? She looked around for her T-shirt, but stopped. Why cover up now?

"Last night was amazing. Truly. But, it's not something we can repeat."

"Why not?"

"Because you live four hundred-plus miles away.

Because my son thinks you're his uncle, and the idea of his mother and his uncle fooling around would probably freak him out."

"But what if we tell him I'm his father?"

Lisa swallowed. "I've been thinking about that Joe and I'm not sure we should."

"What?"

"Well, I mean, how can we know for sure if you are or you aren't? You and Patrick were twins. You share the same DNA, right? And we're assuming that Patrick was sterile, but you haven't had any other children, either. Have you?"

He punched his pillow as if it had wronged him, but when he looked at Lisa he appeared composed, "No."

Drawing a breath for courage, she said, "Well, why put Brandon through the emotional trauma—especially considering his proclivity for drinking and his whole teenage angst thing—if you're just going to go back to L.A. and resume your normal life? Do you see what I mean?"

"I get your point," Joe said, his voice icy. "But I don't agree with it."

Lisa tried to keep her disappointment from showing, but he touched her cheek and said, "I'm tired of lying about my life, Leese. I'm thirty-five years old. In my twenties, I was on the fast track to fame and fortune, but that track ran out. I'm back to doing what I started, making little movies about issues that grab me. I don't have to live in L.A. to do that."

He ran his fingers through his hair in a manner she

found totally endearing. "I'm thinking about moving home, Lisa. Permanently."

She was too shocked to speak. "But you had a reviewer call you the next Orson Welles."

His chuckle sounded bitter. "The trouble with listening to what people say about you is you start to believe it. When it became clear that I wasn't the genius Orson Welles was, I tried to make up for it by strengthening my connections. Which is where Paulette came in."

Lisa lifted her head to look at him. "That sounds too cold and calculated to be you."

"Things like that happen all the time in Hollywood. Ours was a mutually beneficial alliance, at first. I still had enough name recognition to make the red-carpet interviews. But then my fifth movie got canned."

"Panned? Like by reviewers?"

"Nope. Never made it that far. It's still sitting on a shelf in some Hollywood vault."

"Why?"

He let out a sigh. "It was a black comedy about a group of bumbling terrorists who accidentally set off World War III. Unfortunately, its scheduled release date fell two weeks after 9/11."

"Oh. Oh!"

Joe shook his head and quickly added, "I'm not complaining. Really. I lost a friend that day. My first roommate in college was on the plane that hit the Pentagon. He'd been in Washington the week before testifying about inner-city business opportunities for minorities. He was the kind of guy who made a difference in the world. Gone. Just like that."

Lisa slid her leg across his and squeezed closer. "I'm sorry."

"Yeah. Me, too. I couldn't argue about the movie, but I'd been counting on the profits to fund two other projects I had in the works. Then my dad died, and I sort of quit returning calls."

"Sounds like depression."

He nodded. "Probably was. Only I'm a Kelly. We don't do depression or addictions or anything that requires some kind of inner reflection or, God forbid, therapy."

His tone held irony...and raw pain. Lisa nuzzled her nose against the skimpy triangle of chest hair between his pecs. "I'm not a licensed therapist, but I do have a minor in psychology."

"And carpentry," he said, tweaking her ear.

"There you go. First, I rip down your defenses then build healthy, healing structures in place of them."

He chuckled and covered her hand with his. "You're good. I feel better already. Perky, even."

Lisa moved her leg so it covered the body part under discussion. "We're not done talking yet."

He rolled his neck. "I was afraid you were going to say that. Can we finish talking over breakfast? I'm starved. Must have been all that exercise you put me through last night."

"Avoidance behaviors..." she said, shaking her head.

He laughed. "Okay. Okay. The fact is I never really fit in in Hollywood. I'm a small-town guy who loves making movies about people. Real people."

"Can you make a living at that?"

"I don't know, but the industry has changed. Anybody who wants to do what I do can buy a desktop editing program for seven hundred dollars and set up shop. There are boutique editing houses all over the country. If you're good at what you do, people will find you."

And Joe was good at what he did. She knew that. She'd seen all his movies, even though she'd lied about not seeing the last one.

If he was serious about moving back to Worthington, that meant they might have a chance to build a real relationship. Maybe even one her son could come to understand and appreciate.

She gave in to temptation and ran her tongue over the soft, flat tip of his nipple. "Last night was really lovely. I wish you'd come home sooner."

"I doubt if you would have liked me very much. For a while there, I was really full of myself. Shallow, egotistical."

Like Patrick, Lisa thought with sudden clarity.

Patrick's death had created a vacuum that Joe had, in a way, stepped in to fill. He'd picked a fight with his father, treated Lisa with uncharacteristic disdain and turned his back on his family. All behaviors more befitting Patrick's personality than Joe's.

"If Mom had called me and said she was going to

sell Joe's Place, I probably would have swept into town like a conquering hero and sold it to the highest bidder without thinking twice about your situation or Brandon's."

"You'd have done that? Sold the place then left without finding out what any of us wanted?"

He nodded, his expression sad. "Oh, I might have asked, but in the end I'd have done whatever was expedient and had the best result on the bottom line. I know that makes me look like some kind of caricature of a bad guy…"

"Snidely Whiplash."

"I beg your pardon?"

Lisa ran her index finger over the wrinkle in his brow. "Remember the summer you worked at the dinner theater in Jamestown? One night you filled in for the villain."

"That's right," he snickered softly. "The melodrama. People threw popcorn at me."

"The more prepared brought peanuts."

His eyes opened wide when the meaning behind her words sunk in. "You and Patrick."

She tried to look innocent, but her grin must have given her away. He wrapped his arms around her and rolled, so he was on top. "I could have been blinded," he growled, going for her exposed throat.

She let out a muffled scream then in a falsetto said, "Why, Snidely, what a big gun you have."

AN HOUR OR SO LATER, Joe stumbled into the kitchen in search of coffee. Normally, he'd make tea, but considering their lack of sleep, they might both benefit from a jolt of caffeine.

Lisa was perched on a chrome-and-red-leather stool. She was dressed in baggy denim overalls and a yellow top. He detoured to give her a long, satisfying kiss. "I missed you in the shower."

"Yeah, well, I remember what happened last night when we took a shower together. We ran out of hot water we were in there so long."

He couldn't deny that. Just one night in Lisa's arms and he was acting like a lovesick teen. "Is there more of that coffee somewhere?" he asked, trying to regain some dignity.

Before she could answer, the phone beside her rang. "The carafe is by the toaster," she said, picking up the phone. "Cups in the cupboard above it."

"Hello?"

Thinking the caller might be Brandon, Joe watched her face as she listened to the voice on the other end of the line. "Uh, no. Brandon's still with Maureen. How's everything going with you? Did you have a good flight?"

Her mother.

The flush on Lisa's cheeks intensified. Apparently, Constance had overheard Lisa talking to someone and wanted to know who was present with her daughter so early in the morning. Joe was curious how Lisa planned to handle this—and any future public questioning.

"Well, not that it's any of your business," Lisa said testily, "but it's Joe."

Joe was both surprised and relieved.

"No. Yes. Mother," Lisa said sharply. "I don't know."

Lisa looked at Joe and rolled her eyes. He wanted to kiss her. Instead, he poured himself a cup of coffee then walked to the sliding glass door and looked out. He could hear Lisa's one-sided conversation, but instead of listening, his mind was racing.

He'd just spent the night with Lisa. He'd made her breathless and excited. And, damn it, a part of him still felt guilty.

"Good grief," Lisa said, hanging up the phone. "She has a lot of nerve asking me questions about my personal life. Oh, well, at least she likes Jerry's family and they like her. We can be thankful for small miracles, right?"

Joe tried to smile, but he knew he'd missed the mark when Lisa slid off her stool and walked to where he was standing. "What's the matter?"

"Nothing."

Lisa looked at him for several seconds, then she held out her hand. "Come on. We're going to my special place."

He knew where she meant, but something in her tone made him nervous. "Why?"

"We're going to work on your schemas."

"I don't like the sound of that."

She opened the door. "Of course, you don't. It

means you finally have to be honest with yourself. And your brother."

Joe took a sip of coffee and scalded the roof of his mouth. "I can't. I'm injured."

She gave him a stern look that probably made teenage boys quake in their boots. Joe gave in. He remembered her mentioning something about this psychological theory. His family never put much stock in such things, but in the name of research, Joe had participated in several group sessions that dealt with grief. He thought they'd helped. Not enough, but some.

A few minutes later, he and Lisa were seated on the shaded patio. He was resting in the chaise, his ankles crossed. Lisa sat on the bench just across from him.

"Don't look so skeptical. We're just going to talk," she said. "We each did the whole guided-imagery thing in psychology class, and I felt it helped me deal with my feelings about my father, but since I'm not a professional, we won't try anything elaborate. Okay?"

"Okay."

She sat forward, the way he'd been sitting yesterday. "Have you ever heard of schemas?"

"Not till you mentioned it."

"Well, basically, they're coping behaviors. As a kid, we learn that if we do A, we can avoid the unpleasant results of B."

"Huh?"

"For me, I never wanted to rock the boat where my relationship with a man was concerned because if I did, he might leave."

Joe let out his breath. "Your father."

"Exactly. And Patrick."

Joe sank back against the cushion. *Of course.* She'd taken all sorts of crap from his brother but remained loyal. The few times they'd broken up had been Patrick's doing, not because Lisa was the one to walk away.

"Wow. That's pretty insightful," he said.

She made a wry sound. "Yeah, well, knowing what drives you is only part of the therapy. You still have to confront the person behind your schemas."

"What if that person is dead?"

"Sit back. Close your eyes. And I'll show you."

"I don't know, Lisa. Communing with the spirits isn't my idea of a good time."

"This isn't a seance, Joe. It's just a way of looking at your life and drawing some understanding of why you do what you do."

He closed his eyes and rested his head against the cushion but that didn't mean he was relaxed.

"Now, picture your brother. Any age. Just how you remember him best."

Joe felt his heart rate increase. He swallowed hard then tried to do as she asked.

He recalled some old film footage he'd run across a few days earlier. Patrick at a track meet in Snelling. Sixth grade. Before Lisa. Joe had been chosen as an alternate in case someone got hurt. He'd been sitting around, totally bored until another kid's mother had let him use her video camera.

"You and Patrick were polar opposites," Lisa said. "I know that sounds like a cliché, but it's true. You are water. Deep, cool, connected to the earth. Patrick was energy. Bright, fast, dangerous at times."

At the track meet that day, Patrick had beaten nearly every competitor. Afterward, he'd mugged for the camera, boasting about how good he was. He'd also told everyone that the reason Joe hadn't run was that he knew he'd get beaten. "He's a loser," Patrick had said.

Joe's throat went dry and he couldn't swallow.

"You can see him pretty clearly, can't you?" Lisa asked.

He nodded.

"Then, tell him how you feel."

Tell him I felt embarrassed when he belittled me in front of my friends? And stupid when I cheated to give him a better grade? Or that I wanted to beat the shit out of him when he kissed you in front of me?

Joe opened his eyes. He could feel the sweat collecting under his arms. "This is crazy. I don't want—"

She cut him off by putting her hand on his forearm. "I know it seems like a waste of time, but we're almost done."

"What else is there? I told him he was a rotten excuse for a brother. I wasn't perfect, either. Big deal."

"You have to hear him say whatever it is that you always wanted him to say."

He shook his head. "That's too creepy for me." He

started to get up, but Lisa smiled that all-knowing smile of hers. The one he hated, and loved.

"Okay. Take off. I'll see you later."

He hesitated. He knew Lisa, and he knew she'd never let him live this down if he didn't at least pretend to cooperate.

"Fine." He sat back and crossed his arms and ankles. He took a deep breath and let it out, then tried to refocus on the image of Patrick.

What do I need Patrick to say?

The one thing he never would have said if he were alive, of course. A shiver passed through Joe's body and suddenly Patrick was there, sporting the cocky grin that had gotten him in so much trouble in his life.

I was a pretty crappy brother to you, Joe, but I always loved you. You knew that, right?

Joe felt Lisa's hands grip his. "You have to give yourself permission to believe what he's telling you, Joe, because Patrick's actions were the product of certain schemas, too. It's what he did to protect himself."

Joe squeezed his eyes tight. He wasn't going to cry in front of Lisa, but a second later he heard a small sob and felt her arms around his neck. And when her face pressed against his, he wasn't sure whose tears belonged to whom.

CHAPTER TWELVE

"WE'RE AMAZING," Lisa said, stepping into the main hallway so she could survey her and Joe's efforts. The doors to the side-by-side restrooms both stood open. The walls of the men's side, which Joe had painted, were sage green. The walls of the ladies' room were persimmon. "Maybe I should have majored in interior design."

Joe held up his paint-splattered hands and eyed them with obvious distaste. "I wouldn't go that far, but not bad for an afternoon's effort by a couple of amateurs."

"Who are you calling an amateur?" she asked, threatening him with her brush, which was still wet with shiny orange-colored paint.

"Just a slip of the tongue," he said with a suggestive leer.

Their playful banter, although separated by a common wall, had made the hours fly by. They'd kept up a running dialogue, discussing everything from politics to movies to Lisa's need to psychoanalyze people. Lisa realized with a painful tug that she loved Joe's mind, almost as much as she loved his body. Which, she decided, she might still have time to enjoy one more time before her son and Maureen returned.

Although she'd awoken with every intention of returning their relationship to a non-physical plane, something had happened when she'd pushed him into a little introspection. The moment had pulsed with intensity and had possibly provided the emotional healing she'd hoped for. She wasn't sure exactly what Joe had experienced, but she felt closer to him, and that closeness was intoxicating.

"Let's clean up."

Without waiting to see if he followed, she picked up her bucket, roller and pan and started for the rear door of Joe's Place. They'd set up a hose and temporary workbench in the small exterior courtyard everyone called the beer garden.

"Eventually, I'd like to do a little stenciling around the top of the wall," she called out as she walked. "Like the ivy in my bedroom. That turned out nice, don't you think?"

"Huh?"

She looked over her shoulder. Joe was a few steps behind, but his focus seemed fixed on her derriere. Lisa shook her head. What could he possibly find attractive about a female butt in sloppy overalls? Then it hit her that she'd been lusting after his body all afternoon, too, and he was dressed in a funky set of what Brandon would have called "dog shit brown" coveralls that Martin had left hanging in the office.

"We're pathetic," she muttered, shaking her head.

"I beg your pardon," Joe said, reaching past her to hold the door open so she didn't smear paint on the knotty-pine paneled walls. The billiards room had originally served as a storage facility until Joe's father had bought a pool table.

The exterior door served as the building's emergency exit and was equipped with a push bar required by the fire marshal. This quick escape feature meant the door remained unlocked to people inside the building, but if it closed behind you, you had to either go around to a different entrance or bang loudly enough to be heard by someone inside to open it. Or, you wedged something in place to keep it ajar, which is what Lisa did with a leftover chunk of two-by-four.

Once outside, she took a deep breath of clean, fresh air before explaining what she meant. "Don't play innocent. We've been exchanging lustful glances all day. This, after a night of almost nonstop sex. I know what my excuse is—I'm making up for lost time, but you can't say that. You and Paulette were a hot item for five years, right?"

He turned on the water spigot then joined her by the storm drain so their messy splatters didn't hit the building. "A slight exaggeration," he said. She could tell he wasn't comfortable talking about the subject. "And we spent most of our last year together fighting."

"Which can lead to passionate making up, I'm told," Lisa added. "Jen's marriage has been an emotional roller coaster. She calls her three kids 'makeup' babies."

Joe chuckled. "I've never heard that expression before. But in my case, any de-escalation of tension between Paulette and me only came about after several weeks of mutual sulking."

Lisa tried to look sympathetic, but Joe's bemused expression told her she hadn't been successful.

"If you want to fight, I'm game," he said, a coy look in his eye.

Lisa swished her brush back and forth under the spray of the nozzle that Joe was directing downward. "What would we fight about? We share the same taste in movies and books, although you really don't know what you're missing until you give fantasy a try." Lisa had been surprised that Joe had never read anything in the genre.

He snickered. "I promised to read one, even though I have to warn you, vampires aren't my thing."

She focused on removing every speck of orange paint from the bristles of her brush. In college, care of tools had been an important part of each project's grade. And considering the price of a good brush… She lost track of the thought when she glanced up to find Joe grinning.

"What?"

"I was just wondering what you thought of wet T-shirt contests."

Lisa didn't like where this was leading. "I think they're messy and demeaning to women. Not the kind of thing I want to promote at the bar. Why?"

"Because I like them." His dimple appeared. "And I have the hose."

He turned the nozzle on her, catching her full on the chest.

Lisa tried to jump back, but her heavy boots made her clumsy. She landed on her butt on the wet concrete. Sputtering in shock, she could barely talk. "You big jerk. I ought to…"

Joe was laughing so hard he had one hand—the hose hand—resting on his knee while he used the back of his wrist to wipe the tears from his eyes. Lisa felt a surge of adrenaline. Her bucket, which was filled to the brim with coral-colored water, sat at her feet. She scrambled to her knees and picked it up. One well-directed heave sent a peach tsunami straight at Joe.

"Oh, crap," he coughed. "You fight dirty."

"You started it."

Lisa stood up, plucking the wet fabric away from her bare skin. Her overalls felt like soaked cardboard. She looked at Joe who was facing her. The hose still gurgled in his hand, but Lisa could tell by his expression he was done playing.

Two adults giving in to old needs. Constance had stated her blessing on the phone that morning. Lisa hoped Maureen and Brandon would be equally accepting—if she and Joe decided to go public with their feelings. In the meantime, they still had a couple of hours before Joe's mother and Lisa's son were due back.

"Toss the brushes in the bucket and put some water on them to soak. We can finish cleaning up later."

The glimmer of lust in Joe's eyes told her he had

the same idea. "We need to get out of these wet clothes, right?"

"Absolutely. Might get chilled. Huge health risk." She opened the door and Joe quickly followed.

Once they were both inside the darkened interior— the billiard room hadn't qualified for a skylight because of the ornate light fixture above the table—it took Lisa several seconds for her eyes to adjust. The cooler interior air made gooseflesh appear on her bare arms.

"You're cold," Joe said, pulling her into an embrace. "I can cure that."

"Oh, really," she returned, keeping her tone teasing. She used her thumb to wipe a trickle of water from his forehead. "You're a doctor now?"

"No. But I wouldn't mind *playing* doctor." He wriggled his wet, faintly orange brows à la Groucho Marx. Lisa burst out laughing.

"Oh, Joe, I love you," she said, without thinking.

His hold on her tightened. "Do you mean that?"

Did she? Of course. She'd always loved him. But was this the time to tell him that?

"Yes. I do."

He kissed her. Hard. Possessively.

Lisa liked this new aspect of his touch. No, loved it. She dropped the last few shreds of self-protection, which she'd hoped might keep her heart from getting bruised or broken, and returned his kiss with all of the love she felt.

"Wet clothes are harder to remove than dry ones," Lisa said when Joe stopped kissing her long enough look down. He was trying to undo the metal clasp that held her bib overalls in place, and the withered pads of his thumb and forefinger weren't finding much success.

"Now, you tell me," he muttered.

Lisa gently pushed his hand aside and slid the button free. She then stepped away and shed the wet, bulky fabric, exposing the clothing underneath—stretchy running shorts and a T-shirt. Unfortunately, there was no way to completely remove the overalls without taking off her boots.

Feeling as graceless as a hobbled horse, she bunny-hopped the short distance to the pool table and hoisted herself up.

Joe had managed to rid himself of the hideous brown coveralls in record time, no doubt helped by the fact that he could kick off his paint-splattered running shoes with no effort at all. Lithe and nimble in his navy-blue boxer briefs, he dropped to one knee in front of her and took her left foot.

"Did I tell you how sexy I think these boots are?"

The obvious humor in his tone made her heart flip over. "No. You didn't. Do you like power tools, too?"

"Depends on what kind you're talking about," he said with a wink. He tossed her left boot over his shoulder and picked up the right foot. "Certain tools, applied with judicious pressure on just the right spot can be very…entertaining, I'm told."

The right boot made a graceless arc and clunked to the floor behind them.

"Interesting. Too bad we only have one drill in the toolbox. And it's a bit dull."

"I beg your pardon," he said, his smirk so Joe it made her heart turn over.

He stood up. His bare torso looked healthy and powerful. The stretchy navy-blue fabric was molded to his thighs. Even sexier than bare skin, Lisa thought, noticing the way his arousal pressed against the fabric.

Without losing eye contact, he yanked the overalls off in one smooth motion. She balanced on her butt so she could applaud. "Nicely done."

Joe bowed slightly. "Thank you."

"What about the rest of these things?"

With her ankles free, she could spread her legs to accommodate him. He closed the gap between them, resting his thighs against the framework of the table. "I'm sure you'd like that cold, wet T-shirt off, but if you could see what an erotic vision you make, you'd understand why men pay money for this kind of show."

He ran his finger down the front of her shirt, pausing briefly at her taut nipple, which was clearly evident through the material of her bra.

"Well, I'm glad you're happy, but I'm cold and wet. What about your promise to warm me up?"

He worked both hands under the hem of the shirt and started peeling it upward. Lisa lifted her arms, shuddering slightly when her torso was exposed to the air.

Instead of pulling the shirt all the way off, though,

Joe left it bunched around her wrists, then reached behind her to unclasp her bra. Her sexiest bra with the
sculpted lace cups. A part of her wondered if she'd
planned for this moment even though her conscious
mind had said, "No more."

She dropped her hands, still locked together, across
Joe's shoulders and sat up a little straighter. "I'm getting warmer."

"I can tell," he said, before kissing her.

His right hand moved down her bare back, slipping
inside the matching bikini briefs. He nudged her close
to the edge of the pool table so she could feel his body
straining to meet hers.

His left hand circled along her ribs to dip beneath
the lace that loosely cupped her breasts. "Is the front
door locked?" he asked while applying kisses along
her neck.

Lisa cocked her head, grateful that her hair was
tied up. She didn't want anything to interfere with the
pleasure she was experiencing. Seductive beyond reason.

"Uh-huh," she murmured, closing her eyes to ab-
sorb the nuance of his tongue pressed against the place
where her collarbone and neck met. "And if your
mother came back early, she'd use the kitchen door."
She locked her ankles around the backs of his calves
to give herself leverage to wriggle closer. "We'd have
plenty of time to grab our clothes and duck out the
back door."

She nibbled along his jaw, slightly bristly since

he'd left his shaving gear at his mother's house. She paused mid-nibble. "It closed behind us when we came in, right?"

He turned to look over his shoulder. "I think so. No visible crack of light."

She discarded her wet top and took his face in her hands. "Good," she said looking into his eyes. "Because I've always fanaticized about making love on a pool table."

The desire in his hooded eyes made her shiver—from the heat, this time. When she set her mouth on his, Joe's lips were parted and he welcomed her tongue into the warm, wet recesses. She lost herself in his touch, their mutual need. Had she really believed that one night would be enough?

"I love the way you kiss," she said, pulling back for a breath of air.

"I love the way you let me kiss you. Open and generous. The same way you make love."

Lisa knew she was blushing. She wasn't comfortable with such frank talk. "It's not like I know what I'm doing," she said. "I just try to go with what feels good."

"Wise beyond your years," he said working the straps of her bra down her arms. He'd hooked the stretchy material with both thumbs, but his hands were formed to her muscles. "I wish I'd known that about you sooner."

Lisa had pulled back slightly to facilitate the removal of the undergarment, when a sudden rush of light and warm air made her freeze. She looked over Joe's shoulder.

A figure stood in the doorway. A silhouette backlit by bright sunlight. "Mom?"

Shock made Lisa's fingers thick and stupid. She used her hand to flatten her bra to her chest, then she dropped her forehead to Joe's shoulder. She silently muttered a curse word that her son used far too frequently. A completely off-the-wall thought hit her. Maybe Brandon *was* Patrick's child. This was exactly the kind of circumstance Patrick would have reveled in. One fraught with high drama.

"Go back outside, Brandon," Joe said, using his half-naked body to shield Lisa from view. "Your mother and I will be out in a minute to talk to you."

"When we're dressed," Lisa mumbled under her breath.

She looked up to see if he would comply. "Brandon," Joe barked. "Now."

The door slammed with a resounding bang. Not an easy feat given its pneumatic closer. But Lisa could hardly blame the boy for being upset. He'd just walked in to discover his mother nearly naked in the arms of his uncle.

"Oh, God, what have I done?" she cried, covering her face with her hands.

Joe put his lips close to her ear and whispered, "If anyone is to blame, it's me. I should have checked to make sure the door was completely closed. I'm sorry, Lisa."

Lisa sat up straight and reached behind her to re-hook the clasp on her bra. Joe stepped back to give her space to hop down. When her bare feet were flat on the floor, she gave him a quick, tight hug. "Thank you for that. It's nice to know that I'm not alone in this."

Joe put his hand on her shoulder. "I was an active participant—just now and seventeen years ago."

Lisa stepped away to pull on her still wet T-shirt. Now, instead of feeling sexy, it felt obscene. "I appreciate that, but I don't think Brandon will understand or care. Being caught in a compromising position on the pool table isn't exactly my idea of breaking it to him gently." She tugged on her bulky coveralls. "With any luck your mom's here, too."

Joe could think of a lot of things that would qualify as lucky, but having to explain *this* to his mother wasn't one of them. He stopped zipping up the ugly brown jumpsuit to look at Lisa.

"How would that qualify as fortunate?" he asked.

"We wouldn't have to go through this a second time for her benefit." The way her still wet T-shirt clung to her made Joe's body respond. Furious that he had so little self-control where Lisa was concerned, he yanked the metal tab on the end of the zipper upward, nearly imbedding it in his throat.

Lisa finished dressing, but left her shoes off. "Maybe if I'd slept around like my mother this wouldn't have been such a big shock to him."

Joe doubted there was much that could lessen the impact of having a boy's worst fear—that your mother was a sexual being—proven in broad daylight in such a public way. Young men and sex were an unpredictable equation.

He held out his hand to Lisa. "Ready?"

She inhaled deeply as if steeling herself, but instead of moving forward, she stood frozen and said, "Wait. We aren't going to say anything about Patrick until after your mom's wedding, right?"

"Probably the less we say at the moment, the better. I have a feeling he's going to want to do most of the talking."

Joe pushed on the door release and they stepped into the bright light. It took several seconds for his eyes to adjust. When they did, he looked around, praying Brandon was still waiting.

Sure enough, the young man leaned against the rear fender of his car. Arms crossed at his chest, he reminded Joe of his father when the elder Kelly was pissed off about something his sons had done. The image was so vivid, Joe almost burst out laughing.

But he controlled the impulse because he could feel Lisa's tension as they neared her son. She'd put on a brave face inside, but he knew her too well to be fooled. She was embarrassed and worried about how this would affect her relationship with her son.

She wasn't the only one who was worried.

"Do you mind telling me what the f—"

"Stop," Joe said when he felt Lisa cringe. Joe had become inured to crude language after working on various film crews, but he knew Lisa had worked to maintain a higher standard for her son. "Keep it clean."

Brandon threw up his arms. "Oh, that's funny. You two are caught screwing on the pool table and you tell me to watch my language." He glared at Joe and let loose a long, insulting diatribe.

Lisa walked to her son and took his shoulders between her hands. "That's enough."

He pushed her hands away, but he also shut up.

"I realize you're upset. I don't blame you. I once walked in on my mother when she was in bed with a man I'd never seen before. It wasn't pleasant."

She blew out a breath and went on, "But this isn't the same."

"Yeah, I know. It's worse. Joe's my uncle, Mom. This is sick. It's like against the law, isn't it?"

"You know that's not true," Joe said, walking to Lisa's side.

"Well, it should be," the teen said, sending Joe a scathing look that clearly said any relationship they'd established was over.

"Brandon, Joe and I are friends. We care about each other, and we're adults. Sometimes adults have sex. You know that. We've talked about it."

Brandon's lip curled up. "You mean you've preached about it. About abstaining until I met the right girl. Shit, Mom, he's only been back a couple of weeks. Where's *your* self-control?"

Lisa looked at Joe, a plea for help in her eyes.

"Your mother and I love each other, Brandon." Joe

wanted to put his arm around Lisa, but he didn't want Brandon to interpret the action as some kind of macho claim. "We went our separate ways, partly out of respect for my brother, partly because of my work, but now we're—"

"Screwing on the pool table. Yeah, I figured that out on my own." He looked at his mother and said, in a condemning tone, "All this time you acted like some kind of saint, but you're a bigger slut than Grandma C ever thought of being."

He got in his car and started the engine.

The window was open so Joe tried one more time to reach him. "Brandon, if you'd calm down and listen, we could explain." *Or try to.* He touched Brandon's shoulder, but the boy stepped on the gas. Joe pulled back his hand to avoid losing it.

The tires made a squealing sound when they hit the pavement. The roar of a gunned engine shattered the quiet of the Sunday afternoon in downtown Worthington. Lisa stared after him, tears flowing down her cheeks. "Oh, Joe, what if he doesn't come back? What if he…"

Her question drifted into space, but Joe knew what she meant. If Brandon reacted as Patrick would have in such a circumstance, he'd drink. And then, because rules didn't apply to the Patrick Kellys of the world, he'd drive.

BRANDON DROVE WITHOUT THINKING. He didn't care where he wound up as long as he was far, far away from his mother and his uncle. His uncle.

"Why him?" he muttered under his breath. Brandon had liked Joe—until this happened. But the idea that Joe and his mother *loved* each other freaked him out. What if they got married? Would Joe make them move to L.A.? They'd have to sell the bar, of course. His grandfather's legacy.

Damn. He and his mother had a good thing here in Worthington. They didn't need some jerk who'd barely even taken the time to visit when Brandon had been a kid coming along to ruin things now.

Then he remembered why he'd been in such a hurry to find his mother. He'd wanted to tell her the news: Grams had decided to call off her wedding.

Brandon didn't know what part he'd played in that decision, but he and his grandmother had had a long talk on the drive over to San Francisco. Mostly, Brandon had listened as Grams had rambled on about what marriage had been like with Grandpa Joe.

The two of them had kinda grown up together, she'd said. "We didn't know we were poor and struggling. We still had fun. We'd go fishing or walk in the park. Or dance in the living room to our little hi-fi. Being with someone you want to spend the rest of your life with shouldn't be such a big production, should it?"

Although he hadn't been listening too closely, he knew that some of her complaints with Gunny came from his sons insisting that both Maureen and Gunny sign prenuptial agreements that kept their assets separate if they died.

"Of course, we're going to die. Everyone dies,"

she'd said with such conviction Brandon's stomach had turned over. "But if we've committed to be with each other through the good and the bad then what business is it of theirs who we leave our money to?"

Brandon had to agree, but mainly because he wouldn't mind inheriting a little of Gunny's wealth. If he had money, his mother wouldn't have to work so hard. Brandon had always known growing up that he was different from most of his friends. He didn't have a dad and he didn't have as much money as they had to spend on stuff. The discrepancy hadn't been that big a deal. He had a grandfather who filled in and always slipped him a couple of bucks that Brandon wasn't supposed to tell his mother or grandmother about.

Brandon missed his grandfather. A lot. Gramps had been the one person who'd really seemed to "get" him. He had listened and hadn't preached. And he'd always had something good to say about Brandon's dad.

His mother never talked about his dad anymore. If fact, sometimes she seemed mad at him. Was that because of something Joe had said?

Maybe Joe had been talking to his mother before he'd come. Maybe making a movie about Joe's Place was an excuse to worm his way into Brandon's life. Maybe the Mandy Moore photo and the music CD were bribes.

Brandon reached into the CD wallet that was on the passenger seat. Driving with one hand, he flipped through the plastic sleeves until he found the brightly colored disk Joe had given him. Without a second thought, he sent it flying out the window.

A horn honked. In his rearview mirror, Brandon saw a familiar car. A chopped Toyota with extra-wide tires. Metallic purple with red-and-yellow flames on the hood. Rory's older brother's car. Rory was behind the wheel with Winston in the passenger seat.

Brandon pulled over and the low rider pulled along-side him. "Hey, man, what's up? You cruised right past us back on Cherry without even looking."

"Sorry. Had a fight with my mom."

"The ultrafine Lisa gave you grief?" Winston asked in disbelief.

Brandon's friends had been lusting after his mother almost since they were old enough to get a woody. He knew she was young and pretty, but that didn't mean Brandon ever wanted proof of some guy screwing her.

"Where you going?" he asked. "I got some beer in the trunk." He'd "borrowed" a case from his grand-mother's storeroom last week when he'd planned to at-tend the all-school kegger. But then Joe had asked him to help edit some film, and Brandon had fallen for the ploy. Of course, now, Brandon knew that all Joe had wanted was for Brandon to make it easy for him to get to Brandon's mom.

"Really?" Rory asked. "Cool. How 'bout we go to the lake?"

Brandon pictured the photograph on his mother's dresser. Her and Joe and Brandon's father. At the lake.

"Cool. Lead the way."

CHAPTER THIRTEEN

EIGHT HOURS, Lisa thought, pacing from one end of the kitchen to the other. She shot a glance at the clock. Eleven. "Where are you, Brandon?"

She'd left messages with most of his friends—none would admit that they'd seen Brandon or spoken with him all day. Two of the boys, Rory and Winston, were unaccounted for, too. Rory's sister said he was at Winston's. Winston's mother said he was at Rory's. Neither seemed too concerned. But Lisa was.

She was angry, too. Mad at herself for letting humiliation keep her from acting more parental. "I should have taken away his keys and made him talk to me."

But, no, she'd let him go. Her personal schemas had taken over. And, now, history was on the brink of repeating itself.

The thought made her stomach heave. "No. Not Brandon. This isn't happening."

She started toward the phone, intending to check on Joe. He was at his mother's house, where Lisa had asked him to wait in case Brandon called for a ride—not that that was likely to happen now that Brandon considered Joe the enemy, but she'd felt they both needed the time apart to think.

The phone rang just as she reached for the receiver.

"It's just me," Jen said. "No word yet?"

"No," Lisa said, her voice thin and reedy.

"Want me to come over?"

"Good heavens, no. All this angst wouldn't be good for the baby. Brandon will turn up. Drunk, probably," she added under her breath.

"Well, jeez," Jen said. "Sounds to me like he was looking for a reason to get tanked. You're a woman, Lisa. You're entitled to adult desires." Lisa had given Jen a toned-down version of the story—that Brandon had walked in on his mother and Joe kissing.

"Thanks for the support, pal. I appreciate the call, but I'd better hang up. We don't have call waiting."

"Okay. Just promise you'll let me know when he gets home. Safely," she added authoritatively.

"I will."

"And quit blaming yourself. You're good at that whole martyr thing, but it doesn't work this time. You're the parent. He's the kid. You are entitled to a life. He's only going be around full-time for another year. After that, you'll be alone. Alone, Lisa. If Joe can make you happy, then I say go for it."

Lisa tried to smile but couldn't quite pull it off. "You're a good friend, Jen. I love you."

"Me, too, you." Something in her tone told Lisa that Jen had more to add. "Um…you weren't naked, were you?"

Almost. "I'm hanging up, now."

"Ohmygod," Jen shrieked. "You were." Jen's bubbly laugh was the last thing Lisa heard as she replaced the receiver on the hook.

Shaking her head, Lisa walked into the main hallway leading to the bedrooms. A collage of framed photos—Brandon from birth to seventeen—captured her attention.

She touched his baby picture. The photo taken at the hospital didn't do justice to the thick black hair he'd been born with. Maureen had told her it was a family trait and not to worry because it would be replaced by a lighter color. She'd been right. Brandon had been a towhead most his life. Only when his hormones had kicked in had the color darkened to a shade similar to Joe's.

Tears filled her eyes, blurring the rest of the images. "I'm so sorry," she told the serious boy in the most recent shot. "I really made a mess of things, didn't I?"

So much for my storybook ending, she thought with a sad smile. She loved Joe, but she couldn't choose him over her son. That's what her father had done. He'd picked another daughter to love. Lisa wouldn't do that to her son.

JOE STARED OUT the kitchen window. Through a small gap in the fence, he could see the yellow glow from the lights at Lisa's house. So close, but he knew they were separated by a whole lot more than a fence.

She'd made it quite clear that she didn't want his

help—or even his shoulder to cry on—while she attempted to find her son.

Her son. And that's what Brandon was. Joe hadn't contributed a dime to the boy's welfare or the cost of raising him. He would have, of course. If Lisa had asked. But she'd been too independent and proud to consider it, even if she'd thought Joe was Brandon's father.

And there was still the matter of proof. Joe didn't know much about genetics, but he'd once heard a mystery writer talking about a plot involving twins. She'd said that twins had different fingerprints but shared the same DNA. Did that only apply to identicals? Should Joe insist they undertake whatever testing was required to prove paternity? The thought of the emotional turmoil this would create for his family made him want turn around and go back to L.A.

The sound of the garage door going up alerted Joe to his mother's arrival. He'd left a message on her cell phone in case Brandon turned to his grandmother for help, but she hadn't called him back.

Joe opened the door for her. "'Bout time. I was beginning to worry. Why didn't you answer your cell phone?"

She dumped her purse on the counter. "I forgot the charger. The battery is dead. Besides, the service is spotty at the lake, anyway," she said with a tired attempt at a smile.

"You were at Gunny's?" Joe hadn't thought to call there because Gunny was supposed to be in Napa.

"Yes. Didn't Brandon tell you what happened?"

"No."

"That's funny. When we got back from our trip and found both houses empty, we figured you and Lisa were at Joe's Place. He went there to find you."

Oh, he found us, all right. "We only saw him for a minute. He didn't mention you."

She seemed shocked. "Really? He didn't tell you the wedding is off?"

Joe nearly tripped over his feet. "What?"

"Come and sit down. I'm exhausted." She walked into the family room. Joe followed. They sat down on the sofa, side by side. "I'd been wrestling with this problem for weeks, but I didn't know who to talk to. No offense, son, but you've been a bit preoccupied. Brandon it turns out was the perfect sounding board. At seventeen, life is very black and white.

"He asked me if I loved Gunny the way I loved your father. I told him I didn't but that a second love wasn't meant to hold the same kind of fire and passion."

What if your second love is really your first? She went on before he could ask the question. "And Brandon said, 'Then why bother, Grams? Why don't you just hang out and travel together?'"

Her inward-looking smile seemed to say there was more to the issue, but before Joe could ask, she added, "The more I thought about it, the more I decided he was right. I called Gunny this morning from the motel. We had a long talk on the phone, but he said he wouldn't take no for an answer until we met face-to-face."

Joe touched her shoulder supportively. "I'm sure that couldn't have been easy for you."

"It wasn't, but I owed him that much. He's a good man, just not the right man for me."

Joe understood all too well. "So, you and Brandon came home early."

"We stopped at the outlets in Tracy and I bought him some fancy new shoes he said were hot." Her smile seemed surprisingly benign considering what she'd been through. "Then I drove around for an hour or so, thinking. I knew it would take Gunny a while to get home from Napa."

She looked at him apologetically. "I'm sorry I didn't let you know where I was. I should have called the bar as soon as we got back, but I couldn't face Lisa. She's put so much time and effort into arranging this wedding…."

"Mom, Lisa adores you. She just wants you to be happy. That's all that matters to me, too. How did Gunny take it?"

She clasped her hands in her lap. "Not well. Fortunately, his son from San Francisco—the one you met—showed up. He made his father see that Gunny and I didn't have enough in common—" she frowned as if remembering the scene "—by which he meant *money,* of course—-to make a successful marriage."

Joe covered her hand with his. "Mom, nobody ever thought you were a gold digger."

"Oh, I know, but deep down I always knew his sons didn't think I was good enough for their dad. And, in all honesty, they were right."

"Mom," he protested, squeezing her hand. "You're an amazing person. Gunny would have been lucky to have you in his life."

Maureen squeezed back. "Thank you, dear. I appreciate your support. But what I meant is it wasn't fair to Gunny that I didn't love him as much as he deserved. I think he loved me, or maybe he just needed someone to take care of again, but regardless, the feelings were one-sided. You can't build a strong and healthy marriage unless both parties are emotionally committed to each other."

The truth of that statement resonated deeply in Joe's head. *Marriage. Committed.*

"Anyway," she said, brushing her hands together. "The wedding is off. I need to call Lisa, but it's late. Maybe, I should wait until morning. There's a lot of stuff to cancel."

Joe put his hand on her knee to keep her from rising. "Um, Mom, something happened."

Her eyes opened wide. "What? Did you and Lisa have a fight?"

Joe let his gaze drop to the floor. "Just the opposite actually. Lisa and I were…um…making out when Brandon came into the bar. He saw us."

"Oh."

"He drove off in a huff. Lisa's afraid he might be somewhere with his friends…drinking."

His mother groaned softly and she put her head against his. "And you haven't heard from him since? Oh, dear."

Both were silent a moment, then Maureen said, "If you and Lisa are together, why isn't she here?"

"She went home to use the phone. She's been calling his friends, and she wanted me to wait here—in case Brandon tried to get in touch with you."

They were both silent a minute, then Maureen asked, "He doesn't know that you could be his father, does he?"

"No, thank God. And I've pretty much made up my mind not to tell him."

His mother looked shocked. "Never?"

He rested his elbows on his knees. Running one hand over the tense muscles in his neck, he let out a long, frustrated sigh. "I don't know. Lisa and I talked about how to handle this but nothing was decided."

Where before Lisa had seemed to treat the issue with some degree of inevitability, after Brandon's blowup she'd changed her mind completely, saying, "I don't know if I can do this, Joe. Turn Brandon's life upside down. Your mother and I both painted a pretty rosy picture of Patrick whenever we talked about him to Brandon. A little boy wants to think his daddy is larger than life—and that's easy to do when he's just a memory. If Brandon was this upset seeing us together, can you imagine how well he'd take the news that the man he thought was his father was actually a liar, as well as a drunk?"

Joe shook his head. "We're not sure telling the truth would be in Brandon's best interest. He'd have to take a DNA test, and it might not prove anything. So, why rock the boat?"

His mother shifted sideways to look at him. "Because you love Lisa. You always have. It's why you were with her behind Patrick's back, even though you're an honorable man and the guilt probably tortured you for years."

It still did.

"That's the reason you were with her today, right?"

Joe nodded. He was done lying to himself. He loved Lisa. She was the only woman he'd ever loved.

"Brandon is an adult, Joe. And wise beyond his years. Shouldn't he, at least, have all the facts so he can make an informed choice in the matter?"

"It's Lisa's call. She knows Brandon better than I do. I'll support her decision." Even if it meant denying what was in his heart.

He jumped to his feet and started to pace. "What pisses me off most is even from the grave Patrick is running the show. God, I wish he were alive so we could end this stupid competition, once and for all."

Earlier that morning, at Lisa's, Joe had felt a kind of closure, as if he and Patrick had made up and put the past behind them. But for the past few hours, Joe had been filled with fury.

"After he died, I only wanted to remember the good things about him. But when Lisa told me that he'd lied to her, I started remembering the other side of his personality. Petty, demanding, selfish."

Maureen shook her head. "He was human, Joe. Patrick may have acted confident and boastful, but you know as well as anybody that was a sham."

Her words stopped him. "I thought I knew him, but now, I'm not so sure. Why did he lie? Why didn't he talk to me about what Lisa and I did? She told him when she found out she was pregnant, and he said it didn't matter. But, obviously, it did. He went out and got drunk and drove his car into a canal."

His mother looked sad. "Is that what you think happened?"

"Yes."

"Well, you're wrong. He wasn't upset about you and Lisa. He was celebrating. I know because he called me a few hours before the accident and told me he'd just gotten a promotion. His own route and delivery truck. He planned to take Lisa house hunting the next day."

Joe vaguely remembered hearing his mother tell him that the day of the funeral. But he'd blocked it out. For some reason. Guilt? Shame? Fear that he'd be asked to step into a life he'd always eschewed?

"After Patrick died, Brandon was my ray of hope. He's the reason I didn't give up after your father died. I had to go on because I knew how sad my grandson would be if I let go. I couldn't add to his pain."

"You have a special bond with him," Joe said, trying to keep the envy from his voice. "He needs you."

"He needs you, too."

Joe rolled the tight muscles in his neck. "Maybe as

his uncle who brings photos of starlets, but not as the man who wants to marry his mother."

His mother made a bright, happy sound. "You asked Lisa to marry you?"

He shook his head. "No. I wish I had. Seventeen years ago."

Neither spoke for a few minutes. Then Joe asked the question that had lingered in the back of his mind for as long as he could remember. "Mom? Is there a chance that the nurses mixed Patrick and me up when we were born?"

She looked at him, frowning. "What do you mean? You were the only set of twins born that month."

"No. I meant is it possible that Patrick came out first, but in the post-birth mayhem somebody put the wrong wristband—or whatever—on me."

She took a deep breath and slowly let it out. "Of course not. Why does it matter?"

He shrugged his shoulder. "It doesn't. Not at all, but when I was looking through some old footage a little while ago, I ran across a piece where Patrick and I were talking about being twins. He said that he'd read that first-born children were leaders and second children were the peacemakers. He was sure the nurses had mixed us up."

His mother had a bemused look on her face. "How strange. But he was wrong, because you had pitch-black hair. Your Grandmother Kelly called it the black Irish legacy. And always claimed first-born sons gave the gene to first-born sons. Patrick's hair was so fair he looked bald."

She blinked suddenly and let out a small gasp. Joe looked at her with concern. "What's wrong?"

"Nothing." Then she smiled. "Where are those photos of Brandon you were scanning?"

She clambered to her feet and hurried to Joe's makeshift editing desk. She picked up the album marked Brandon and flipped open the first page. "Black hair. Just like yours."

Joe's knees went screwy and he sat down heavily in his chair. "I...I don't have black hair in my baby pictures."

She nodded. "I know. It all fell out before we could get photos taken. Patrick's delivery was difficult. The doctor even called for a priest. By the time I left the hospital, you and your brother were both a week old. And money was tight."

Joe's heart was beating erratically but he made himself draw a deep breath. "This doesn't prove anything, Mom. A coincidence. A fluke."

She put her hand on his shoulder. "I didn't give it much thought when Brandon was born. We were still grieving for Patrick and Brandon's birth was the one bright spot in our lives. But after Lisa started acting so strange, I remembered thinking that Patrick must have shared the firstborn gene because you were twins."

"That could be it, Mom. We just don't know. We might never know."

"Then you and Lisa owe it to yourselves to be honest. With each other. And with Brandon."

She turned and started toward the kitchen. "I'm going to make coffee and call Martin. He's pretty handy in an emergency." Glancing over her shoulder, she said, "Go to Lisa's, son. She shouldn't be alone at a time like this."

CHAPTER FOURTEEN

LISA OPENED THE DOOR at his knock. "Any news?"

He shook his head. "No, but Mom's back. She'll man the phone in case he calls. She thought you might need help pacing. A flagman or something."

His lame joke didn't raise so much as a hint of a smile. "Can I come in?"

She opened the door wide enough for him to enter. The kitchen was well lit but it felt cold and empty, as if Lisa's soul was searching for her son. "How 'bout a cup of tea?"

Her shoulders lifted and fell. She'd changed out of her wet clothes, he noticed. She was wearing stretchy black capris and a rose-colored T-shirt that said Chicks Rule on the front. Joe wanted to hug her, but instead, he filled her kettle with water from the tap and told her about his mother's decision to call off the wedding.

"Really?" was all she said.

He walked to where she was standing and picked up her hand. It was ice cold. "Lisa, snap out of it." He chafed her hand between his until she looked up at him, puzzled and a bit put out.

"What do you want from me? My son is missing. I don't care about your mother's wedding. Brandon is all that matters at the moment."

"I agree, but you're not thinking about him. You're remembering the night Patrick died." She swallowed and jerked back her hand.

"No, I'm not."

"Yes, you are. I know because I was thinking the same thing. And blaming myself. The same way you are. But that's going to stop. Right now."

She flung her hands wide. "How, Joe? How do you turn it off? What if history repeats itself? What if Brandon—"

Joe gathered her into his arms and squeezed hard. "That isn't going to happen. Because Brandon *isn't* Patrick." *He isn't even Patrick's son,* he almost added but didn't.

Lisa started weeping, great anguished sobs that nearly broke his heart. He prayed harder than he had in many, many years that his prediction would hold true.

Her face was pressed to his shoulder and he tenderly stroked her hair. "It's going to be okay, Leese. Honest."

They stayed like that until a shrill whistle alerted him that the water was boiling. He helped her sit at the table and gave her a tissue from a box he found on the counter.

A few minutes later, they were seated across from each other, two cups of tea in front of them. "Are we going to talk about what happened today?" she asked.

"No. We'll probably laugh about it some day—way, way down the road. But for now, I think we should pretend today never happened."

Her lips almost smiled, but she picked up the cup and blew into it, instead. "Then why are you here?"

"To ask you to marry me."

The cup wobbled, spilling hot liquid over her fingers.

Joe pulled Lisa to her feet and led her to the sink where he held her hand under the faucet. "Talk about poor timing," he said, shaking his head. "Was that the worst proposal in history or what?"

When she looked at him, tears glistened in her eyes. "Just unexpected. Where did that come from?"

"The heart."

He opened a couple of drawers until he found a clean towel and gently wrapped it around her fingers. "I realize I'm seventeen years late, but I love you, Lisa. I always have. You know that, right?"

"I'm not sure what I believe, anymore. My brain is a mess. My emotions are even more screwed up."

"Then, don't answer me. Let things settle. We'll clear the air with Brandon and look at the long-term later. But I've made up my mind to stay in Worthington. I want to spend time with Mom, finish my movie and, if Brandon will let me, get to know him better."

She didn't say anything, but she didn't appear mortified or fearful. Emboldened, he added, "And court you. I might even buy a white charger—or an SUV, whichever impresses you the most."

Her smile was tremulous at best, but it gave him hope. And a man could slay dragons if he had hope.

They returned to the table and drank their tea in silence until the phone rang. Lisa grabbed the receiver.

"Hello? Brandon?"

Joe hoped it was the kid, but when she shook her head, he sat back. She listened in silence for a moment then said, "Okay. We'll be right there."

His chest ached from holding his breath.

"That was your mother. Martin just called. He found Brandon. He's safe. Drunk, but not behind the wheel, thank God. They'll be here in fifteen or twenty minutes."

LISA CHECKED THE CLOCK. Again. Time had decided to crawl while she waited in Maureen's kitchen. She could hear Joe in the family room on the phone. He'd volunteered to call Jen and Brandon's friends to let them know Brandon was okay.

Lisa and Maureen were sitting across from each other at the table, not unlike the way Lisa and Joe had been when he proposed. *He proposed.* There was an irony here that almost made her laugh out loud. Her mother had called not an hour earlier with the same news.

"Lisa, you won't believe what just happened. Jerry proposed to me. On the beach. He gave me a ring and everything. Can you believe it?" Constance had cried, apparently not catching the anguish in Lisa's voice when she'd answered the phone.

Lisa had congratulated her and tried to sound up-beat but had obviously fallen short in her effort because Constance had asked, "What's wrong? Do you think I'm a fool for accepting? With my track record, who am I trying to kid, right?"

"No, Mom," Lisa had answered, making herself step back from her own problems. "I'm sorry I sounded so down. I had a fight with Brandon this afternoon and he still isn't home, but that'll work out." *I hope.* "I'm thrilled for you. Really. Jerry is great and I had a hunch he was the one. When's the wedding?"

They'd talked for a few minutes—her mother, still, obviously on cloud nine. Lisa was happy for her mother, she honestly was, but she was worried, too. Would Constance's past eventually undermine Jerry's trust?

"Do you think it's possible to ever escape our past?" Lisa asked aloud.

"What do you mean, honey?"

"Mom called a little while ago. Jerry proposed to her. He wants to get married right away."

"That's wonderful," Maureen exclaimed. "I'm so happy for her."

"Me, too," Lisa said, "but I'm afraid her past will get in the way of any lasting, happy relationship."

"Oh, pooh. That was small-town gossip. Your mother is a good friend and a wonderful nurse. She might have been a little wild when she first moved to town, but people came to understand her once they got to know her."

Lisa shook her head. "Maureen, they called her Connie Made 'Em. I used to be embarrassed to go to school because I knew people were talking about her behind my back."

Maureen walked to the cupboard. She opened the door and took out an extra cup then walked to the refrigerator and extracted a container of cream. She arranged the two things beside the coffee carafe then looked at Lisa and said, "People talk. It's human nature, I suppose. I once asked Joe how he stood listening to all the stories people told him, the petty jealousies, the backstabbing."

"What did he say?"

"He said it was his job to let his customers get whatever was bothering them off their chests, but he didn't have to repeat it. And he never did. Not to me, anyway."

Lisa smiled. Joe Sr. hadn't been a saint, but at times he had been wisdom personified. "I miss him," she said. "He was good to me. A surrogate dad."

"I know. And he adored you. And Brandon. Your being here helped make up for losing both his sons."

Lisa took a deep breath and lowered her voice, her gaze on the doorway. "Joe asked me to marry him tonight."

Maureen dropped the dishrag she was using to wipe the counter and rushed to where Lisa was sitting. Tears sparkled in her eyes. "Oh, my word. You and your mother in the same day. How wonderful is that?"

Lisa swallowed hard. "I haven't given him an answer."

"Oh," Maureen said softly. "But you love him. I've seen it in your eyes. And he's crazy in love with you."

Lisa put her arm around the older woman's shoulders. "I know. You're right. But we have this history between us. Patrick. And Brandon. I screwed up once and ruined so many people's lives…."

Maureen jerked back and looked at her. "What are you talking about?"

"I slept with Joe…when I was going steady with Patrick. Maureen, that's exactly the kind of thing my mother would have done. It was wrong, and when I found out I was pregnant, I told Patrick the truth. He didn't seem freaked out at the time, but the closer we got to the wedding, the more he drank. I didn't blame him. Who would want to marry a woman you couldn't trust?"

"Oh, Lisa," Maureen cried, wrapping her warm, motherly arms around her. "You've blamed yourself all these years and I never guessed. Probably because I was doing the same thing. My son killed himself. Not on purpose, I know, but the end result was the same, and it was my fault because I didn't make him get help."

"You're both wrong."

Lisa's breath stopped. She and Maureen turned to look at Joe, who was standing in the doorway. "You're taking responsibility for something you had no control over. My brother was an alcoholic. He suffered from a disease that owned his actions. He wasn't able to deal with his addiction and it killed him.

"When I was making *Dead Drunk,* I talked to a lot of people who'd lost a loved one to drunk driving. Believe me, there's never a shortage of guilt to go around after this kind of accident. But the only person who had an option that night was Patrick. He chose to get behind the wheel, knowing he'd had too much to drink. Because to admit that he was incapacitated was unthinkable, it was un-Patrick."

Lisa felt an odd release. Almost as if Patrick had chucked her under the chin and said, "Told ya." Maureen made a protesting sound, but Joe wasn't done. He took his mother's hand and led her to a chair.

"Mom," he said, kneeling beside her. "I loved my brother, but he wasn't a saint. He wasn't even a good brother at times, but he was human. And that's okay. What happened isn't anybody's fault and I'm tired of beating myself up over it. Patrick wouldn't have wanted that."

Joe gave Lisa a wink he knew she'd understand. "Well, he might have liked the attention. For a few years. But, now, it's time to move on."

He took a breath and let it out. Lisa had a feeling he was about to repeat his proposal for his mother's benefit, but the sound of a car pulling up stopped him. He looked at Lisa and got up. "Team effort? Or do you want to talk to him alone first?"

Lisa hesitated for a heartbeat then she put out her hand. "The two of us, I think."

Joe told himself not to read more into her gesture than she'd intended, but he couldn't prevent his heart rate from escalating. He squeezed her fingers supportively and led the way to the door.

They paused on the stoop as Brandon's car pulled into the driveway with Martin behind the wheel. No passenger was visible. Lisa looked at Joe questioningly, but he had no answer.

As they walked to the car, Joe was vaguely conscious of the background noises, dogs barking, cars honking, a distant train whistle—stuff he would have thought too clichéd to be used in one of his movies. The temperature had dropped at least fifteen degrees from the afternoon but his inner turmoil made him impervious.

The door opened and Martin got out. Even before Joe could frame the question, Martin pointed to the back seat.

Joe and Lisa stepped closer. Brandon was sprawled face down, one arm on the floor. His mouth was open and a puddle of drool darkened the wine-colored upholstery.

"He isn't wearing a seat belt," Joe said, realizing the moment he said it that he sounded like a fool. Or a father.

Martin let out a raspy guffaw.

Joe was glad it was too dark for either Martin or Lisa to see him blush. He let go of Lisa's hand to shake Martin's. "I don't know how you pulled this off, but I thank you from the bottom of my heart."

Martin looked from Joe to Lisa and said, "My cousin works for the irrigation district. They've been having trouble with teenagers partying at a couple of the lakes around here. When he spotted some boys drinking, he called me."

"Why you?" Lisa asked. She made no move to open the door.

"He recognized Brandon's car."

Joe looked at the unremarkable sedan. "How?"

Martin didn't look as though he was going to answer, but then he said, "Your mother used to drive this car."

The import of that statement hit Joe squarely. *He loves her. All these years. He's always loved her.*

Sadness hit Joe. He knew Martin well enough to guess that the other man had never made his feelings known while Joe's father was alive. He was too honorable. And after Joe had passed away, he'd probably wanted to give Maureen time to heal. Then Gunny had stepped in.

But he felt joy, too. Because he knew something Martin didn't.

"You think you waited too long to declare your feelings, don't you, my friend?"

Martin made a snarling sound and glanced toward Lisa, who looked at Joe, curiously.

Joe went on. "While you were being considerate of Mom's feelings, letting her grieve for her husband, Gunny elbowed in and beat you to the punch. Right?"

Martin straightened proudly. "Maureen has chosen another. I want her to be happy."

Joe wondered if the real reason behind his mother's

sudden change of heart was connected to her feelings for this man. He'd sensed something between them when he'd first come home, but then he'd pushed the idea out of his mind because he'd been too wrapped up in his own problems.

"Actually, Martin, she's 'un-chosen' him," Joe said, placing his hand on the man's shoulder. "She called off the wedding a few hours ago."

Martin didn't appear to believe him. "What? Why?"

Joe nodded toward the car. "Ask him. Apparently, Brandon helped her make up her mind. Or you could just ask Mom. She's in the kitchen."

Joe felt an odd tremor pass through his friend. Hope, perhaps? The possibility of being given a second chance to be with the woman he loved? Joe was still praying there was a little more of that going around.

Martin looked at Lisa and said, "He isn't that drunk. Mostly confused and upset. He told me about finding you together."

"We didn't plan this, but…"

"'Bout time, I'd say," Martin muttered softly. "You two have had a thing for each other ever since you were too young to even think about sex. Are you going to do something about it this time?"

Joe looked at Lisa. "Are we?"

When she didn't answer right away, Martin walked to her side and said softly, "You can't say he never asked."

With a deep sigh, he stepped back and added, "I'll

leave you two alone to figure it out. I need to talk to Maureen. I made enough mistakes in my life without letting opportunity pass me by a second time."

Opportunity. Mistakes. Joe knew all about those.

"What are we going to do, Joe?" Her long, pale lashes blinked rapidly to keep back tears. Such a tender heart. He'd wounded it in the past, but she was too strong to let a few battle scars keep her from living. She was as courageous as any warrior.

He looked at the sleeping boy then checked to make sure Martin had taken the keys out of the car. Decision made, he took her hand and started leading her toward the house. "Five minutes. Just give me five minutes to prove that you and I belong together. Brandon's safe. Mom can keep on eye an him through the kitchen window. This is between us, only. Okay?"

She looked skeptical and didn't seem anxious to leave her son passed out in the car, but in the end, she followed him into his makeshift editing studio.

He pulled over a spare chair so they were shoulder to shoulder in front of his extra-wide laptop, which displayed a split screen. "I was working on this while you were making calls and pacing," he told her.

He clicked on a file. A moment later, an image appeared on the full-size television monitor to her left. "This is raw. Completely unedited. And after you've seen it, I'm going to delete this file and destroy the original."

Lisa looked at him questioningly. "Why?"

"Because we might never know who Brandon's biological father is. He has a certain image of Patrick, and I don't want to ruin that for him. What's here doesn't affect him, it's only important to you and me."

He hit the play button.

The image of a laughing young girl came on the screen. The color was washed out, the picture grainy, but there was no mistaking Lisa at age seventeen.

"The lake," Lisa said, as the scope of the shot opened up to include water, a dock and a group of young people standing around in swimsuits. Several other girls, including Jen Jensen, had their towels wrapped around their hips. Lisa was wearing a two-piece suit. The bottom half was a skimpy swath of navy blue, the top a stylized version of the American flag.

"How patriotic of me," she murmured, blushing.

The voice of a narrator, Joe, came through the speakers. "Here we are. Worthington High's most illustrious students playing hooky. Kinda makes you fear for the future, doesn't it?"

Joe thought he sounded very young. "Watch closely and you will see the one bright spot in this group of less-than-illustrious stars. A supernova in a galactic vacuum."

Joe felt a blush of his own. "Dreadful commentary, I know. But, hey, I was a dumb ass who thought I was brilliant."

"I always thought you were brilliant, too," Lisa said softly.

He couldn't tell what she was thinking, but the pain

in her eyes was too intense to take for long—like watching an eclipse with ordinary sunglasses. He returned to the screen.

"This, good viewer, is our resident goddess." The camera zeroed in on Lisa. Her long blond hair—streaked from a summer in the sun. She walked a bit pigeon-toed in oversize rubber thongs that she'd borrowed from someone. She crossed the dock to where Patrick was sitting with his legs dangling above the water. He wore wraparound sunglasses and held a beer bottle.

She paused as if sensing Joe's attention and looked straight at the camera. She smiled and lifted her right hand to wave. Her left arm hung loosely at her side, which was closest to Joe's brother. Her boyfriend.

What happened next took place so fast, Joe knew Lisa missed the actual cause, but she saw the effect because she gave a little gasp of surprise. One second a happy, smiling Lisa was standing there waving, the next she was in the water, spitting and sputtering.

"Watch closely," he said, dragging the mouse to rewind the action. He adjusted the speed and replayed the scene.

This time, Patrick's role in her fall became apparent. He'd grabbed her hand and yanked downward. She'd had nowhere to go but into the water.

"It wasn't until I watched at this speed that I realized how close you came to dying," he told her.

Lisa leaned closer to the monitor. "I fell into the water. It's not like I was going to drown."

Joe turned to face her. "Watch again. Look where your head is."

Her fingers were linked tight. Joe watched her face as she stared at the screen. He knew the moment she saw what he meant. When Patrick had pulled on her arm, she'd been completely unprepared. Her body had snapped like a Raggedy Ann doll. When she'd gone over the edge of the dock, the back of her head had come within inches of a metal cleat that people used to tie up their boats.

"Oh, God..." she murmured. "How come I don't remember this?"

"There's more. It might come back to you."

He adjusted the controls to play the footage in real time. The camera went sideways. The recording continued. Obviously, Joe had reacted by dumping his camera on what appeared to be a picnic bench. He came into view, racing down the incline to the dock.

He dove into the water and splashed toward Lisa. Patrick stopped laughing when Joe helped Lisa toward the shallow boat launch. Words were exchanged, but the camera only picked up the sound of the wind blowing. To this harsh orchestration, Patrick jumped to his feet, tossing his bottle angrily. He tore off his sunglasses and hopped into the waist-deep water.

Once Lisa was safely surrounded by her friends, Joe attacked Patrick with a fury that made Lisa sit back sharply. "Oh, no...oh, Joe," she cried, grabbing his shoulder as if to stop the altercation.

She winced when Patrick landed a solid blow to

Joe's cheekbone. Joe's feet went out from under him and he fell backward into the water. Patrick, obviously seeing his chance, pounced on his brother, holding Joe's torso under water. Three male friends pulled Patrick off.

"Why did he go off like that? All you did was help."

Joe sighed. "Because I called him a stupid son of a bitch. Pat couldn't stand to have someone correct him or point out that he'd done something wrong. Especially if that someone was me."

Joe turned off the unit then swiveled his chair to face hers. "Patrick was my brother and I loved him, but at times he could be an arrogant, self-centered bastard. I never wanted to admit that. And when I watched this, I realized something important."

He paused until she looked him in the eye. "I let his needs take precedence over yours, and for that I'm eternally sorry. I always knew you were the best thing he had going for him." He touched her face. "But when I saw this tape, I realized that he didn't deserve you."

Her bottom lip disappeared beneath her top teeth. Unshed tears glistened in her eyes. Emboldened by the look of compassion and love he read in her eyes, Joe moved closer. "Maybe I don't deserve you, either. I wasn't there for you—or Brandon," he added, gesturing with his chin toward the front of the house, "when you needed me. I was never honest with myself or with you about how I felt. But, Lisa, I want to change that. I can't imagine a future without you in it."

The raw vulnerability in Joe's face was something Lisa had never witnessed before. His honesty touched her deeply, but she wasn't sure how to express the turbulent emotions bouncing through her brain.

She'd been shaken by the video. She recalled the little drama all too clearly now. Just before summer break. She hadn't spoken to Patrick for two weeks after that, but he'd apologized with tears in his eyes. And she'd forgiven him. Just like she had after other, equally distressing, incidents.

Had she erased those bad memories to build up Patrick for her son's sake? Or because remembering meant admitting that she'd chosen the wrong brother for the wrong reason—security. Joe, the boy most likely to leave Worthington. Patrick, the one most likely to take over Joe's Place.

Even now, Lisa thought, Joe wasn't a safe bet. His work could easily take him far away. But she wasn't an insecure young girl anymore. She was a woman in love, and home would never be home without Joe.

She placed her hand along his cheek. He pulled it to his lips and kissed her palm.

"Let's go get Brandon," she told him. "We need to talk about what happens next…as a family."

CHAPTER FIFTEEN

BRANDON FELT LIKE CRAP. The inside of his mouth was dry and sticky, like one of his friends had stuffed it full of cotton balls while he'd been passed out. And his head felt like someone was beating on a drum inside his brain. There was a good chance he might throw up, too, but none of that seemed to matter to the four adults sitting around the table.

"I said I was sorry. What more do you want?" he asked, giving his mother a look he knew she'd understand. He'd probably never be able to forget seeing her and Joe going at it on the pool table.

His stomach heaved, and he swallowed hard.

"We want to talk about what happened this afternoon," she said.

"Well, I don't. It sucked finding you like that, you know? It was…gross." He couldn't even look at Joe without feeling like he should punch him out or something.

And the worst part was he liked Joe. *Had liked him.* Having Joe around was kinda like having a dad. Only now that was screwed up, too.

"It was unfortunate timing on both our parts," Joe said. "You weren't prepared to see us that way because Lisa and I weren't prepared to talk about how we feel about each other. But we are now."

"I don't wanna hear it."

His mother made a sad noise. Brandon couldn't look at her so he glanced at his grandmother. "It's never easy for a child to admit that his mother is more than just a mother," she said. "Ask Joe. All I had to do was tell him I was getting married and he came racing back home." She looked at her son, who was sitting very close to Brandon's mother, and winked.

"But you broke up with Gunny. Didn't you?" Brandon asked. So much had happened in the past twenty-four hours, he wasn't sure he even knew what day it was.

Grams took his hand. "Yes, dear, that's over. Gunny's son and daughter-in-law are moving him to Napa. Where there are more eligible women to pick from."

Her smile said she wasn't too sad about the whole thing. Then she looked over her shoulder at Martin, and Brandon got the feeling he was missing something. "What?"

She squeezed his hand. "Later," she said softly. "First, let's get this settled between you and Joe and your mother."

Brandon was tired of worrying about his mother. He wanted her to be happy and get off his case. If Joe was the guy who could make her happy, then did it really matter if he was Brandon's uncle? Rory and Winston thought the idea was kinda twisted, but what did they know?

He let out a heartfelt sigh and said, "Why can't my family be normal? Just once."

Joe sat forward. "Define normal. I grew up in a home with two parents who loved each other—and their twin sons. My brother and I had a great childhood, but that didn't mean we didn't have problems. Patrick drank. I hid behind a camera."

Brandon looked up, drawn to his uncle's brutally honest tone. "You have a choice, Brandon. You can blame your future decisions on your childhood, which from the photos and home movies I've been looking at appeared to be pretty darn happy," he said. "Or you can take responsibility for your life and face these kinds of issues head-on."

The serious look in Joe's eyes never wavered as he added, "But either way, your mother and I love each other. We always have. That doesn't mean we didn't love Patrick. My feelings for him will never change. He's my brother. But I need Lisa in my life. And if you'll let me, I'd like to be a part of your life, too."

Brandon looked at his mother. He could tell she was waiting for him to say something.

"Are you guys gonna…like…get married?"

She kinda gasped, but then she smiled and looked at Joe. "Yes," she said. "We are. There's a lot of that going around at the moment."

Brandon didn't know what she was talking about

but Joe apparently did. He let out a gruff laugh and kissed her. A long, full-on-the-mouth kiss.

Brandon dropped his head to his arms. "Oh, sick. Can I go now?"

His grandmother stood up, put a hand on his shoulder and said, "Come on. Martin and I will walk you home."

"Grams, I know the way."

"Of course, you do, but I want to tell you a little story."

He tried not to groan, but one got past him. Martin laughed and took Brandon's elbow, the same way he had when he'd shown up at the lake. Brandon didn't even try to resist. Who knew the old man was so strong?

"Listen to your grandmother, boy. It's a story I think you'll like."

Brandon stumbled to his feet. He gave his mother a pleading look, but she was staring at Joe, who had his arms wrapped around her. *Oh, man...*

"It's the story of two brothers who loved the same woman," Grams said, her loud voice echoing off his hungover brain cells. But when she added, "It has a very happy ending," he gave in and listened. Maybe Martin was right. Maybe this was one story he wanted to hear.

JOE FELT LISA LET OUT a long, heartfelt sigh as his mother, Brandon and Martin left the room. A few seconds later, the sound of the door closing made her relax against him.

"Wow. Talk about drama. Is this day ever going to end?" she asked, snuggling against his chest.

"Oh, yeah," he said. "Although upstairs in my bed would probably be pushing my luck."

She shook her head and looked up at him. "Always the joker."

Tears sparkled in her eyes. He kissed her—just a soft, quick peck meant to reassure her that things would get better. "Sorry. Conditioned reflex, but I was serious when I proposed to you. Did you mean it when you said you'd marry me?"

"Of course," she murmured, drawing his head down so their lips were touching. She kissed him until the background noise faded to black, then added, on a whisper, "You heard your mother. How else could we live happily ever after?"

EPILOGUE

LISA CLOSED HER EYES and tried to seal every image into her memory. The vivid pink and orange gerbera daisies on the tables inside the banquet hall. The dramatic, wind-swept cypress trees framing the ocean vista beyond the knoll where her mother and Jerry were standing. The harpist. The minister, who had been a childhood friend of Jerry's, had flown in from Boston for the ceremony.

And although she couldn't see them, Lisa knew Martin's nephew's salsa band was setting up nearby.

When the minister cleared her throat and said, "Friends, welcome to this joyous occasion," Joe took Lisa's hand in his and gave a gentle squeeze. She looked into his beautiful eyes that reminded her so much of Brandon's, then leaned across the small distance between them and said, "We're next, you know."

His lips curved upward, ushering in the notorious Kelly dimple. "October can't come soon enough."

They'd given themselves three months to recuperate from this wedding, but they both knew the time would fly. Look how much had happened in the month since their engagement.

Constance and Jerry had returned from the East Coast and promptly moved in together. Since both wanted an outdoor wedding—and given the heat of the summer in the Central Valley, they'd started looking for a spot on the coast. A cancellation had opened up at Seascape in Aptos and they'd grabbed it.

Since Jerry had hired a professional wedding planner, Lisa had had time to help Joe put his house in L.A. on the market and arrange for a mover to pack up his belongings, which would stay in storage until they could move into the new home they'd just bought— from Gunny of all people.

Once the dear man got over his disappointment of not marrying Maureen, he'd given Joe and Lisa an excellent price on his lakeside home. After signing the papers, the first thing Lisa, Joe and Brandon had done was rush down to the dock and pose for a picture.

A gift for the bride and groom, who now stood facing each other. A tearfully blushing Constance in a lovely, demure, white tea-length gown and her silver-haired prince, Jerry. Maureen and Martin were the only attendants.

Maureen and Martin were talking marriage as well, but both had assured Joe and Lisa they weren't rushing into anything. They'd decided to give living together a shot first. As Maureen jokingly told Lisa, "With your mother dropping out of the gossip-generating business, someone has to give our customers something to talk about."

Although she'd given Maureen the option of buying back a share of Joe's Place, both Maureen and Martin insisted they were content to be "extremely" silent partners, but promised to help out any time Joe and Lisa needed a break.

After all, once Joe got his office moved, he'd need time to finish his movie, which was turning out to be a very moving tribute to a man and his dream. Lisa had a feeling *Joe's Place* was going to touch a chord with anybody who fondly remembered a neighborhood hangout. He might even have another hit on his hands.

Lisa was busy, too. Still remodeling. It kept her from worrying about Brandon. He wasn't drinking anymore, but he was in love.

She leaned forward to sneak a peek at her son. His date for the wedding, Nikki Jean Cho, was quite vocal about her belief that alcohol and drugs killed artistic vision. Lisa wasn't sure how her son had managed to snag this amazing, black-haired goddess, but according to Jen-Jen, who had just given birth to a new baby daughter, the actress Mandy Moore played some role in the courtship. Lisa believed the attraction stemmed more from Brandon's rapidly escalating skill behind the camera.

Joe whispered, "What are you thinking?"

"How strange it is the way everything worked out. Did you know Michael and Christine are here?" she said, nodding toward the Bjorgensens. "I thought Gunny was in Holland."

"He is," Joe said. "Mike told me they didn't want there to be any hard feelings between our families."

He craned his neck to look around. "Nice turnout, but I think most of the other guests are hospital staff. Now would not be a good time to get sick in Worthington."

Thinking about doctors reminded her of the talk she and Joe had had with Brandon a few weeks earlier. Joe had left the decision of whether or not to tell Brandon about the uncertainty surrounding his paternity to her. And after a great deal of soul-searching, Lisa had decided she didn't like keeping secrets from her son.

They'd sat him down and laid out the brutal facts. Brandon took the news with surprising maturity. He and Joe discussed their options at length and even did some research online. Finally, Brandon announced their mutual decision. "We ordered a paternity test kit, Mom. Identical twins share the same DNA, but Joe and Patrick were fraternal. Joe and I both think it's better to know the truth than always wonder."

They didn't have the results, yet. But Lisa sensed the experience had brought both of her men closer. Which made her extremely happy considering *her* news.

She'd intended to tell Joe later, when they were alone, but the serenity of the moment called to her. She motioned him closer and put her lips to his ear. "I took the test this morning," she whispered. "We're pregnant."

Lisa could only see half of Joe's face. The side with the infamous Kelly dimple. So she knew he was smiling. A smile that made her heart turn over. When he looked at her, there were tears in his eyes. He mouthed the words *I love you*, as her mother and Jerry exchanged their simple, heartfelt vows.

Lisa kissed him, then rested her head on his shoulder. He moved his hand to touch her belly tenderly. They'd talked about this possibility, but neither had expected it to happen so fast. Blinking back tears of her own, Lisa smiled. She knew that some things—the best things—were meant to be.

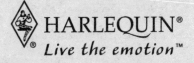

HARLEQUIN®

AMERICAN *Romance*®

is happy to bring you
a new 3-book series by

Dianne Castell

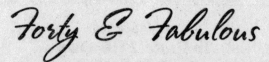

Forty & Fabulous

Here are three very funny books
about three women who have grown up
together in Whistler's Bend, Montana.
These friends are turning forty and are
struggling to deal with it. But who said
you can't be forty and fabulous?

A FABULOUS WIFE
(#1077, August 2005)

A FABULOUS HUSBAND
(#1088, October 2005)

A FABULOUS WEDDING
(#1095, December 2005)

Available wherever Harlequin books are sold.

BLACKBERRY HILL MEMORIAL

Almost A Family
by Roxanne Rustand
Harlequin Superromance #1284

From Roxanne Rustand,
author of *Operation: Second Chance*
and *Christmas at Shadow Creek*,
a new heartwarming miniseries,
set in a small-town hospital,
where people come first.

As long as the infamous Dr. Connor Reynolds stays
out of her way, Erin has more pressing issues to
worry about. Like how to make her adopted children
feel safe and loved after her husband walked out on
them, and why patients keep dying for no apparent
reason. If only she didn't need Connor's help. And if
only he wasn't so good to her and the kids.

Available July 2005 wherever Harlequin books are sold.

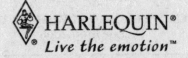

HARLEQUIN®
Live the emotion™

Montana Standoff

by Nadia Nichols

Harlequin Superromance #1287

Steven Young Bear is ready to fight
the good fight against the mining
company whose plans threaten to
destroy a mountain. Molly Ferguson
is fresh out of law school and
representing the other side. Steven
and Molly are in a standoff!
Will love bring them together?

Available July 2005
wherever Harlequin books are sold.

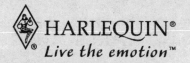

COMING NEXT MONTH

HSRCNM0605